Thomas Jenner

That Goodly Mountain & Lebanon

by Thomas Jenner

Thomas Jenner

That Goodly Mountain & Lebanon
by Thomas Jenner

ISBN/EAN: 9783337287528

Printed in Europe, USA, Canada, Australia, Japan

Cover: Foto ©Andreas Hilbeck / pixelio.de

More available books at **www.hansebooks.com**

THAT

GOODLY MOUNTAIN & LEBANON,

BY

THOMAS JENNER,

SECOND EDITION, REVISED.

LEBONAH'S WELL.

London:

HAMILTON, ADAMS, & CO.,

PATERNOSTER ROW.

1874.

THAT

GOODLY MOUNTAIN & LEBANON:

BEING THE

NARRATIVE OF A RIDE THROUGH THE COUNTRIES

OF

JUDEA, SAMARIA, AND GALILEE,

INTO

SYRIA,

IN THE MONTH OF AUGUST, 1872,

WITH

YOUHANNAH EL KAREY,

OF NABLÛS.

BY

THOMAS JENNER.

SECOND EDITION REVISED.

London:

HAMILTON, ADAMS AND CO.,

PATERNOSTER ROW,

—

1874.

CONTENTS.

APPENDIX No. 1.

ARABIC PHRASES.

APPENDIX No. 2.

LINES BY THE AUTHOR.

LIST OF ILLUSTRATIONS.

PREFACE TO THE SECOND EDITION.

———◆———

REFERRING to the journey narrated in the following pages, several friends have said to me, "I suppose you have no wish to go again?" This proposition, however, I could only subscribe in the spirit with which the fox pronounced the grapes to be sour.

Yet, although the occasion for repeating the journey in person is, like the vocative case of *ego*, wanting; the rapid disposal of the first edition of two thousand copies of "That Goodly Mountain and Lebanon" affords me the opportunity of doing so with the pen. The work will be found to have been revised throughout in several respects, in all of which improvement has been my aim.—Reader, I wish you *bon voyage*.

J

9th November, 1874.

PREFACE.

In offering another book on Palestine and Syria to the reading world, I feel that no apology is called for on the ground of the previous exhaustion of the subject, for in that I no more believe than I pretend to the achievement; while, whatever is needed on account of the defects of my little quota, added to that which has gone before; the fact of its being required unfits me for making it. For, why should I extend a book of many shortcomings, with a page or two devoted to the enumeration of those which are evident to myself?

As to the disadvantages under which I have laboured in the writing, it is sufficient that they are known to those of my readers who are also my personal friends. But, of my advantages I may, and justice requires that I should, speak. My best thanks are

due to several who have cheerfully helped
me as amanuenses, and readers of "copy" or
" proof."

The title I have chosen from the words
of Moses in Deuteronomy iii. 25. I am
aware that many Bible students accept
"That goodly mountain, *even* Lebanon," as
the correct reading, but the majority consider that two distinct mountains are referred to (as is certainly the natural sense
of the English version), and that these are
none other than Mount Moriah (on which
the Temple was built) and Lebanon. To
this, the common view, I have adhered, and
used the passage in its generally accepted
sense of—The lands of Palestine and Syria,
spoken of under the metonymy of the
names of their principal mountains.

The majority of the woodcuts are from
drawings on wood, by some of the ablest
artists, after my sketches, and may be distinguished by bearing the monogram "J,"
and the date when they were taken. In

selecting the other illustrations I have used a corresponding care.

Of Appendix No. 1, Mr. Catafago and I can truly say, "*We* did it;" while I can as truly add, "Mine was a *wee* share."

In Appendix No. 2, I have collected such of my jottings in verse as are directly associated with the scenes or incidents of the journey. To these, with the hope that, by the Lord's blessing, (without which nothing is good) my book will not have been written in vain, I will only add the following :—

ACROSTIC.

T here's a land, 'tis the fairest that rivulets nourish,
H er stones furnish iron, her mountains yield brass ;
A land where the vine and the fig-tree do flourish,
T here flow milk and honey which none can surpass.

G od gave unto Israel this land to inhabit,
O n before them the hornet He sent to destroy ;
O utcasting, in judgment, the Hivite and Hittite,
D efending His people, their blessing His joy.
L ong time in the desert their manners provoked Him,
Y et conquest and praising He made their employ.

M oved not by their sins from His word to their fathers,
O r aught to forego which His love had devised ;
U pon them descendeth, while daily each gathers,
N ew manna from heaven. E'en this is despised.
T he rock, at His bidding, them water provideth,
A nd all of their need is supplied by His hand ;
I n front, by the pillar, Jehovah them guideth,
N or fail they to enter the fair promised land.

A nd there, in the fulness of time, is presented
N one other than God in the flesh manifested,
D escending from glory to die on the tree.

L o ! scattered and driven, beneath the whole heaven,
E ach one upon whom was the judgment called down
"B e vengeance outpoured on us and our children,
A cross who appoint Him, and thorns for a crown."
N one the less shall His mercy by them yet be tasted,
O n Olivet's mount, when His feet shall have rested,
N o more to forsake Him, shall Israel return.

J.

London, 24*th November*, 1873.

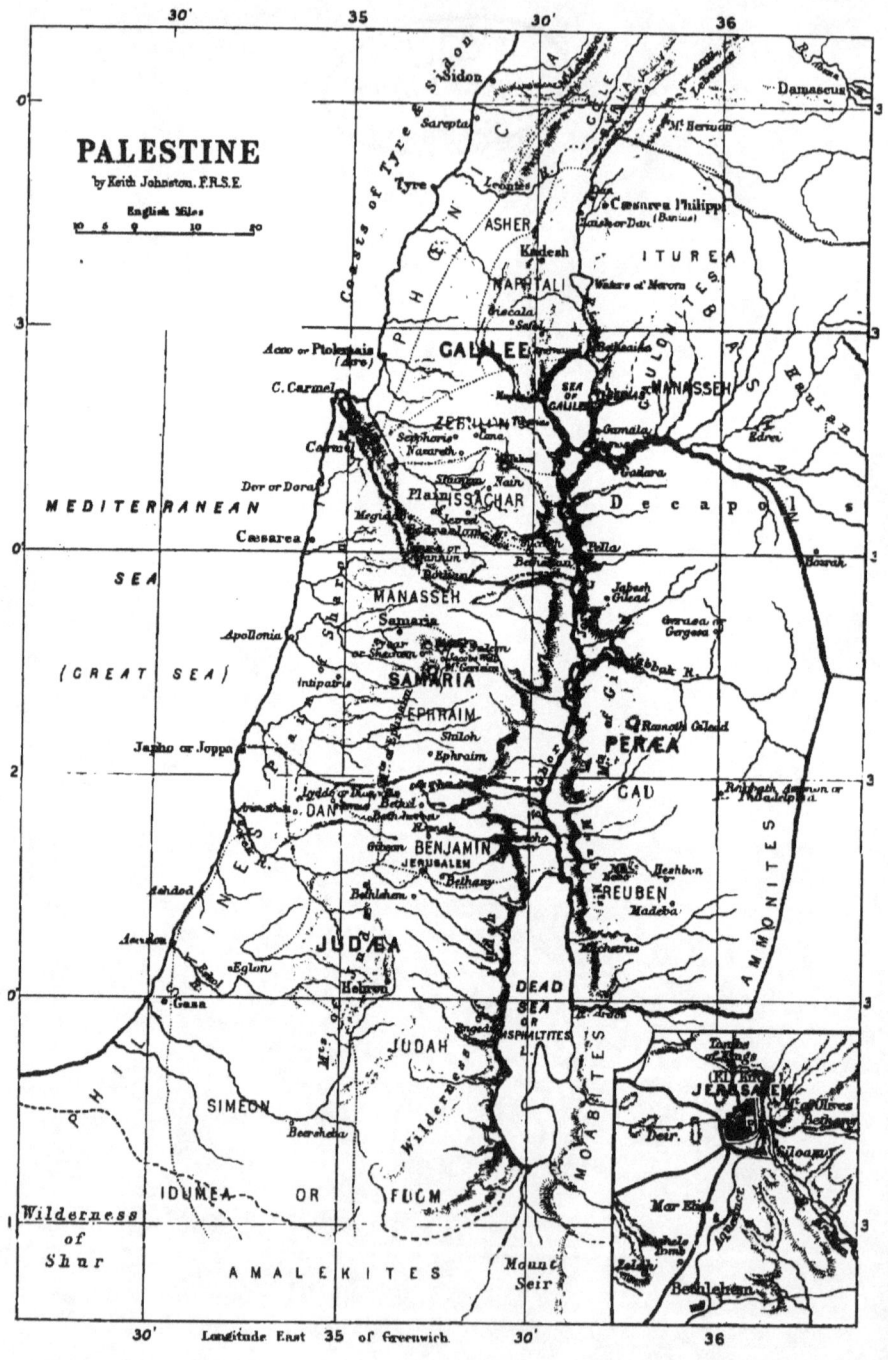

That Goodly Mountain and Lebanon.

CHAPTER I.

LONDON TO BRINDISI.

" For the next fortnight I expect to be travelling as fast as I can to Jerusalem," are words which I remember addressing to some of the children of my Sunday school, assembled the last evening in July 1872, and which were more than fulfilled, as, a fortnight after, I spent my third evening in the ancient capital of the land of Israel. On the morning following the school meeting,

Thursday, August 1st, I left London. At the Cannon Street station were three friends who I knew took a prayerful interest in my journey, and by whom I was enabled to send a last message to my family.

Familiar scenes were passed as the train hurried on to Dover; whence, as the steamer got away, I noticed the foam marking her way across the sea. Thus it is with travellers across the sea of life :

B

the path we trace is not only known to Him who searcheth the heart, but even by our fellow-men our ways and example are noticed. So Longfellow speaks of "Footprints on the sands of time":—

> "Footprints, that perhaps another,
>   Sailing o'er life's solemn main,
> A forlorn and shipwreck'd brother,
>   Seeing, shall take heart again."

Landed at Calais, I soon entered the train, and, after a little delay, was on my way to Paris. At Amiens the porters announced, "*Vingt-cinq minutes d'arrêt,*" which enabled me to take some refreshment. From the train, as well as in Paris, I observed many instances of destruction to public and other buildings wrought by the late war.

Leaving by the night train, and running through Mâcon soon after daylight, in a few hours more I obtained my first view of the Alps with their terraces of vines, carried from the feet to considerable heights up the mountain sides, the rich growth of trees, the snow-covered tops, and the cascades leaping and pouring into the valleys beneath. Through such lovely scenes of nature, I hastened towards one of the most recent of the achievements of human skill and labour—the Mont Cenis tunnel.

A short distance before reaching the tunnel, the

train stopped and the travellers were requested to
alight, a landslip from the mountain side having
buried a portion of the railway. The luggage was
transferred to mule carts, and we (the passengers)
went on foot to the other end of the obstruction.
Several peasants walked with us, earning a little
by carrying some of our smaller parcels. One
woman I noticed especially, who sought for gain
not only by her industry, but also by telling some
pitiable story—whether it was that the landslip
had involved her in the loss of friends or property,
through not understanding her *patois*, I did not
discover, but all the circumstances together enable
me to accompany the poet in the stanza :

> "I've been among the mighty Alps,
>   And wandered through their vales ;
>   And heard the honest mountaineers
>   Relate their dismal tales."

In the course of this walk, we passed other
peasants to whom the landslip had proved a source
of gain, as we saw them splitting some pieces of
slaty rock, which had been brought down, into
slabs for roofing their cottages ; while at the point
where the line was again clear, another had opened
a buffet under a canvas awning, where he and his
industrious wife were selling bread, butter, fruit,

and small beer. The railway company had improvised a waiting room out of some tarpaulins
stretched over an apple tree which one of the
officials, with the light-heartedness usual in his
countrymen, called ' *Le bureau de tente.*'

After we had waited a few minutes, greatly enjoying the Alpine air and scenery, the train from
Italy came up, and we and our luggage took the
place of the newly arrived.

Again setting out, we were soon perceptibly
rising high above the level of the valleys through
which we had been running, and having attained
by means of zig-zag slopes to the height of 4050
feet above sea level, as appeared from the instruments carried by a fellow-traveller, in a rather
humid atmosphere of 67° temperature, we entered
the great tunnel, the passage through which occupied seventeen minutes. Emerged on the Italian
side, the train descended similar slopes to those by
which we had risen to its entrance.

Having looked on the pleasing Italian land-
scapes, so often and well described, we reached
Turin about an hour after sunset, where a small
break in the journey again occurred, to our
comfort.

Having taken refreshments and a ticket, I

4   BUREAU DE TENTE.

entered the Italian night train for Bologna, two
of my new travelling companions being fellow-
countrymen, and the rest French and Italian.

Perhaps the circumstances of night travelling
are specially calculated to set one noticing the
national and other characteristics of one's companions. I confess that such was the effect upon
me. Our compartment was fitted with four
double seats, and, as we were seven in number,
only one of us had the double accommodation.
In him I recognised an Englishman and addressed him with, " *Monsieur est Anglais, je crois ?*"
Being affirmatively answered, I rejoined, " *Et moi
aussi.*" Although his position compared so favour-
ably with ours, he proceeded to complain, in
honest English, of the want of accommodation,
the inconvenient heat of the carriage, &c. My
reflection was that while in many things which
are good and right, the Englishman commonly
excels, he does so too in the equivocal property of
grumbling. Nor was this the only occasion
during my journey when this propensity of my
countrymen was brought to my mind.

As the night wore on, the French, Italian, and
English compliments, questions, and complaints
sank into a common silence, disturbed only at very

occasional intervals till we reached Bologna, where we changed for the South Italian line. The train was ready to start as soon as the passengers and their luggage could be transferred from ours. This being done, my proneness to make comparisons was subject to less temptation, as from this point to Brindisi my companions were all Italian.

Soon after dawn we had the Gulf of Venice in view on our left, and the Apennines on our right. The aspect seaward and landward was alike of the most lovely character as we ran through Sinigaglia and came to a few minutes' rest at Ancona.

Here and at other stations this day I made unsuccessful attempts to get breakfast or luncheon, and was thankful for the provision made before reaching Turin, the preceding evening, in the purchase of a small bottle of the country wine and a few biscuits which, with the addition of a little fruit bought in Ancona, was my diet for the day, until, at midnight, I got supper in the Great East India Hotel, Brindisi. Nor do I think my want of success was wholly due to my own awkwardness, as a native fellow traveller from Bologna to Brindisi fared no better, and did not despise some of my *biscuits à vanille* in the absence of more worthy food. And now, to confess, wo two, while sole occupants of the carriage for an hour or more, illustrated the common ability of English and Italian to grumble under certain conditions.

As we advanced southward, the bathers in the Adriatic, with their coarse broad-brimmed steeple-shaped hats, the olive trees, the vines, differing in the style of their training from those we had seen in France and especially from some we saw after-wards, when homeward bound, in the Burgundy district; these successively came under notice, also the peasants at the railway station offering for sale :

till both daylight and twilight having departed, the anxiety to reach our *ultima Thule* increased.

Under these circumstances I had fallen asleep, and was awakened by a shake of the shoulder from an official who had entered the train while in motion and said something in Italian, which, with returning consciousness, I rightly guessed and said : " *Ah ! Monsieur, vous demandes mon billet, le voici.*" Whether he replied, " *Grázia, Signore,*" or no, I either did not notice or have forgotten, but the confirmation which my *compagnon de royage* gave of my impression that we might now prepare to alight was very cheering, and the train soon stopping, with mutual wishes for " *Bon royage,*" we parted.

As I was being driven to the Great East India Hotel, among the objects which drew my attention in the dim light, as we passed by a landing place, was one that I thought I recognised as a pile of 68 lb. shot, but a closer regard and inquiry proved it to be a heap of water melons. Things are not always so bad as they seem at first.

By midnight I was seated, taking my supper in the hotel, with the promise of a bath at 7 a.m., and I need hardly say how delightful it was, for the first time since Thursday morning, to undress, wash, sleep, and bathe.

Brindisi I explored but very little, for it being Lord's-day, I felt small inclination to visit its classical, ecclesiastical, or other relics, and contented myself before breakfast with a stroll along the quay, where the winkle catcher and a few bathers were all I met.

The excellent arrangements of the hotel demand, I think, a passing word which I would express thus, " Everything very good." My worthy host (M. Bruschetti) was very communicative and ready to second the *timide avis* which had been given to me, not sparingly, before leaving England. To explain : some of my friends, notably a gentleman who had resided four or five years in Syria, sought to dissuade me from attempting the journey during the heat of August. This good friend had even suggested to my wife, that the desire of obtaining a grave in Palestine had influenced me in the choice of time. Such reasoning from so high an authority was of course notable; but a confutation was at hand, from our family physician, himself once a resident for a longer period in the same climate. While admitting the considerable heat which I might expect to encounter, he gave as his opinion that by avoiding, when practicable, the mid-day exposure, and conforming to the diet of the country, I might hope, with the blessing of God, to escape those ills which some had not been backward to foretell as the penalty of my rashness. Seated beside mine host in the lobby of the hotel, I was interrogated somewhat thus :

Host.   Where do you intend going?

J.   To Palestine and Syria.

H.   What! at this season?

J.   Yes! at this season.

H.   But you will find the heat too great.

J.   I hope not.

H.   Take my advice, and stay in Europe till between November and January, and then take your journey into Palestine; it will be much safer.

J.   But I have made my arrangements.

H.   Very true; but if you should die, of what use would your arrangements be?

J.   Well, I hope to make the journey now, and in three or four weeks' time to revisit you in as good health as you see me at present.

H.   If so, I shall be *très-content*.

J.   *Merci, Monsieur.*

There being another English traveller in the hotel, we arranged to dine together, and so broke a little from the foreign and fashionable elements around, as we talked freely of those homelier and more profitable scenes with which we were both familiar.   By this time the P. and O. boat "Massilia," Captain Christian, was moored alongside the quay, awaiting passengers for Alexandria. At the hour of sunset a juvenile military band arrived, marching and playing, and took their stand on the quay. They played for an hour or more, and I took the opportunity, after expressing to the master my admiration of the performance of his pupils, to ask him to accept from the humble author, some lines which speak of "a river that's flowing of pure living water." This he did with Continental politeness.

Now were to be seen priests and people, the élite and mediocre of Brindisi, promenading and enjoying the swellings of the music, the tide, and the evening breeze. *Quant à moi*, I felt drawn to the British steamer which was to be my home for about three days; so taking leave of mine host, I ordered my goods to be removed on board the " Massilia," and saw them duly stowed in my cabin.

My outfit comprised three flannel shirts, six pairs of socks, &c., a tourist's suit in Scotch tweed and one in brown holland, a Scotch bonnet, and a broad brimmed hat with thick linen puggaree. My *necessaries* of the above class were carried in two saddle-bags. I took also a Scotch plaid, macintosh coat, and a sun umbrella; a portable filter, thermometer, camera and dry collodion plates (the latter I essayed to use but once, and then without success): a portmanteau, containing twelve Arabic copies of each of the Gospels, two or three dozen knives and scissors, key-rings, &c.

Beside these I had a small tent well fitted to shelter two people. This I had purchased on the strong recommendation of the friend whose advice with respect to delaying the journey I have already mentioned, but it did not accompany me beyond Nablûs, and was not once used, though I trust that in the hands of those with whom I left it, it will yet be very useful, in which case I too shall be *très-content*.

There yet remain to be mentioned a case of medicines, two brandy flasks, sketch-book, water colours, note-book, and pocket Bible. One of the brandy flasks I found broken the first time of opening my portmanteau, but this was nothing serious, as about three-quarters of the contents of the other were brought home; the medicines were not opened, except at the time of a little sea-sickness, the residue being left behind for others. The same with two pots of Liebig's extract, and the balance of a tin of cocoa essence. Thus relieved of the care of sundry things which were found to be unnecessary, I had the more room to spare for a few relics which I was desirous of bringing to England from the Holy Land.

VIA APPIA—NEAR ROME.

13

CHAPTER II.

HAVING been introduced to my berth and taken a stroll on the "Massilia's" after-deck, I made good acquaintance with my new quarters in a night's sleep, from which I was not fairly roused until the wash-deck donkey pump, which happened to be fixed near my berth and was started every morning at 5 o'clock, by its rapid and noisy alternations, bade me think of the engagements of another day.

Though not fairly roused till this hour, I had not been altogether unobservant of the coming on board of the arrivals from England by the last opportunity, to whom the breakfast hour brought me an introduction.

About 7.30 a.m., the steamer put out from Brindisi; when a German fellow traveller pointed out to me the ancient Roman column, standing where for centuries, if not millenniums, it has marked the termination of Via Appia, the commencement of which was at the Forum of Rome. To the Christian, Via Appia must always be interesting in connection with the journey of the

Apostle Paul towards Rome along that highway from the place called "the Three Taverns." (Acts xxviii. 15.) The Latin name for Brindisi was Brundusium.

Our steamer carried the Bombay mail, and among my companions were several of Her Majesty's Indian civil servants returning to duty after furlough; there were also a colonel and his daughter in the company, and in addition we had French and Armenian companions.

Going into the saloon after breakfast to attempt some writing, I was soon drawn into conversation with a gentleman whose society I shared a good deal afterwards, I trust not altogether un-profitably. The same evening we paced the deck together till after the night-watch had put out the cabin-lights, so that we had to turn in, in the dark. Our good captain, when duties did not prevent, was always ready to do and say anything that would contribute to our comfort and entertainment.

Notwithstanding the after-deck awning and other palliatives, it was not difficult to appreciate somewhat the warmer climate of the Mediterranean as compared with England.

I think it was on Tuesday, the 6th of August,

that several of us were upset by the motion of the
steamer, but not seriously, except in the case of a
French boy whose suffering was considerable, and
painful to witness. On that day, between 2 and
3 p.m., we were off Cape Matapan.

Wednesday, 7th, 7 a.m. In sight of Candia,
that is, Crete, an island well suited to direct our
thoughts and reading to the voyage of the Apostle
Paul when he, too, sailed under Crete. (Acts
xxvii. 7.)

We expected at this time to fall in with the
homeward bound P. and O. steamer, but she
seems to have passed us in the night; however
at 8.45 a.m., just before the ringing of the
breakfast bell, we were passing the Austrian
Lloyd's steamer "Aurora." Being a screw, she
compared unfavourably with us for steadiness.
The compensating action of paddles is sufficiently
well established and too obvious to require any
explanation.

As she neared us, she ran up the Austrian flag
to the gaff, which was responded to by our hoisting
the ensign, and when abreast of each other, the
three times dipping and hoisting was a sufficiently
pleasing incident to entertain one, like myself,
witnessing this international courtesy for the first
time.

The particulars of the ship's run posted outside the captain's cabin each day at noon, assumed, of course, a growing interest. The following is a copy, completed to the hour of noon of the day (Thursday, 8th) we reached Alexandria.

Date.	Lat.	Long.	Run.	Distance from Alexandria.
August 6	36 26 N.	21 35 E.	246	520
7	33 48	25 23	244	276
8	31 26	29 18	245	31

Thursday, August 8th, 1.13 p.m. Sea gulls. We are not far from port. The Egyptian coast is in sight. As we near the harbour, the native pilot boats, the harbour improvement works, the Khedive's flour mills, appearing in the distance like a number of tarantulas, and the palace on the shore, deserted since the fire, but still a magni-

ficent pile, are among the features of Alexandria
which first strike one's notice.

We took a pilot on board, and proceeded at
easy speed, the pilot standing beside the captain
on the bridge, and an able-bodied British seaman
on either paddle-box heaving the lead, so that we
had every human assurance that we should not
run upon a sand-bank.

These pilots, in their swift-sailing, clean-painted
boats, which they handle with great dexterity,
give a favourable first impression of the race to
which they belong, and of which the acquaintance
with other types is so soon to be made on shore.

The steamer having been brought to an anchor,
was visited by the Custom-House and quarantine
officials; and being reported "all right" we
were at liberty to land. And now, individual
interests begin to assert themselves above those
which are common to all. Friendships contracted
on board claim a farewell shake of the hand, with
a promise, in some cases, to write. "Good bye,
Captain; whenever I need to cross the Mediterranean I shall be happy to do so on board any
steamer you may be commanding."

Captain. "I should be very happy to take
charge of you; good bye!"

c

Never having landed in Alexandria before, but
having heard much of the pitiable position of
the newly-arrived among the Arab boatmen and
donkey boys, I sought the kind assistance of my
German fellow-traveller — who had drawn my
attention to the Roman column at Brindisi, as we
left that port, and continually, during the voyage,
contributed information which he had obtained
by his readings of books and men—who was well
accustomed to the business of landing, and made
with him the compact, as did also another, that
we should land together, he paying the boatman,
and we to reimburse him in our shares.

Thus favoured, I reached the landing-place
with a minimum of trouble and expense; but here
we were separated, while my things were taken
to *theirs*, and I put on shore on *my* side of the
Custom-House.

I produced my passport to an official, and was
by him referred to another for instructions.
After a few questions, I was told that I must
apply for my passport next morning at the
British consulate (French, as on most of these
occasions, being the medium of conversation);
but I urged the value of time in my case, and
the necessity which lay upon me to leave next
morning for Jaffa.

While thus pleading my own cause, I was accosted from the other side by a smart-looking man, in a costume half Arab, half Greek (he was a dragoman), thus:

D. " You English gentleman ?"

J. " Yes."

D. " My business to look after English gentleman."

J. "Then will you please to look after me?"

Upon this he addressed the Custom - House official in about three quarters of a page of Arabic. Without further parley, my name was marked in the list, my passport returned, a ticket to frank me through the gate was put into my hand, and with my dragoman for a guide, I was led up to a bench loaded with travellers' goods of all descriptions, including, as I soon discovered, every one of my own. I pointed out to the dragoman which were mine, and, instructed by him, a porter soon placed them all together, and a few words having passed between the dragoman and an official which, from the strangeness of the tongue in which they were spoken and the general confusion, I could neither understand nor guess, I saw the porter was loading himself with the things (indeed he exceeded his duty, for he had included some one

else's portmanteau), and was on his way to the
outer gate. (These men carry great weights,
passing a rope round their load, and supporting it
against the forehead by a noose, the running end
of which they hold in their right hand.)

I pointed out the porter's mistake to the dragoman but was told not to trouble myself, and we
passed through the gate to the carriage. The
strange portmanteau was returned by the porter,
and, I having once more counted my things, we
drove away through the bazaars of Alexandria.

Now, I could realise that I was in the *East!*
The drawings of Roberts and Bartlett, and the
descriptions of several writers had prepared me to
recognize many of the features in the scene; but,
however true the picture or description, there
remains much to be supplemented by experience:
the solidity and movement of the objects, the
changing expressions, the temperature, the sounds
and odours of the eastern city.

So rapidly had one novelty succeeded upon
another, that we had passed through two or three
streets before I was sufficiently collected to recall
and remark to my dragoman that the Custom-
House officers had not examined my things.
"No," said he, "that what me for; I give them

bakhsheesh; they no look at your things." In another moment or two I said, " But I have not told you which hotel to take me to."

D. "Oh! I know; British Hotel."

The truth is he had been down to the landing-place and ascertained more facts concerning me than, in the confusion of things, I had managed to remember about myself. Reaching the hotel and stowing the luggage, he proposed a donkey ride. In this again he was right; the recollection of luncheon on board the steamer was still sufficiently good to last me for two or three hours.

Thereupon he went into the square to choose donkeys. Before we reached the stand, the boys began to clamour for us to take their animals, and, but for my dragoman with his stick and words of authority, I should, no doubt, have presented for some time that picture of helplessness which one has often heard described. He dealt whacks and pokes upon donkeys and boys till, as if by magic, a space was cleared around the best donkey of the group, which he requested me to mount.

This done, he secured the next best for himself, and with a boy running behind, followed for a short distance by some of the others and the shouts of all, we trotted away through streets and roads flanked with walls, above which palm and other trees were waving, till we reached "Pompey's Pillar."

This monument, which by the critical is referred to the period of Diocletian and not to that of him whose name it has long borne, has a total height of eighty-eight and a half feet, and the shaft is a monolith seventy-five feet long; while to gaze at it from a vantage ground near its base imparts feelings of amazement at the skill and power of its constructors.

A child from a group of Bedouins came to us and offered me a piece of granite, purporting to be broken off the column, which it probably was; but genuine, spurious, or doubtful, I declined it.

From the pillar we turned in the direction of Cleopatra's Needle, a monument of superior antiquity. On our way there, the dragoman proposed a halt at a canteen where bottled English beer was to be obtained. Chairs were placed, and while the storekeeper was opening a bottle, my cicerone slipped off his shoes and flapped the dust from his feet with a handkerchief. He next prepared a cigarette, lighted it, drew a whiff or two and offered it to me; but I was no more amenable to the attractions of smoke than of granite, so, endeavouring to decline his offer as politely as it was made, and taking as much of the ale as I required, I suggested giving the remainder in my glass to the donkey boy. My dragoman, however, ruled that ale was not good for donkey boys, and that if I really did not wish for more, he would not decline it himself.

Thus recruited, we re-mounted and continued our way to Cleopatra's Needle. This is also pronounced to be a misnomer; the obelisk, which is about seventy feet high, being referred to the period of Rameses the Great.

The donkey boy watched his opportunity, when the dragoman's attention was drawn away, to make a gentle but persuasive request for *bakhsheesh* while the dragoman did not fail to assure me of his own qualifications, the testimonials he could produce, and how happy he would be to take charge of myself and all the family to almost any part of Africa or Asia, and began to enumerate the languages which he could speak. I remarked, "You have Chinese sometimes passing through Alexandria?"

D. "Oh! yes; I speak Chinese."

J. "*Haou pang yiu ya tsing tsing.*"*

* 好 朋 友 呀 請 請. How are you, my good friend?

D. " Yes, Chinaman say, ' *Chin chin.*' "

J. " *Sien sang shwo Kwan hwa mo ?*"*

D. "I no talk much Chinese."

He expressed the hope that I would furnish him with a testimonial, adding, " English gentleman ask me what is my name? I say ' Adam :' you know, Adam, the father of everybody! English gentleman ask me, ' Adam what?' I say, 'Adam, Eve ; you know, the mother of everybody.' " I understood him that these were his metaphorical names, from which it was to be inferred that whoever employed him as their dragoman, he would be as good as father and mother to them.

Having ridden beside one of the mouths of the Nile (if under that name we may speak of the canal), looked at the boats, and visited a friend in the city, we dismissed the donkeys and strolled back to the hotel. I told Adam that I should not require his help again till next morning, and having given me his fatherly counsel not to trust myself away from the hotel without my Mentor, which advice I willingly acted on, he took leave and I prepared for dinner.

How great the luxury to get rid of coat and

* 先生說官話麼. Do you speak Mandarin ?

waistcoat, pour water into the basin, plunge the face therein, find the sponge and get a wash.

This done, the sofa beside the opened window, which admitted the sea breeze, not too cool to be safe, proved so alluring that I took to it, leaving the outer garments where I had hung them.

Scarcely had I stretched myself there when, with a shrill hum, mosquito number one announced himself, and settled on my forehead. I brushed him off, but either he returned or another came to the attack ; so I abandoned the situation, dressed and repaired to the dining room.

The table at which I sat was chiefly occupied by North British mechanics in the employ of the Khedive, whose work lay principally in the Egyptian fleet and the Khedive's steam yachts. As I was able to inform them of the arrival in England, before my departure, of one of their number by whom I had been recommended to the hotel, I was the more speedily at home, and, my appetite having been considerably sharpened, the new situation did not, after all, compare very badly with the former. I must have been unusually tired, for not long after dinner I yielded to an inclination for the greater quiet of my room, where, before I suspected, I fell into a sound sleep,

from which awaking and finding that an hour or
two had slipped away, I returned to the coffee
room, said good night to those whom I met, and,
with an *Ebenezer* and a *Hallelujah*, settled myself
for the night within the mosquito curtains.

Thoroughly refreshed, I was down stairs by
6 a.m., the time appointed for Adam to accompany
me to the bath. His ideas of punctuality, however, gave me an opportunity of musing on a
morning in Alexandria. The goats going about
to be milked at the customers' doors, the examples
of nations and creeds which I was not expert
enough to recognize and name, and many other
things engaging my attention.

Through this vista of the unknown, I at length
discerned Adam approaching. My rebukes and
his apologies being duly given and received, we
were soon taking a Turkish bath, the first of four
which I had in the East, the other three being re-
spectively in Nablûs, Damascus, and again in
Alexandria.

I was not quite a stranger to this form of bath ;
my English experience therewith had not yielded
much benefit, but with respect to those I took in
Egypt, Palestine, and Syria, the good which I
each time derived was of the most unmistakable

kind. The most luxurious of them all was that
in Damascus, so I will leave further remarks till
we reach the City of the Damascenes, when, perhaps, faithful memory will record her praises.

From the bath we directed our steps, to the
American Mission premises, and were very kindly
received by the missionaries. About half an hour
after our arrival, school was opened with a hymn
and prayer in Arabic; after which it was my privilege to address the dear children a few words
from the text, "God is love;" the missionary
interpreting the same to them. Some of the boys
knew English sufficiently well to sing a verse or
two of a hymn, copies of which were distributed
among them.

Time pressing, I took my leave, a copy of the
Arabic hymn book from which the first hymn had
been sung, being presented to me as a memento of
my visit.

Hymn (being a paraphrase of Psalm xxiii.) sung
by the children of the American Mission School,
Alexandria, Friday, August 9th, 1872. Tune:
an adaptation of "Happy Day!"

> "Arraboo yaràani fala,
> Yaàozooni sheion wala;
> Wafi makani khoodraten
> Yurbudni rabu-l-ola.

Yaroodu nafsi hadian,
Kalbi elihi sooboola;
Fafi zilalil mowti in
Masheitoo la akhsha-l-bala.

Aasahoo maâ ôokazihi,
Hooma yuâazianini;
Rahmatahoo wa khyrahoo,
Lildahri yatbaâanini.

Bildohni rasi kad tala,
Wakad sakani murwiyan;
Famasakni fi bytihi,
Tool-ul mada mohtamiyan."

While the address was being given, Adam stood
waiting at one of the doors, and a veiled woman
appeared listening at the other. The accompanying sketch I made from memory after leaving the
school, on board the steamer.

We next called at the office of the Austrian
Lloyd's steam-ship company, to engage my place
on board the Jaffa boat, and as her time for leaving
was 11 a.m., it was necessary to use all possible
despatch in returning to the hotel, where I made
a hasty breakfast, during which Adam was most
useful and zealous in trussing up my things and
stowing them in the carriage; so, having settled
with the landlady, we set out for the quay.

28   MISSION SCHOOL—ALEXANDRIA.

On our way, I noticed a money changer's stall, so stopped the carriage and asked Adam to get me small change for a five-franc piece; this he did, but I was struck with the impalpable lightness of the little silver pieces which he brought me, in contrast with the respectable piece I had given for them. My intention in obtaining the change was that I might be furnished with small *bakhsheesh* for such examples of the Arab boys as I might meet in Jaffa and elsewhere.

Leaving all fiscal arrangements to Adam, I was soon on board the Austrian steamer "Urano," where, having obtained my ticket (I had not sufficient money with when I called at the office earlier in the day), stowed my things and settled with Adam, he left me, promising to watch for my return, and shortly after we were steaming out of the harbour.

CHAPTER III.

BEING the only passenger on board the "Urano" who had engaged first class, I should have been rather solitary but for the different rules of the Austrian Lloyd's steamers as compared with the P. and O. In the latter service it is forbidden for second-class passengers to use the after-deck for promenade, but in the Austrian Lloyd's and French Messageries' boats this rule does not obtain; so that I had a few companions, notably two Romish priests, an Italian corn merchant, and an Italian student. A very amiable Arab also joined us sometimes; this man accepted a copy of one of the Gospels in Arabic from me, and, in spite of the strangeness of our tongues, we endeavoured to discourse.

The student was my principal companion. It was exceedingly interesting, though painful, to contemplate the groups of Mahometans and Jewish pilgrims on the middle deck; to see the latter poring over their Hebrew books, while denying "Him of whom Moses in the law and the pro-

phets did write, Jesus of Nazareth " (John i. 45),
and the former, at the hour of prayer, spreading
their mats and garments, and, their faces toward
Mecca, with unshod feet, going through their
prostrations and bowings and the repetitions of
their prayers.

The Mahometans pray five times in the day :
first at day-break, secondly at noon, thirdly in the
afternoon, fourthly in the evening, and fifthly at
the first watch of the night.

At dinner I occupied the honourable seat on the
captain's right, for the sufficient reason that there
was no one else to take it. Italian is the official
language on board the Austrian steamers ; but
having no acquaintance with it, I availed myself
of the international French, the utility of which I
soon proved.

On board the English boats, to which my experience had been hitherto confined, all wine is
ordered through the steward. On the table was
some which I noticed the captain, doctor, and first
officer, my only dinner companions, helped themselves from, and, suspecting that I was free to take
some too, to make all plain sailing, I addressed
the captain, " *Cela est-il pour moi, Capitaine ?*

Captain. " *Ah ! certainement, Monsieur*," passing
me the wine.

The first officer, though reserved in manner, was evidently a man of a kind disposition ; for, after breakfast and dinner, he would be seen repairing to the side of the after-deck and handing to some of the children among the Arab deck passengers in the gangways below, some fruit which he had saved for them from the table ; indeed, in speaking to me about them he was unsparing in his praises of their *" instinct très naturel."*

The first evening on board, the stars shining very brightly, the young Italian and I were drawn into conversation upon astronomy. Naturally *ursa major* and *ursa minor* took a principal place in the dialogue, which led to his inquiring, " *Que dit-on en anglais pour ' ours' ?*"

J. " Bear" (spelling it with English and French pronunciations of the letters B, E, A, R, Ba, ā, ah, ar). This done, we advanced to *"ursa major,"* greater bear, and *" ursa minor,"* smaller bear. At about this point, the first-class passengers' tea-bell rung, so they responded and their companion sought his separate entertainment.

I had not long returned to the deck after tea, before I was rejoined by my friend with the confession, *"J'ai déjà oublié le mot anglais pour 'ours,' "* so the lesson had to be gone over again.

33   PORT SAID—ENTRANCE TO SUEZ CANAL.

Saturday 10th, 6 a.m. Looking out of my cabin window, I espied the breakwater of Port Saïd, constructed of manufactured stone blocks, similar to some which we had seen in the Alexandrian harbour improvements.

While I was dressing, we were steaming at easy speed between the outworks of that great engineering achievement—the Suez Canal; until, the steamer being anchored, she commenced discharging some of her cargo and loading with other.

Having taken coffee, the young Italian and I landed for an exploration of the port. We made our way through the streets and purlieus, over road and sand, passing a small camp of Bedouins, to the lighthouse, from the gallery of which I took a sketch of the entrance to the canal, with our steamer and the Turkish guard-ship.

The ascent of the lighthouse tower is made by means of two hundred and eighty stone steps, and the light is produced from a monster magneto-galvanic machine, worked by a six horse power steam engine; the engine and instruments being in duplicate, so that if any part be under repair, the light may not be suspended. I was told that the working expenses are found to be so high,

that it is contemplated superseding the electric
with an oil light.

We returned to the boat and were rowed a short
distance into the canal, passing the engineers' and
other sheds on shore, and being amused by the
great porpoises (the largest that I saw in the
Mediterranean) rolling about.

Again on board the steamer, the rest of the day
passed much the same as the one before, saving
that I made the acquaintance of the Romish
priests. Port Saïd presents at one view, some of
the greatest diversities. The camel ("ship of
the desert") unloading into the Arab craft, the
Bedouin from his native wilds, extending his
wanderings to this vicinity of Western civilisation,
the flags, the people and customs of many nations,
the important engineering works for construction
and maintenance of the great highway, and the
coming and going of monster steamers, with the
modern Pharos and its electric revolving light, to
guide them to its entrance.

At 4 p.m., the steam ship, "Agra,"* captain

* As this page is in type, a telegram announces the loss
of the "Agra," through striking on rocks outside the harbour of Galle, when on her sixth voyage homeward from
Calcutta, under the command of Captain John Gibb. No
lives lost.

35   ARAB SETTING HIS WATCH.

Alexander Boyd, homeward bound from Akyab, with a complete cargo of rice, dropped her anchor, and shortly afterwards another English steamer followed in her wake.

At 5 p.m., we left the port, entering upon the last portion of our outward-bound voyage, at a very delightful period of a truly bright day. As the sun was on the point of disappearing, I was interested in watching our amiable Arab friend setting his watch to 12 o'clock. This circumstance naturally brought to my mind many scriptural references to the calculation of time, from the words in Genesis i. 5, "And the evening and the morning were the first day," to those in Acts ii. 15, "These are not drunken as ye suppose, seeing it is but the third hour of the day." (About our 9 a.m.) And in the next chapter, verse 1, "Peter and John went up together into the temple at the hour of prayer, being the ninth hour." (About our 3 p.m.)

Sunday 11th, 6 a.m. In sight of the coast of Palestine—the land promised to Abraham and to his seed after him, where is the mountain upon which was the trial of his faith, where Isaac and Jacob dwelt in tents, and into the possession of which the children of Israel were led under Moses and Joshua, to drive out thence the Canaanites and other inhabitants when the iniquity of the Amorites was full. The land of the judges and the kings; of David, the "man after God's own heart," and of Solomon his son, where the prophets delivered their messages, and where, in the fulness of time, Christ was born. How soon I may hope to tread the soil of that land and contemplate the words and ways of Him by whom came grace and truth, in the scenes where those words were spoken an those ways displayed!

The telescope is now frequently in demand as,

THE CARRIER DOVE OF PALESTINE.

first the general coast line, then some of the principal features of tree and rock, then of buildings, camels, and men, come into view. I exchange parting words with the Roman Catholic priests, and make my luggage all snug, ready for removal.

At 8 a.m., we are putting into Jaffa roadstead when a dove settles on the bow-sprit. Who could be so devoid of sentiment as not to hail it as a harbinger of peace from that country where our peace was made ? (Col. i. 20.)

Breakfast over, and the steamer brought to an anchor, the official communications with shore having first been made, the Arab boats are seen coming off in quest of employment. The glass is now directed to them, in expectation of recognising a familiar face. The boatmen swarm the deck, clamorous to be engaged. I take leave of the captain, young Italian, and first officer, and at last yield to the persuasions of an Arab and tell him that I am expecting to meet a Mr. El Karey.

Arab. Mr. El Karey is on the shore waiting for you; you mean Mr. El Karey of Nablûs?

J. Yes

The agreement is made, I conduct the boatman to my cabin, and call over the number of my

packages, " 1, 2, 3, 4, 5, 6," he and his man carry
them to the boat and I follow.

Scarcely have we pushed off from the steamer
than I am addressed from another boat: "Are
you Mr. Jenner?" "Yes." "Mr. El Karey
asked me to fetch you in this boat." "But I have
made a bargain with this man." "Very well;
then I will come into yours." In such circumstances, hearing your own name has a more than
ordinary effect. Mr. Floyd, for such was the name
of my interrogator, told me that Mr. El Karey
was fully expecting me, my letters having caused
him to look for me by the particular steamer in
which I had come.

As we neared the shore, it became evident that
we were to pass between two rocks, divided by
only a narrow channel, but the lusty Arab boatmen
pulled us through without any disaster, and very
soon we were sufficiently near the crowded quay
for me to pick out from a multitude the familiar
countenance of my dear friend, Mr. El Karey.

Having landed, and made and answered inquiries
for the welfare of friends in Nablûs and London, I
must introduce him to the reader. This I do in
an extract from an appeal on behalf of his mission
kindly furnished to me by Dr. Landels.

"Youhannah El Karey, the son of an Arab who was a member of the Greek Church in Nablûs, was at twelve years of age sent to the Protestant school in that place, where he was instructed in the truths of the gospel. He remained there between two and three years, when, owing to the persecution which arose against Christians at that time, he removed to Jerusalem, where he came in contact with the American baptist missionaries and was, by Mr. Jones, one of their number, baptized in the pool of Siloam. Although engaged in business and not formally connected with the mission, he took part in the work of the missionaries, by reading the word of God among his countrymen. While thus employed he met with the Rev. John Mills, F.R.G.S., of London, who has ever since taken the deepest interest in him. Feeling the want of a better education than he had received, especially in theology, he came to this country in 1859, and through the influence of Mr. Mills and other friends who had met him in Palestine (all of the Welsh Presbyterian Church) was admitted to the Baptist College, Pontypool, where he remained for about three years, and afterwards studied at Regent's Park under Drs. Angus and Davies for about a year and a half."

I was now under the guidance, not of father Adam, but of brother El Karey. His first act reminded me of the good Samaritan (I do not say it irreverently), for he set me upon his own beast and took me to an inn.

Mounted for the first time on an Arab horse, and being as unused to the mode in which they are usually handled, as he was to the English style of a taut rein, we made our way rather awkwardly through the streets and bazaars of Jaffa. These bazaars are exceedingly narrow, and show no distinction between roadway and footpath; passengers, mounted and on foot, and loaded camels push their way along, without any rule as to which side of you they pass. Add to this the shouts which were directed from all sides, and my utter inability to comprehend or reply, excepting at a hazard and in a barbarian tongue; imagine these things and in a measure you can appreciate my new situation.

At length (not so long as it seemed) we passed out of the town, and our party gathered more closely together, while I received a little instruction in the management of the rein for an Arab horse; so, in a little better order we reached the American Consulate.

It had been arranged that I should dine here,
Mr. El Karey adjourning to the house of Mr.
Floyd, with an understanding that I should rejoin
him after dinner. These arrangements were not
such as I should have made, but if the wisdom of
the plan was equal to the kindness of the intention,
then assuredly they were much better; and certainly the recollection of the hour spent with the
family and friends of the consul, is a very happy
one. As arranged, I rejoined Mr. El Karey at the
house of Mr. Floyd, of whom I take this opportunity to speak. He is a German, residing in one
of the houses of the American colony, and a dragoman, holding several excellent testimonials, including that of one of my personal friends who
formed one of a very large party that he accompanied officially. I have also heard the highest
opinion expressed of his qualifications for conducting travellers through the country, of the
justness of which I am further convinced by his
acquaintance. His name is Rolla Floyd.

Thus recruited, Mr. El Karey and I retraced
our steps to Jaffa. By the sandy roadside, just
outside the city, was a group of beggars, one or
two of them blind, and one, from the appearance
of his hands, I took to be a leper. Thus am I not

only in the land, but in the circumstances which surrounded the Son of man, who came to seek and to save that which was lost, at whose word the blind received their sight, the lame walked, the lepers were cleansed, the deaf heard, the dead were raised, and to the poor the gospel was preached. (Luke vii. 22.)

The pitiable voices of the blind men, their up-turned faces and outstretched hands presented most strikingly the scene outside Jericho when Jesus passed that way. "And as they departed from Jericho, a great multitude followed him. And, behold, two blind men, sitting by the way side, when they heard that Jesus passed by, cried out, saying, Have mercy on us, O Lord, thou son of David. And the multitude rebuked them, because they should hold their peace: but they cried the more, saying, Have mercy on us, O Lord, thou son of David. And Jesus stood still, and called them, and said, What will ye that I shall do unto you? They say unto him, Lord, that our eyes may be opened. So Jesus had compassion on them, and touched their eyes, and immediately their eyes received sight, and they followed him." (Matt. xx. 29—34.)

" Blind Bartimeus at the gates
Of Jericho in darkness waits ;
He hears the crowd ; he hears a breath
Say, " It is Christ of Nazareth ;"
And calls, in tones of agony,
'Ιησοῦ ἐλέησόν με !"

We passed by the cemetery and re-entered Jaffa. In connection with this cemetery, Mr. Floyd mentioned to me a recent circumstance which seems sufficiently apposite to the Old Testament expression " gathered to their fathers," to justify its insertion. A small party of Bedouins from a distance came to the place, bringing on one of their camels the dead body of a member of their tribe. They opened an old grave, and, uncovering the bones of its occupier, carefully laid them aside and interred the body of the recently departed, then replaced the bones of his father, as they stated them to be, filled in the earth and returned to their tribe.

We made our way to the house of a christian Arab, one who had formerly been an instrument of good to Mr. El Karey. He received us very cordially, and after the hot and dusty walk, it was exceedingly pleasant to rest on the divans in an airy apartment, with the windows opened sea-

. ward, and to speak together of Him whom through grace we owned as our common Lord and Saviour.

During the conversation a servant entered, bringing on a tray three tumblers ; in the first was some quince jelly, in the second some tea-spoons, and in the third some water.

These being offered, evidently for my refreshment, I felt a little perplexed as to the proper mode of partaking, so ventured on the safe experiment of sipping the water. My moderation evidently amused those who witnessed it, not excepting the maid servant. In my confusion, Mr. El Karey came to my aid, saying, " Here, my brother, let me shew you." So with one of the spoons he took a little of the jelly and then drank some water. The method was imparted in one lesson ; I followed his example, and, as the delicious jelly yielded to the water, it set free its sweetness which was combined with, and followed by, the pure cold water in a most refreshing way. Nehemiah viii. 10, was instantly and spontaneously brought to my mind, and I said, this must be what is referred to in scripture under the expression, "Drink the sweet." "Exactly so," said Mr. El Karey, " that is how we understand it."

45   HOUSE TOPS—JAFFA.

Through one of the windows of this room we had a view over part of the city; on one or two of the roofs I noticed a pile of old pottery, and on a wall adjoining, a pigeon was pluming his wings, which at once reminded me of the following paragraph from the pen of Miss Whately.

"The roofs are usually in a great state of litter, and were it not that Hasua (the seller of geeleh) gets a palm branch and makes a clearance once in a while, her roof would assuredly give way under the accumulation of rubbish. One thing never seemed cleared away, however, and that was the heap of old pitchers, sherds, and pots, that in these and similar houses are piled up in some corner; and there is a curious observation to be made in connection with this. A little before sunset numbers of pigeons suddenly emerge from behind the pitchers and other rubbish, where they had been sleeping in the heat of the day or pecking about to find food. They dart upwards and career through the air in large circles, their outspread wings catching the bright glow of the sun's slanting rays, so that they really resemble shining 'yellow gold.' Then as they wheel round, and are seen against the light, they appear as if turned into molten silver, most of them being pure white

or else very light-coloured. This may seem
fanciful, but the effect of light in these regions
is difficult to describe to those who have not seen
it, and evening after evening we watched the
circling flight of the doves and always observed
the same appearance." "Though ye have lien
amongst the pots, yet shall ye be as the wings of
a dove covered with silver and her feathers with
yellow gold." (Ps. lxviii. 18.)*

Our entertainer accompanied us to the reputed
site of the house of Simon, the tanner, by the sea-
side. In the court was a well, and Arabs engaged
in drawing water. Three or four venerable stones,
of an appearance which seemed to justify their
claim, were pointed out as a portion of the house
in situ.

I confess to attaching sufficient interest to the
tradition, that it was here the messengers from
Cornelius, the centurion, came, as he had been
instructed by the angel to send for one Simon,
whose surname was Peter, who should tell him
words whereby he and his house should be saved
(Acts x.), to cause me to pluck a leaf or two from
a fig-tree growing on the spot.

* "Ragged Life in Egypt," pages 32, 33.

I stepped somewhat heedlessly upon a mat, and was rather summarily requested to withdraw, as it was spread for the purpose of prayer, and not having put the shoes from off my feet, I might not tread there. Of course I immediately respected this request, coming though it did from a Mahometan; while the place of prayer so set apart on the house top, at the reputed scene of Peter's vision, was specially calculated to bring to my mind the incidents recorded in Acts x. To such a retreat from the physical and vocal strife of shipmen and tanners, merchants and labourers, camels and asses (if we may judge the past from present scenes) did the Apostle of the circumcision (Gal. ii., 7) betake himself. Here was he removed from the observation and thoughts of the multitude below; but not of the unseen multitude above (who desire to look into the things made known by the gospel. 1 Pet. i. 12.) One of their angelic number is sent to Cæsarea, not to tell Cornelius how he may be saved; the heavenly messenger is only commissioned to instruct Cornelius where he shall find one from among his fellow men who will tell him the glorious news. While these things are being accomplished and the messengers from Cornelius are making their way to the house

of Simon the tanner, Peter also is the subject of a
heavenly revelation, and by the vision of the sheet
let down from Heaven, wherein were all manner
of four footed beasts of the earth, and wild beasts
and creeping things, and fowls of the air, he is
taught that he must not call anything common or
unclean which God hath cleansed. His prejudices
broken down, he accompanies the messengers on
their return to Cæsarea and from his lips do the
Gentiles also, as the Jews at Pentecost (chap. ii.),
hear, and by the power of the Holy Ghost, receive the word of God.

We parted from our friend and returned to the
house of Mr. Floyd. As a night's journey was
before us, we were glad to pass an hour on bed
and sofa.

Soon after we had re-assembled, two Christian
teachers and five of the children from Miss
Arnott's Mission Schools came to visit us. They
sang some Arabic hymns very sweetly, and I
think all felt we had a very happy meeting. The
simplicity of the children's cheerful faces and native dress, the Christian demeanour and conversation of their teachers, the sweetness of the
singing, and withal the happy surprise of having
Sunday school come to you, contrasting with the

previous Lord's day's experience in Brindisi, where you could not even go to school, produced a happy impression that will not easily be forgotten.

After they had left, and as we were taking tea, at the moment the sun was setting, the muleteer announced himself, bringing the luggage-mule and my horse, and attended by his master's son, riding upon an ass. He was directed to the American Consulate for the luggage, and while he was loading the mule, we found opportunity to read together Psalm cxxi., in which are these words of happy assurance, "The Lord is thy keeper; the Lord is thy shade upon thy right hand. The sun shall not smite thee by day, nor the moon by night. The Lord shall preserve thee from all evil: he shall preserve thy soul. The Lord shall preserve thy going out and thy coming in from this time forth and even for evermore," and we commended ourselves in prayer to Him who is there set forth as the help of those who put their trust in Him.

> Through the day Thy love hath spared us,
> With Thy presence we are blest;
> Through the silent watches guard us,
> Let no foe our peace molest.
> Jesus, Thou our guardian be,
> Sweet it is to trust in Thee.

E

Pilgrims here on earth and strangers,
　Dwelling in the midst of foes ;
Us and ours preserve from dangers,
　In Thine arms may we repose.
And when life's short day is past,
　Rest with Thee in heaven at last.

CHAPTER IV.

JAFFA TO JERUSALEM.

WE were on the point of starting, when it occurred
to me that, although sufficiently clad for the temperature at the moment, I should find my brown-
holland coat an inadequate defence against the
colder air of night. In this opinion I was supported by others, whereupon the mule had to be
partly unladen, as the tweed coat could not otherwise be obtained.

About an hour after sunset we got upon the
road. Our course first lay between the extensive
gardens of Jaffa, but it was already too dark for
me to form a very distinct idea of their luxuriance, and although the grapes and figs of which
I had partaken during the day were such as to
give me a high estimate of those celebrated gardens, I was singularly unfortunate with respect
to the oranges; the only one I ate being about as
much inferior to the average examples which reach
the English market, as accounts lead us to
imagine their being superior. There was no
time to make a further proof and like, most of

my readers I too depend upon imagination. The moon, which was near her first quarter, had set early in the night and, as many clouds were in the sky, it was a decidedly dark season.

A short distance beyond Jaffa, a sycamore tree by the roadside was pointed out to me, and, as we did not meet with the sycamore afterwards, this was my only opportunity for observing its characteristics. Dr. Kitto cautions us against confusing it with the sycamine tree, both being mentioned by the same evangelist. (Luke xvii. 6, xix. 4.) The Doctor and other writers identify the sycamine with the black mulberry (συκαμενία), while all are agreed that the sycamore is the *Ficus fatuus* (wild fig). The tree still abounds in Egypt; and in Palestine it used often to be planted by the roadside, in which situation we found this specimen. The prophet Amos says (chap. vii. 14), "I was no prophet, neither was I a prophet's son; but I was an herdsman, and a gatherer (dresser) of sycamore-fruit;" referring, no doubt, to the practice of cutting or scraping the fruit and letting out the watery matter, without which operation it will not ripen. Its frequent location by the roadside and its wide-spreading branches render very natural and easy to be imagined, the circumstance of Zaccheus climbing into its top (Luke xix. 4); while from his elevated retreat, as Nathaniel from his beneath the fig-tree (John i. 48), each found his blessing in coming out to Him who is the true Vine. (John xv. 1.)

Our little party sometimes straggled and sometimes held together; of course I kept near to Mr. El Karey, whom, to avoid so frequent a repetition of his name, I will also call "my companion." My companion, then, and I kept as well together as the disparity in mettle of our horses would allow. The one he rode was, in this respect, much superior to mine, which was with difficulty kept from dropping to the rear. Having neither spurs nor whip, I asked the muleteer to furnish me with a substitute, which he soon did, in the shape of a reed from the roadside.

Thus we kept our way along the Ramleh road, passing now and then another traveller, till we reached a spot where a little group had halted and, having lit a fire, were preparing coffee.

They proved to be Jewish pilgrims, one or two of whom had been deck passengers on board my steamer. They were on their way to Jerusalem, and, one of their number falling ill, they were making the coffee for his comfort.

I had no remedies accessible without unloading
the mule, so (as on reflection it appears to me)
we acted an intermediate part between those of
the Priest and Levite on the one hand, and the
Samaritan on the other, toward the man who had
fallen among thieves. (Luke x.) We consulted
as to whether there was anything we could do,
and decided to continue our course; so, expressing our hopes for the success of the coffee, we
passed on.

In due time we reached Ramleh, which was on
our right, and were saluted by the baying of one
or two watch-dogs.

Ramleh is identified with Arimathea of the
New Testament, which is so honoured by its association as the native place of Joseph, who
begged the body of Jesus, and, having received
such a sacred trust, placed it in the new sepulchre in the garden (John xix. 38—42). From
the several Evangelists we learn that Joseph was
at the time a resident in Arimathea, a rich man,
an honourable counsellor, who had not consented
to the counsel and deed of those who condemned
the Lord, who waited for the kingdom of God
and was a secret disciple of Jesus. Thus, in one
of the counsel which resolved upon his death, as

RAMLEH.

afterward in the centurion who commanded the soldiers that crucified Him, the Lord had witnesses ; in Nicodemas, too, and one of the malefactors that was crucified with Him. In the lowest depths of His humiliation, as recited in Phil. II., when He came to death, "even the death of the cross," His heavenly glory laid aside, and the clouds gathered round Him; through their thickest folds did the glory of His grace shine out and penetrate some hearts. The new tomb at Jerusalem also illustrates the desire which operated with the Jews, whatever might be the place of their abode, to be buried at Jerusalem, a desire which reappeared in Christian times, as in the case of the German emperor, Frederick Barbarossa, of the Crusades.

A short distance past Ramleh, on account of the temperature and exercise, our thirst prompted us to inquire for water, but we found that the muleteer had no supply with him ; however he encouraged us to hope that we should, ere long, find a well, roadside fountain, or, at the least, a bush of the prickly pear, with the fruit of which we might cool our throats ; but, notwithstanding two or three reminders to continue his search, he failed of success, when after an hour or two of waiting, relief came from an unexpected quarter.

The darkness of the night greatly limited the range of our observation, and with scarcely any notice, our party was suddenly increased to eleven: seven horsemen (who proved to be the Governor of Ramoth Gilead, the Mufti of Nablûs and five attendants) fell in with us. Thus recruited and in such good company, a little fresh energy seemed to be imparted to our horses and our-selves, as if by induction, from the good steeds of our new companions and their riders.

We were soon offered the wished-for draught; one of the horsemen unfastened his girdle, to which was attached a goat-skin water bottle, and handed it to me. I did not need any instruction, as in the parlour at Jaffa when the sweet draught was offered ; but lifting the flexible bottle to my mouth, notwithstanding its instability and the movement of my horse, I took a good draught without spilling, and returned the bottle to its owner, at the same time asking my companion to convey the thanks which I was unable to express in the vernacular of the country, and to speak a word to my benefactor about the water which if a man drinks he "shall never thirst." (John iv. 14.) Neither could I fail to reflect, that as the Arab thus willingly shared his draught with a fellow

traveller, so should the Christian be at least as
ready to speak a word for Jesus and His salvation
to a fellow traveller to that bourne whence none
return.

> " Singing for Jesus, singing for Jesus,
> Trying to serve Him wherever I go ;
> Pointing the lost to the way of salvation,
> This be my mission, a pilgrim below ;
> When in the strains of my country I mingle,
> When to exalt her my voice I would raise ;
> 'Tis for *His* glory whose arm is her refuge,
> Him would I honour, His name would I praise."
>
> PHILLIP PHILLIPS.

Mr. El Karey was naturally a good deal engaged conversing with the Governor and the
Mufti, whilst, being an entire barbarian in speech
to the rest of the party, and my horse requiring
more than a graceful, not to say comfortable,
amount of urging, I found some improvement in
allowing him to move at his own speed for
awhile, which I could now afford to do for a
longer period, falling some distance to the rear.
The white turbans of the Governor and Mufti
could be discerned a good way off,* and when the

---

* This incident reminds me of the following, recounted
by Josephus (Wars, book 5, chap. vi. 3.) Respecting the
missiles hurled by the Romans from their engines, he says,

limit of this distance had been reached, we fetched up our lee-way in a *bond fide* trot, which was far preferable to the repeated urging, walking, and ambling every minute.

The country we crossed was diversified with

" Now, the stones that were cast were of the weight of a talent, and were carried two furlongs and farther. The blow they gave was no way to be sustained, not only by those that stood first in the way, but by those that were beyond them for a great space. As for the Jews, they at first watched for the coming of the stone; for it was of a white colour, and could therefore not only be perceived by the great noise it made, but could be seen also before it came, by its brightness; accordingly the watchmen that sat upon the towers gave the notice when the engine was let go, and the stone came from it, and cried out aloud, in their own country language, ' *The Son cometh*;' so those that were in its way stood off, and threw themselves down upon the ground, by which means, and by their thus guarding themselves, the stone fell down and did them no harm. But the Romans contrived how to prevent that, by blacking the stone, who then could aim at them with success, when the stone was not discerned beforehand, as it had been till then; and so they destroyed many of them at one blow." The above expression " *the Son* cometh " has given rise to much conjecture. 'Ιός (an arrow) has by some been put forward as the true reading, in preference to υἰὸς (the Son), while among those, by far the greater number, who adhere to υἰὸς as the unmistakable word of the original, some have thought that there was here a reference to the word of Jesus *the Son* of God, in Luke xix. 43, 44.

cultivation and wilderness, plain and hill and ravine. Many places of interest are pointed out from this road, but, though I preserve a distinct recollection of its diversities of scene, the darkness of the night and frequent separations from my companion, prevented my receiving such deep impressions, and recording them, as might otherwise have been the case. I should, however, be very unobservant, or my journal very incomplete did I not mention the chorus of the frogs on the plain of Sharon, nearly the whole night through.

Monday 12th, 2.30 a.m. We halted by the road-side, at a place where two or three Arabs were attending a fire and other accommodation for travellers. They brought some mats which the light of the stars and the glimmer of an oil lamp shewed to be, in respect of cleanliness, little if at all better than the bare road.

We dismounted and stretched our tired limbs upon them. The Arabs prepared coffee, fetched water and fed the horses, while we and our fellow travellers shared our stores of bread, grapes and figs. Thus we supped, and men and horses were recruited by an hour's rest; then at 3.30 a.m. we broke up our bivouac and re-mounted.

About 4 a.m. we were passing by a village, with, what appeared to me, some important ruins by the road-side. Just then the cock crew, which brought to my mind those periods of the night referred to by our Lord in Mark xiii. 34, 37 : "The Son of man is as a man taking a far journey, who left his house and gave authority to his servants, and to every man his work, and commanded the porter to watch. Watch ye, therefore, for ye know not when the master of the house cometh, at even, or at midnight, or at the cock crowing, or in the morning. Lest coming suddenly he find you sleeping. And what I say unto you, I say unto all, Watch." And in Luke xii. 38, "And if He shall come in the second watch, or come in the third watch, and find them so, blessed are those servants."

Then, we remember that as the Lord had foretold, it was before the cock crowing that Peter denied Him for whose sake he had said he would lay down his life. "And the Lord turned and looked upon Peter, and Peter remembered the word of the Lord, how he had said unto him, Before the cock crow thou shalt deny me thrice." (Luke xxii. 61.) And am I incapable of denying my Lord ? Alas ! how often do I discover a

heart like Peter's; how little and how feebly do
I confess him before men! Let me, then, not be
regardless of the cock crowing, as if I needed not
the prayer which was made for Peter, and the
answer to that prayer that my "faith fail not."

The account of Peter's denial as recorded by
St. Mark, compared with those of the other
evangelists, presents one of those seeming dis-
crepencies which generally, on examination, yield
most striking and profitable instruction. We
there read (ch. xiv., v. 30) that "Jesus saith
unto him, Verily I say unto thee, that this day,
even in this night, before the cock crow twice,
thou shalt deny Me thrice." It is well known
that the cock invariably crows more loudly a little
before day-break than during the earlier watches
of the night, and this period, just before dawn,
is still commonly designated " *the* cock crowing,"
and in keeping therewith the other evangelists
relate in a general way these events which St.
Mark recounts with more exactness of detail;
while as connected with Peter we may doubtless
learn that they whose consciences are heedless of
first and gentle appeals, and flee not those things,
such as self-indulgence and the fear of man,
which bring a snare, require a louder voice to call
them to repentance.

We had now reached the hill country of Judea. My companion pointed out to me a hill on our left, behind which lay the reputed site of Emmaus. As we advanced, the hill-riding became more and more tiring, and I noticed as the last hour or two before day-break wore on, that sleep asserted its claim on my companion, whose eyes would not keep open, and his posture became more and more stooping, till a jolt compelled him to re-erect himself, but only to a speedy relapse.

Morning light revealed to me the goodly aspect of men and horses in our companions of the night, in a way which the lamp at the midnight halt had not enabled me to appreciate. I exchanged salutes with one or two as well as I could, and finding they were inclined to lessen speed, we left them in the rear, and continued our way over hill after hill, till the sun rose upon us, passing very near to *El Neby Samuil*, the tomb of the prophet Samuel.

Shortly after sunrise the heat prompted me, like Æsop's traveller, to divest myself of the tweed coat, and hang it on the front of my saddle. I was quite unprepared for the extent of hill country to be crossed before coming to the

mountains which lie immediately around Jerusalem. At last, about 6.30 a.m., Mr. El Karey,
who was a little in advance of me, reined in his
horse, and when I came up with him I found, as
his manner had made me suspect, that we were in
view of a walled city.

El K. What do you see before you?

J. A mosque.

El K. Well, that is not a mosque but the
Russian convent. Over there what do you see?

Turning in the direction to which he pointed,
I recognised what pictures had made me familiar
with, and said,

"That is the Mosque of Omar."

"Yes," said he, "and this is Jerusalem, the
city of the Great King."

We were at the point where Jewish pilgrims
and Crusaders have, so many and so often, fallen
down and kissed the ground. In this we did not
emulate them, but the view of the city was accompanied by a flood of thought, too full to be expressed, even feebly, by words.

On the right was Zion, the city of the King, on
the left Moriah, where used to be the temple, its
services and offerings, which foreshadowed the one
great offering on Calvary, whose courts were so

JERUSALEM FROM MOUNT OF OLIVES.

often trodden by the feet of the Son of God who taught in the temple. (John viii. 20.) Here, when eight days old, He was presented before the Lord, and aged Simeon, taking Him in his arms, made the divinely-taught confession to Him who is God's salvation. (Luke ii. 25-32.) Here, at the age of twelve, He was found sitting in the midst of the doctors, both hearing them and asking them questions. (Ver. 46.) Here He vindicated the honour of His Father's house from the doings of them that bought and sold in the house of prayer. (Matt. xxi. 13.) Here they brought to Him one taken in a sin, for committing which, Moses in the law had said that such should be stoned, and tried Him with " What sayest thou ?" Did He make light of the sin ? God forbid ! Did He then order the carrying out of Moses' sentence? Wherein would He then have exceeded Moses? Nay, He enjoined conditions which He only could have fulfilled. " He that is without sin." Besides Himself was there one ? From the eldest unto the last, not one. The accusers gone, and the accused left before the sinless One, did He condemn? Hearken ! " Neither do I condemn thee" (grace), "go and sin no more " (and truth, John i. 17). " For God sent not His Son into the world to condemn the world ; but

that the world through him might be saved."
(John iii. 17.)

This is Jerusalem, beautiful for situation, whither the tribes went up, but now the stranger dwells there and Israel is exiled, "a nation scattered and peeled." (Isa. xviii. 2.)

We passed on in view of El Mascobia (the Russian church, convent and hospital, all in one building) towards the Jaffa gate, though we did not then enter the city, but kept to the western outskirts over against Mount Zion, and stopped our horses about 7.30 a.m. at the gate of the house of Mr. El Karey's christian friend, Mr. Audi Azam. The household servant, Monsoul, took charge of the horses, and we entered beneath the hospitable roof of our friend and christian brother.

Thus, in twelve hours, we had come from Jaffa, with only the interval of one hour during which we were dismounted, and by the exercise in the climate, and, in my case, on a native saddle, the form of which adds considerably to the tiring of a European, we were both sufficiently fatigued to gladly accept the rest that was now at our disposal.

Soon after our arrival had been announced, our kind "Gaius" (who, however, reminded me of the patriarchal Abraham, rather than of the "well-beloved Gaius," whose character he well sustained nevertheless) appeared, and my companion went forward to meet him. They saluted each other with words of affectionate greeting, kissed each other, and then mutually placed the head over the right and left shoulder of each other, four or five times alternately. This is the manner of salutation among the dearest friends, as we find it in Luke xv. 20 : " But while he was yet a great way off, his father saw him, and had compassion, and ran, and fell on his neck, and kissed him."

Various forms of salutation are practised in the land. A servant saluting his master extends his hand, the master does the same, and the servant, touching the master's right hand with his own, kisses his own fingers where they have touched his master's, places .them on his breast and fore-head, in expression of his devotion of heart and mind. Equals who are on terms of ordinary acquaintance, place their hands first on their breasts, and then on their foreheads, at the same time repeating words of salutation, such as "Good morning, sir."* The dearest friends salute as already described. To those who have witnessed these things and, in their measure, those whom such descriptions as the foregoing enable to imagine them, the marked difference, between the touching of hands, the servile signs

* نِهارِكْ سَعيد‎ *Nehair-ak saâid.*

and postures, and the ardent and repeated em-
bracings and proofs of gushing affection, bring
out very vividly the returning prodigal's miserable thought of being made a hired servant, and
the father's joy in receiving him as a son, once
dead and now alive again, once lost, but now
found, to wander no more for ever.

While in Mr. Azam, Abraham was thus clearly
brought to mind ; in his good wife, Sarah was as
distinctly suggested ; while the worthy Monsoul,
the household servant, supplied the part of Eliezer
of Damascus.

About half an hour after we had dismounted,
bread was placed before us, which Sarah had
hastened to prepare.   (See Gen. xviii. 6.)   We
sat down to eat of it and one or two dishes which
followed ; such as *lebn* (curdled milk), olive oil,
egg fritter, &c., placed successively in the middle
of the table, into which dishes we dipped our
bread, while Eliezer with his arms bared (see Isa.
lii. 10), watching the hand of his master (Ps.
cxxiii. 2), who was sitting with us at the table,
was prompt to bring water, coffee, or whatever he
saw we needed.   At the end of the feast we se-
parately repaired to the side of the room, where
was a wash-hand basin, and Monsoul poured water
over our hands. (See 2 Kings iii. 11.)

CHAPTER V.

RECRUITED by this hospitality, we left the house and entered the city by the Jaffa gate, going first to the Mediterranean hotel, as I had a little commission to execute with the worthy host there. From the roof of this hotel, on a second visit, we obtained a view of many of the interesting features of the city, especially Hezekiah's pool.

We next directed our steps to the Jews' place of wailing, where are the ancient stones *in situ* which they regard as belonging to the court of the temple, and which is the nearest approach they are permitted to make to the sacred site.

We entered by a narrow approach, and witnessed the spectacle mentioned by nearly all visitors to Jerusalem. There were three or four aged men and one woman ; one or two of the number were reading their sacred books, and the others pressing themselves against the stones in apparently deep grief.

I gazed awhile on the touching scene, so fraught with scripture memories. How plainly it told of

HEZEKIAH'S POOL.

70

the separation of the children of Israel from other nations by the Lord who delivered them from the house of bondage and brought them into the good land; but they forgat Him and "they tempted and provoked the most High God, and kept not his testimonies" (Ps. lxxviii. 56), "and his servants some they beat, and some they killed, and when, last of all, he sent his son, they took him, and killed him and cast him out of the vineyard." (Mark xii. 8.) Now are they dispersed among the Gentiles, a nation scattered and peeled.

Who can behold the scene before us, and not recognize the city which was for the people, and the people who were for the city? But now strangers inhabit their inheritance, and their houses are turned to aliens; "the elders have ceased from the gate, the young men from their music." (Lam. v.)

After contemplating this sad spectacle for awhile, I drew near to scrutinize one of the stones, and found that my steps had been followed by a young Arab who, with all imaginable impertinence, came up and offered to break me off a lump of one of the stones if I would give him *bakhsheesh*. I need hardly say that I did not accept his offer; but the fearlessness with which it was made, and

PLACE OF WAILING.

the silent endurance on the part of the aged sons
of Abraham, of this insult to the venerable stones
which they regard with so much sacred affection,
brought with great vividness to my mind Luke
xxi. 24 : "Jerusalem shall be trodden down of
the Gentiles, until the times of the Gentiles be
fulfilled." Her afflictions have been great and
long continued, and shall yet be greater (Luke
xxiii. 28—31), but in the end she shall know His
grace whom she refused and pierced. (Zech. xii.
10.) In her shall His word be fulfilled : "Weeping may endure for a night, but joy cometh in
the morning." (Ps. xxx. 5.)

We next went to the wood-carvers' bazaar, in
quest of relics for friends in England, the selection of which occupied us a considerable time. In
the East much time is commonly sacrificed to the
sellers' custom of asking much more at the first
than they are willing to accept ; and bringing a
bargain to fair terms is very often a tedious process. It proved to be so on this occasion, my
companion attending to my interests. Another
fruitful cause of delay was the circumstance that
Mr. El Karey was known to many of the inhabitants, and much time was consumed in making
salutations according to the usages of the country.

Delays of the latter kind remind one of the words of
our Lord when sending forth the seventy disciples,
two and two before His face, into every city
and place whither He Himself would come, "Salute
no man by the way." (Luke x. 4.) How this
should remind us, who know His name, to seek to
live as the servants of a Master whose business
requireth speed and faithfulness, and the opportunity for doing which will soon have passed away.
We understand this easily enough in our own
things ; but, alas! how little do we remember it
in the things which are Jesus Christ's, if one may
speak for others.

During this day's walk I was interested in noticing the camels, many of which we passed, some
kneeling to be loaded, others on the road with
their immense burdens. I was little prepared for
the almost savage complaints which the animal
appeared to make, as the burdens were bound to
his saddle, swaying his head alternately right and
left, exposing his teeth, and uttering the most
miserable noise. Indeed, when passing one under
these conditions in a very confined space, I thought,
if I did not make, the child's inquiry, "Will he
bite ?"

It has been truly said of the Arab, that he is

74   A STUDY.

seen to the best advantage at a little distance. His free and stately carriage, the graceful style of his garments, and all that makes up his noble presence, is then unspoiled by the discovery, which a closer view makes, of want of cleanliness in person and dress. The same may be said of his faithful servant the camel, who for strength, endurance, and practical docility, is perhaps unmatched, but who has some unamiable ways, which would not be suspected by those who had regarded him only from a distance, or seen his general behaviour on the march.

At dinner we had dishes of *badenjan* (egg plant) filled with rice and chopped meat, and other novelties, of which, however, not having made a note, I cannot write with confidence. I soon surmounted the awkwardness which at first I felt, in breaking the bread and helping myself out of the centre dishes, with portions taken between bread and thumb. On this and the following evening, some friends of our host and of my companion came, and we together took supper, the meal of most sacred intimacy, at the season when, the cares and traffic of the day dismissed or subsided, and no interruptions expected, the spirit unbends, and heart opens to heart. Sitting, squatting, and re-

clining, we gathered round the table which was
placed near the divan, spread with the fruits of
the land. What a promise is that which the Lord
makes in Revelation iii. 20, "Behold, I stand at
the door and knock: if any man will hear my
voice and open the door, I will come in to him
and will *sup* with him and he with me."

Mr. Azam's house is approached through a gateway of considerable width, from which to the door
a broad path leads through the garden. This path
is spanned by a wooden trellis, upon which a vine
is trained, and at the time of our visit, delicious
grapes were hanging therefrom. As I contemplated this scene from within doors, or took the
morning or evening air, sauntering between gate
and door, I could but recall the words in 1 Kings
iv. 25, "Every man under his vine and under his
fig-tree;" and Deuteronomy viii. 8, 9, "A land
of wheat, and barley, and vines, and fig-trees, and
pomegranates; a land of oil olive, and honey;
a land wherein thou shalt eat bread without
scarceness, thou shalt not lack anything in it;
a land whose stones are iron, and out of whose
hills thou mayest dig brass.

In the entrance gate was framed a small wicket,
sufficient only for a man to enter, in a stooping

76   UNDER THE VINE AND FIG TREE.

posture, while for the entrance of a camel, laden or unladen, the gate must needs be opened. The former, I was told, is what they call the " eye of the needle," and referred to by the Lord in the passage in Mark x. 25 : " It is easier for a camel to go through the eye of a needle, than for a rich man to enter into the kingdom of God." The same contrivance is by no means uncommon in our own country.

Tuesday 13th, 8 a.m. At family prayer Mr. Azam read from the Arabic Bible, Exodus, xxv. and Mark v., and after breakfast, a fresh horse having been hired for me, my companion and I started across the hills on to the Bethlehem road; we occasionally met men with camels or asses, and women on foot carrying baskets of eggs, live fowls, grapes, and figs, on their way to Jerusalem, and passed others going from the city.

Our road lay over the lovely hill-country of Judea, till we reached Rachel's tomb, which is some little distance from Bethlehem, and in view of the village of Beth-zala. Here we dismounted, my companion resting, and holding the bridles, while I took a sketch of the tomb, which though comparatively modern, is even by the most critical, accredited to occupy the true site of the grave.

What associations there are, on the page of patriarchal history, to which this relic directs the thoughts ! Jacob sent forth to Padan Aram to take a wife from thence, of the daughters of Laban, his mother's brother, and the blessing of Abraham invoked upon him. His night's rest at Bethel ; thence to the well, where occurred the scene of watering the flock, the drawing near of Rachel and her subsequent history from the moment when Jacob saw her, and went near and watered the

RACHEL'S TOMB.

flock of Laban, his mother's brother, until at Ephrath, which is Bethlehem, her soul departed. "And Rachel died and was buried in the way to Ephrath, which is Bethlehem, and Jacob set a pillar upon her grave ; that is the pillar of Rachel's grave unto this day" (Gen. xxxv. 19, 20, see also xlviii. 7.)

From the tomb we went to Solomon's pools, three immense reservoirs which, in the days of the kingdom of Israel, received the water-supply for the city. Beside the upper pool, at which we dismounted, is a fountain attended by two or three Arabs who live in a ruined Saracen castle close by. The water is drawn from this fountain in a copper dish attached to a chain, out of which men and horses drank with great satisfaction.

Having left our horses in the care of one of the Arabs, we went a short distance to the opposite hill-side, where, through a low doorway, we entered a descending gallery, which led us to the true spring-head of this ancient water-supply of Jerusalem. The chamber in which the water was rising, and from which it ran through an underground channel, to the fountain at which we had been drinking, was reached by twenty-six stone steps ; and in its cool retreat, into which daylight entered from above, we opened the store of bread and meat, which good Mrs. Azam had provided, and made our luncheon with it, and some water dipped from the spring by another of the Arabs, who acted as our guide.

We next visited the upper and middle pools; leaving the lower one unexplored. I saw no water in either of these pools, though I understand that at other times in the year there is a good supply; my visit being made in the dry month of August,

SOLOMON'S POOLS.

before the springs are refreshed by the early rains, would no doubt account for their dryness. The bottoms were covered with wild flowers. On the the hill-side are still to be traced the stone ducts through which the water from these reservoirs once flowed into Jerusalem.

Having completed our hasty survey of these remarkable relics, we mounted and turned our horses' heads towards Bethlehem, which in the

Hebrew is בֵּית־לֶחֶם "House of Bread," and in Arabic بيت لحم "House of Meat."

We have already referred to its connection with the patriarchal history. Here also in the days of the judges, when there was a famine in the land, Elimelech, his wife and two sons, left the "house of bread," came to the country of Moab and continued there. After the death of Elimelech and his sons, did Naomi and her daughters-in-law, who were of the country of Moab, return towards Bethlehem; "for she had heard how that the Lord had visited his people in giving them *bread*." (Ruth i. 6.) At her request did one of them turn back, "but Ruth clave unto her" (ver. 14), and said, "Entreat me not to leave thee, or to return from following after thee; for whither thou goest, I will go; and where thou lodgest, I will lodge; thy people shall be my people, and thy God my God. Where thou diest, will I die; and there will I be buried: the Lord do so to me and more also, if aught but death part thee and me." (Vers. 16, 17.) Here she gleaned in the field of Boaz, who gave commandment for her to be favoured, and when the other kinsman, who was nearer than he,

G

declared his inability, he redeemed that which was Elimelech's and took unto him Ruth, whence Obed was born, who was the father of Jesse, who was the father of David.

In the fields of Bethlehem did young David keep his father's flock, and thither was the prophet Samuel sent by the Lord, with the horn of anointing oil, when the ruddy shepherd-boy was

BETHLEHEM.

pointed out as the one whom the Lord had chosen to be king over Israel.

Of Bethlehem also it is written, "But thou Beth-lehem Ephratah, though thou be little among the thousands of Judah, yet out of thee shall come forth unto me that is to be ruler in Israel; whose goings forth have been of old, from ever-lasting." (Micah v. 2.)

Here was the manger, whither the angelic word and the star guided the footsteps of the shepherds and the wise men : here too did the sword destroy, from two years old and under, all the children of Bethlehem. (Matt. ii. 16.)

Another short ride over the hill country brought us to the city of David. On our way we passed and rode through several gardens, in one of which we noticed some one at work, and in due time reached the house of Mr. Müller, a missionary, having a school and orphanage under his care, and who proved to be the industrious owner we had seen labouring in his garden.

We were thoroughly pleased with the admirable arrangements of the orphanage, and it was a lovely sight to behold the good provision of home for the little fatherless ones, made through the love of Him who, though Maker and Lord of all, was in this same city cradled in a manger, and could say, when grown to manhood, "Foxes have holes, and the birds of the air have nests, but the Son of man hath not where to lay his head." (Luke ix. 58.) The school being assembled, we had an opportunity of hearing the children read and answer (not a little to our satisfaction) some questions put to them by my companion.

Conspicuous by the number and correctness of his answers, was a young Bedouin boy. The Lord grant that he, and many such, may be led as first fruits of the children of the desert, unto Him before whom, one day,

> " The desert-dwellers at His beck shall bend,
> His foes them suppliant at His feet shall fling,
> The kings of Tharsis homage gifts shall send,
> So Seba, Saba, every island-king.
>   Nay, all, ev'n all
>   Shall prostrate fall
> That crowns and sceptres weare !
>   And all that stand
>   At their command,
> That crowns and sceptres beare."

Of course we visited the Church of the Nativity, the original grandeur of which is impressed on the mind by its still surviving, though disfigured, columns and arches, and by what remains of the frescoes which once covered the walls. In

this Church there are, I believe, chapels set apart
for the services of the Latin, Greek, and Armenian
sects.

Having made a general survey of the vestibule,
we were joined by one of the Latin priests, who
guided us to the point of special interest : the traditional spot where the Saviour was born into the
world. This is a recess hung with curtains, and
lit by silver lamps, beneath the centre one of
which is a star of polished marble, surmounted
with a belt of silver inscribed with the words,
" *Hic de Virgine Maria Jesus Christus natus est.*"
Opposite to the shrine of the nativity, and at a
lower level, is a grotto containing a marble
manger which occupies the reputed place of that
mentioned in the Gospels. This also is lit by
silver lamps.

The certainty of being in the city, and the
possibility that I was on the very spot, where was
fulfilled the incarnation of the Son of God, could
not fail to revive, in an especial way, thoughts of
the " grace of our Lord Jesus Christ who, though
he was rich, yet for our sakes he became poor,
that we through his poverty might be rich."
(2 Cor. viii. 9.) Adjoining these shrines we saw
two paintings, the work of the Spanish artist

Murillo, portraying the scenes from which they
derive their sacred interest.*

The priests invited us to explore the other parts
of the building, but our desire was to leave, a
choice in which we were not at all disturbed by
the chanting which we could overhear. We
quenched our thirst with some water from the
well within the church, and withdrew.

At my request, we next made search for such
a manger as those inhabitants of the place who
are familiar with the gospel narrative understand
to be there described. We were conducted to a
house, the sitting-room of which was entered by
a door at one end of the building, approached by
a flight of four or five stone steps. At the other
end a slope descended to a chamber beneath.
We entered this lower chamber, and in the far
corner, situated diagonally from the entrance,
were shewn a recessed stone fixed in the wall.
By the joint aid of my eyes and hands, I observed the form and dimensions of the interior of
this manger to be almost exactly those of a cradle.
The situation of the manger beneath the inha-

---

* In disturbances which have since taken place between
the Latin and Greek factions, these paintings are reported
to have come to grief.

bited portion of the house is a feature common to buildings in other parts of Palestine. How vividly did it bring to my mind the circumstances recorded in the Gospels of Matthew and Luke! At the time of the taxing, when the city of David was filled with people, did Joseph and Mary seek a resting place. The chambers for the reception of human inmates being fully occupied, they were only offered the dark underground stable, where the child, being born, was wrapped in swaddling clothes and laid in a manger. (Luke ii. 7.) Thither did the shepherds, thither did the wise men come. There was adoration and worship, with the offering of gifts, gold and frankincense and myrrh; for in that manger lay JESUS the Son of God, Emmanuel, God with us—He who was with the Father, and was manifested unto us.

" Down to this earth He came,
　And loved, and wept, and died ;
' Glory to God, good will to man !'
　His advent angels cried.
Divine, yet clothed in flesh,
　His own-made earth He trod,
He came to do the Father's will,
　To be the Saviour-God.

That will accomplished, now
　He sits in heaven above ;
The church's representative,
　Dear object of His love.

He bears the glory *there*,
    As *here* He bore the rod ;
He died, yet lives for evermore,
    Victorious Saviour-God.

And soon He'll come again,
    To take His church to heaven :
That church, redeemed by precious blood,
    By grace alone forgiven.
How loud her song will be !
    How sweetly will she laud,
Through one eternal, blissful day,
    Jesus: her Saviour-God."   A. M.

We returned from these explorations to the
house of Mr. and Mrs. Müller, where the pleasures of an hospitable table were considerably
heightened by those of christian intercourse and
edification.   Here too, we realized the proverbial
excellence of the fruits and wine of Bethlehem—
thus the "House of Bread" to us, in more senses
than one.   Indeed it was not without thankfulness for the privileges of this visit, qualified
though it was with the regret that it had reached
its close, that we re-mounted for departure.

We chose to return to Jerusalem by the road
which leads up from Hebron, and in making our
way thither, we strayed from the path, and got
entangled in some gardens divided by dry walls,

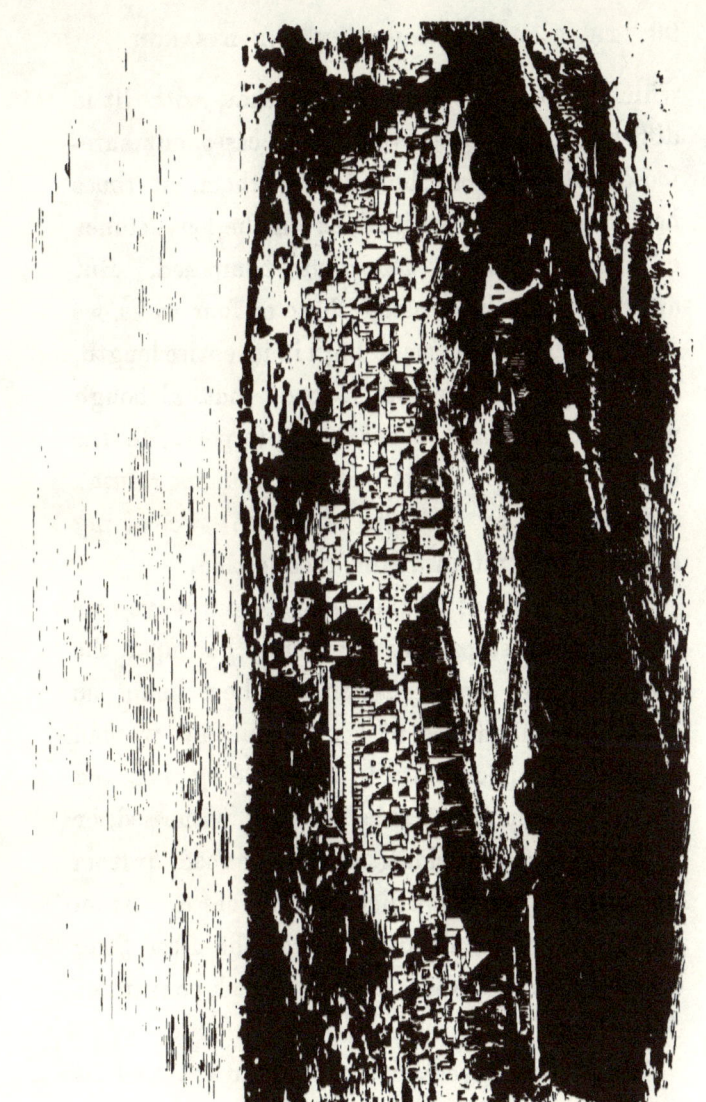

HEBRON.

which were, in places, so low that, with little
difficulty in the first two or three cases, our sure-
footed little barbs climbed over them, at times
balancing themselves and us on the loose stones
of which these low fences are composed. But
after successfully crossing three or four walls, we
came to one which was so high in its entire length,
and the ground beyond so bad, that, although
we dismounted and endeavoured to persuade the
horses to cross, we obtained only a blank refusal,
accompanied by a kick, of which two of my
knuckles still retain a faint recollection.

Thus convinced of the error of our ways, we
retraced our steps, and eventually got upon the
Hebron road for Jerusalem. There being no
longer any likelihood of again deviating, we had
leisure and opportunity to ride side by side, and
converse upon the scenes we had witnessed, or
which met us at various turns in the road, or from
the rising grounds which we traversed. From
one point we obtained a view of the Dead Sea;
at another we passed near the Greek convent of
Mar Elias.

Presently we reached the point in the road, at
which Jerusalem comes into view from a greater
distance than any from which we had yet beheld it.

"Here," said my companion, "is the spot where, it is believed, Abraham lifted up his eyes and saw the place afar off." (Gen. xxii. 4.) It will be remembered that Mount Moriah, on which the temple was afterwards built, is accredited to be the Mount on which "he that had received the promises offered up his only-begotten son." (Heb. xi. 17.) Here then, we may believe the patriarch left the servants behind with the ass, saying to them, "I and the lad will go yonder and worship and come again to you." What must have been the thoughts of his heart as he traversed that long stretch of road, with the place continually coming afresh into nearer view where he was to lay the wood in order and bind thereon his son, his only son, Isaac! And what, too, when his beloved Isaac broke the silence of that hour, with the question, "Where is the lamb for a burnt-offering?" The faith of Abraham confided in Him whose word he was obeying, and whose pro-vision was soon discovered to him in the ram, caught in a thicket by his horns, when, Isaac being given back to him from the dead and the substitute offered up, Abraham called the name of that place Jehovah-Jireh. (Gen. xxii. 14.)

As we drew near the city, the hill of Evil

Counsel came fully into view. The name of this
hill rests on the tradition that it was here, in the

STREET IN JERUSALEM.

country house of Caiaphas, the traitor Judas made
his bargain for betraying the Lord, as He had foretold, saying unto His disciples, " Verily, verily,

I say unto you, that one of you shall betray me"
(John xiii. 21), and when they asked Him, "Lord,
who is it?" Jesus answered, "He it is, to whom
I shall give a sop, when I have dipped it. And
when he had dipped the sop, he gave it to Judas
Iscariot, the son of Simon." (Ver. 26.) After
which was fulfilled that which is written, "Mine
own familiar friend in whom I trusted, which did
eat of my bread, hath lifted up his heel against
me. (Ps. xli. 9.)

CHAPTER VI.

WE now descend into the Valley of Gehenna, where formerly was Tophet and the idol Moloch, passing the lower pool of Gihon, of which (or the water system connected with it) we find mention in the history of the acts of Hezekiah in 2 Chronicles xxxii. 30.

We rode into the valley of Jehoshaphat, and watered our horses at the brook Kedron, near to the village of Siloam, at a place where some of the villagers had brought cattle to drink. A little beyond, we turned to the left under the city wall, to visit the pool of Siloam, the water in which is tolerably fresh, being renewed from a spring which discharges into it, called the "Fountain of the Virgin."

Captain Warren's excavations have brought to light an apparent connection between this pool and certain channels which led thither, from the base of the altar in the temple, but as the excavations were suspended at the season of my visit,

LOWER POOL OF GIHON.

and as I had no other source upon which I could draw for information, I feel incapable of enlarging upon this subject.

To the interest which the pool of Siloam has for every student of the Bible, because of its connection with the miracle recorded in John ix., was in our case added, that it was there my companion, as already mentioned (p. 39), was baptized in the name of the Father, and of the Son, and of the Holy Ghost.

As we continued our way northward along the valley of Jehoshaphat, we passed the sepulchres which bear the names of Zechariah, St. James, Absalom, and Jehoshaphat.

Before the pillar of Absalom we saw the heap of flint stones, which has accumulated from the custom of Arabs and Jews alike, when passing, each to cast seven stones, with imprecations on the name and memory of him who rose in rebellion against the king, his father.

There seems to be great reason for doubting if these tombs have, in each or any case, a real connection with those whose names they bear. There is, however, one interesting feature which they have in common; namely, a mixture of methods and styles of architecture. The lower

POOL OF SILOAM.

H

portions are rockhewn, Egyptian in style, and
surmounted by an addition of masonry in some
Grecian order. A careful comparison of these
features has led some to the conviction, that the
Grecian superstructures belong to a period long
subsequent to the hewing of the rock-cut tombs
proper.

Presuming on the soundness of these inferences,
it has been suggested that the Saviour made direct
reference to these tombs in the words recorded in
Matthew xxiii. 29-31 : "Woe unto you, scribes and
Pharisees, hypocrites! because ye build the tombs
of the prophets, and garnish the sepulchres of the
righteous, and say, If we had been in the days of
our fathers, we would not have been partakers with
them in the blood of the prophets. Wherefore ye
be witnesses unto yourselves, that ye are the
children of them which killed the prophets."

Near St. Stephen's gate we turned to the right,
and crossing the bridge over the brook Kedron,
followed the road up the Mount of Olives, to the
left of the enclosure which marks the traditional
site of Gethsemane.

This, in common with most spots of sacred
association, can establish no higher claim to its
identity than that of (perhaps a great) probability.

VALLEY OF JEHOSHAPHAT.

True it is that here are to be found some venerable
olive-trees; though their claim, often put forward, to be the same that were growing in

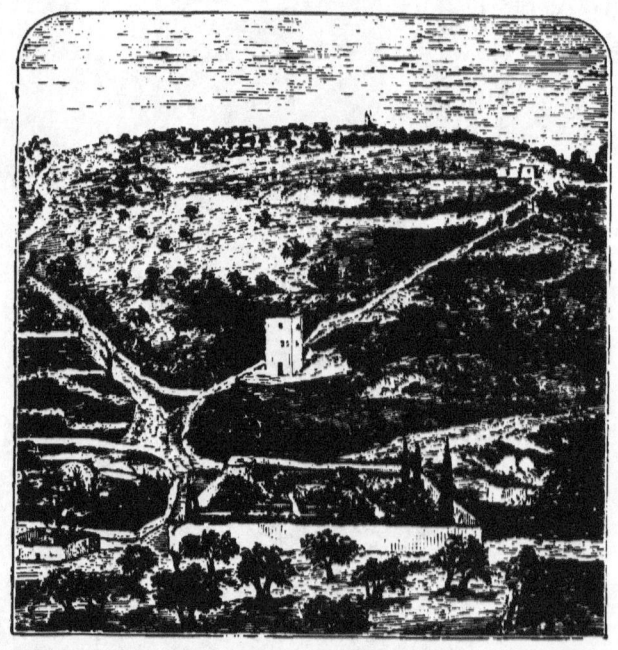

MOUNT OF OLIVES.

the days of the Lord Jesus, is doubtless unten-
able. We learn from Josephus (Wars, 5, xii. 4),
that for the erection of banks around Jerusalem,
Titus caused to be cut down "all the trees that
were about the city," and that his soldiers
brought such materials from a distance of ninety

furlongs. Nevertheless, it is especially true of
the olive that is written in Job xiv. 7-9 : "There '
is hope of a tree, if it be cut down, that it will
sprout again, and that the tender branch thereof
will not cease. Though the root thereof wax old
in the earth, and the stock thereof die in the
ground; yet through the scent of water it will
bud, and bring forth boughs like a plant;" and,
during the existence of the parent tree, the olive
is often found to throw up young plants from the
roots, whence comes the comparison in Psalm
cxxviii. 3, "Thy children like *olive-plants* round
about thy table." Not only, therefore, may the
position be that of Gethsemane, for it is across
the brook Kedron (John xviii. 1), on the side of
the Mount of Olives, opposite Jerusalem, beside
one of the roads to Bethany, and altogether seems
to be entitled to some credence; but the trees
found there may have sprung from the roots of
those beneath which Jesus knelt when, knowing
that His hour was come, having washed His disciples' feet, ministered to them in teaching, and
eaten the passover with them, He went with them
to the Mount of Olives, and, entering into the
garden with three of their number, bade them
watch, and went Himself a stone-cast beyond

and prayed: "O my Father, if this cup may not
pass away from Me except I drink it, Thy will
be done." (Matt. xxvi. 42.) "And His sweat
was as it were great drops of blood falling down
to the ground." (Luke xxii. 44.) Then, although
possessing all power in heaven and in earth, He
surrendered Himself into the hands of sinful
men, and "was led as a sheep to the slaughter;
and like a lamb dumb before his shearer, so
opened He not His mouth." (Isa. liii. 7; Acts
viii. 32.)*

The ground within the enclosure is laid out as
a garden, and attended by monks to whom, however, we did not apply for admission, for the
sufficient reason that the hour of sunset was
drawing very near, and we were anxious to reach
the summit of the mount before that time, to
obtain a view of the city under the favourable
conditions which would then exist.

We reached the summit about half an hour
before sunset and dismounted at a ruinous mosque,
where, leaving our horses in the charge of two or

---

* The Septuagint, Vulgate, and other versions support
the New Testament reading of "*sheep* to the slaughter,"
and " *lamb* to his shearer," which would not, I apprehend,
misrepresent שֶׂיה and רָחֵל.

three Arabs, we were allowed, for a consideration, to climb the minaret stairs and survey the prospect from the gallery.

Here in the quietness of our isolation, we gave ourselves up to the contemplation of the view around us. That which occupied our attention was the whole scene rather than particular points, accredited to be subjects of scripture reference.

From a lower slope of this mount it was that Jesus beheld the city and wept over it. (Luke xix. 41.) Another had wept here before. (2 Sam. xv. 30.) But how different the lamentation! "David went up by the ascent of Mount Olivet, and wept as he went up," in the days of the rebellion of Absalom, on receiving the tidings of whose death, "the king was much moved, and went up to the chamber over the gate, and wept; and as he went, thus he said, Oh my son Absalom! my son, my son Absalom! would God I had died for thee, O Absalom, my son, my son!" (2 Sam. xviii. 33.)

But the lamentation of David's Son was, "O Jerusalem, Jerusalem, thou that killest the prophets and stonest them which are sent unto thee, how often would I have gathered thy children together, even as a hen gathereth her chickens

under her wings, and ye would not!" (Matt.
xxiii. 37.) With reverence we would add, He
cannot say, "O! sinner, would to God I had
died for thee," for He has died and risen again;
but He does say of the careless and scorner,
"Would that thou hadst known, even thou, at
least in this thy day, the things which belong
unto thy peace."

We removed to the eastern side of the gallery,
and truly lovely was the scene which met our gaze.
The shadows of Olivet and the adjoining hills
were cast over the Dead Sea, and on the hillsides
of Moab. Jericho lay between, but concealed
among the hills; the dark bosom of the Dead Sea,
the course of the Jordan,
　　　　　" By its verdure far descried,"
and then the lovely hill-scenery of the land of
Moab, bathed in the soft light of this evening
hour! Pisgah is there, but which it is among
the hilltops we cannot say; yet how the Olivet
view of Moab brings to mind the Pisgah view of
Palestine, which Moses had!

Gladly would we continue these musings, but
a scene of still deeper interest draws us away.

While yet the sun is above the horizon we
would fain look on Jerusalem. There are just a

105   ST. STEPHEN'S GATE.

sufficient number of light clouds to enhance the loveliness of the scene. Towards the left, in the background, is Zion, with the Tower of David. In front is the platform of the Haram, surmounted with the Mosque of Omar, and immediately next thereto is the closed-up gateway, believed to

THE GOLDEN GATE.

occupy the place of the Golden Gate, through which the King of Zion, meek and lowly, entered, "riding upon an ass." (Zech. ix. 9; Matt. xxi. 5.) Further to the right, and near St. Stephen's

Gate, is the accredited Pool of Bethesda; but I must not particularise; to do so would be to repeat the words "reputed," "accredited," "supposed," &c., *ad nauseam*.

There is Jerusalem, with her walls and towers, not as she once was, nor as she will yet be; but it is Jerusalem, and I repeat to my friend as much as I can remember of the lines:

"I WOULD—BUT YE WOULD NOT."

(Matt. xxiii. 37; Luke xix. 41.)

'Tis evening—over Salem's towers a golden lustre gleams,
And lovingly and lingeringly the sun prolongs his beams;
He looks, as on some work undone, for which the time has
    past;
So tender is his glance and mild, it seems to be his last.
But a brighter Sun is looking on, more earnest is *His* eye,
For thunder-clouds will veil Him soon, and darken all the
    sky;
O'er Zion still He bends, as loath His presence to remove,
And on her walls there lingers yet the sunshine of His
    love.

'Tis *Jesus*—with an anguish'd heart, a parting glance He
    throws;
For mercy's day she has sinn'd away, for a night of dreadful woes;
"Oh! would that thou hadst known," He said, while down
    roll'd many a tear,
"My words of peace, in this thy day! but now thine end
    is near;

Alas! for thee, Jerusalem, how cold thy heart to me!
How often in these arms of love would I have gather'd thee!
My sheltering wing had been thy shield, my love thy
    happy lot;
I would it had been thus with thee. '*I* would, but *ye*
    would not.'"

He wept alone, and men pass'd on—the men whose sins
    He bore;
They saw the Man of Sorrows weep; they had seen Him
    weep before;
They ask'd not whom those tears were for, they ask'd not
    whence they flowed;
Those tears were for rebellious man; their source, the
    heart of God:
They fell upon this desert earth, like drops from heaven
    on high.
Struck from an ocean-tide of love that fills eternity.
With love and tenderness divine, those crystal cells o'er-
    flow;
'Tis God that weeps, through human eyes, for human guilt
    and woe.

That hour has fled; those tears are told; the agony is
    past;
The Lord has wept, the Lord has bled, but has not *loved*
    His last.
His eye of love is downward bent, still ranging to and
    fro,
Where'er in this wild wilderness there roams the child of
    woe;
Nor *His* alone—the Three in One, who look'd through
    Jesus' eye,

Could still the harps of angel bands, to hear the suppliant
    sigh ;
And when the rebel *chooses* wrath, God mourns his hapless
    lot,
Deep breathing from His heart of love—" I would, but *ye*
    would not."

The sun disappears and the lights fade, while twilight deepens more rapidly than in England. We look once more over the hill country of Judea, towards the Dead Sea, yet again at the city, and descend the minaret stairs.

Our horses are brought ; we mount and pursue a path along which we are guided by one of the Arabs, to the opposite brow of the Mount of Olives, from which we can look over Bethany.

During this ride I noticed on a path a little above us, a shepherd followed by his flock. His staff was in his hand, and he was calling out, I at first thought, to us, but from the listlessness of my companions, and a close observation of his manner, I discovered that he was calling to the sheep, no doubt by their names (John x. 3), and they followed him. I turned my head once or twice after we had passed them to look again at the lovely scripture spectacle which brought especially to my mind Psalm xxiii. and Thomas Pringle's paraphrase :

"The Lord Himself my steps doth guide ;
I feel no want, I fear no foe :
Along the verdant valley's side,
Where cool the quiet waters flow,
Like as his flock a shepherd feedeth,
My soul in love Jehovah leadeth.

" And when amid the stumbling mountains
Through frowardness I blindly stray,
Or wander near forbidden fountains,
Where the destroyer lurks for prey,
My wayward feet again He guideth
To paths where holy peace resideth.

" Though that dread pass before me lies,
(First opened up by Sin and Wrath)
Where death's black shadow shrouds the skies,
And sheds its horrors o'er the path ;
Yet even there I'll feel no ill,
For my Redeemer guards me still.

" Even He who walked by Abraham's side.
My steps doth tend through weal and woe ;
With rod and staff to guard and guide,
And comfort me where'er I go ;
And He His ransomed flock that keepeth,
Our shepherd, slumbereth not nor sleepeth.

" For me a banquet He doth spread
Of high desires and hallowed joys ;
With blessings He anoints my head,
And fills a cup that never cloys
And nothing more my soul doth lack,
Save gratitude to render back.

"Oh ! still may goodness, mercy, truth,
Attend my steps from stage to stage,
As they have followed me from youth,
Through life's long weary pilgrimage ;
Till He who Israel led of old,
Shall guide me to His heavenly fold."

Though I afterwards saw the sheep with the
shepherd, yet I do not remember to have had
pointed out to me, in all the journey, a sheepfold.
I would, however, remind the reader of the abundance of scripture illustration which is yielded by
a knowledge of its structure and uses.

My information has been added to, in this particular, since my return, by Mr. E. G. Saleeby of
the Mount Lebanon Schools. The Eastern fold,
then, is a square walled enclosure, defended on the
top from the attacks of thieves and wild beasts by
a close set row of thorns. The entrance is by a
single door, of which the shepherd carries the key,
and at night, when the sheep are in the fold, his
place is in a little watch-house close to the door.
The thief will, however, sometimes draw near
when the shepherd, overcome by fatigue and cold,
is slumbering. He will not come to the door, but
to one of the remoter parts, and having removed
some of the thorns, will get over into the fold, and

hand up, one after the other, some of the sheep to an accomplice on the wall ; thus illustrating John x. 1 : " Verily, verily, I say unto you, he that entereth not by the door into the sheepfold, but climbeth up some other way, the same is a thief and a robber."

The watchfulness too of the shepherd, and the dangers he willingly encounters, sometimes sacrificing his life for the sheep, and many other features of the case are deeply interesting and instructive; but I will refrain, especially as I cannot write so fully as I could have wished from my own observations.

With such food for meditation, I followed my companion and the guide ; preferring silence to conversation, but in this I was to be disappointed.

A boy, seeing the guide engaged with my companion, essayed to make a profit out of me. I would gladly have given him a shilling to run away and leave me in quiet, but my ignorance of Arabic put this remedy out of the question. After following for some distance, he began his importunities, which increased in tone and manner as he progressed, till I endeavoured to satisfy him with one of the little silver pieces which I had obtained

in Alexandria through Adam. But this made
matters worse; he ran beside me, holding out the
piece and chattering away in Arabic to the effect,
I suppose, "This piece is current in Egypt, but
not here." I motioned to him, and bade him be
quiet, trying him with the Arabic for "No! no!"
("La! La!") These rebukes were overheard by
my companion in front, who supported them with
a few words which produced a brief cessation,
followed by a running fusillade in an under tone,
which was, if possible, still more distracting. I
gave him a copper piastre but, like a street organ-
ist, the more he got, the more he annoyed me, and
meditation was impossible.

We soon came to a spot commanding a good
prospect of Bethany. There lay the village whither
Jesus so often resorted, where they dwelt of whom
we read, "Now Jesus loved Martha, and her sister,
and Lazarus," (John xi. 6.) We contented ourselves with this view from without, which perhaps,
considering the lateness of the hour and increasing
darkness, was the best to choose.

Hither, from the turmoil of the city and oppo-
sitions of men, did Jesus repair. Here He found a
home, and here was the tenderness of His sympathy expressed in tears, and the fulness of His

BETHANY.

power in the words, "Lazarus, come forth." And he that was dead came forth bound hand and foot with grave-clothes, and his face was bound about with a napkin. Jesus saith unto them, "Loose him, and let him go." (John xi. 43, 44.)

> "The work begun is carried on,
>   By power from heav'n above;
>   And every step from first to last,
>   Declares that 'God is love.'"

Here too, after the miracle, is a scene presented which claims our deepest attention. Jesus is seen in the midst, of whom aged Simeon, when he held Him, as an infant, in his arms, had said by the Holy Ghost, "Behold, this child is set for the fall and rising again of many in Israel; and for a sign which shall be spoken against; . . . . that the thoughts of many hearts may be revealed." (Luke ii. 34, 35.) And were not the secrets of many hearts laid bare at Bethany? For "both the chief priests and the Pharisees had given a commandment, that, if any man knew where He were, he should show it, that they might take Him." (John xi. 57.)

Much people of the Jews came there, but "not for Jesus' sake only." (Chap. xii. 9.)

Judas spake of the waste of the ointment, but "not that he cared for the poor." (Ver. 6.)

115   AN ASS TIED.

But Lazarus in communion, Martha in service, and Mary, with a whole heart, pouring the very precious ointment on His feet, so that the room was filled with the odour (ver. 2, 3), discover hearts that have learned the secret of the Lord, which is with them that fear Him. (Ps. xxv. 14.)

It was indeed a season, as well as a place, appropriate for contemplation (Gen. xxiv. 63), but necessity seemed laid upon us not to loiter. We returned in the same order as we had come, Mr. El Karey with the guide, and my new companion with me. How heartily I wished he would behave, as Pringle describes his,

> " Afar in the desert I love to ride.
> With the *silent* bush boy alone by my side."

On our way back to Jerusalem, we sometimes found it convenient to dismount and lead the horses down some of the most rugged slopes; then, passing by the St. Stephen's and Damascus gates, we came in due course to the house of our kind host.

Wednesday the 14th. After breakfast we paid one or two visits in the city. At one moment, while my companion was engaged in some business, I was interested in seeing "an ass tied," which though a very common spectacle in the cities and villages of Palestine, was now noticed under conditions of leisure, which induced me to make the accompanying little sketch. (Cf. Matt. xxi. 2.)

We went to the Sultan's Khan, where was a glass store, at which Mr. El Karey bought some panes, for repairing dilapidations in his windows at home, and while the purchase was being made I found opportunity to sketch the scene, a novel one to me and truly characteristic of the primordial customs of the unchanged East; the camels laden and unloading, the asses in all positions, not excepting that of strolling on the top of the wall, which was reached by a stone staircase.

This morning, we passed through and surveyed the St. Stephen's and Damascus gates, and having been joined by Mr. Azam and another native friend, and secured a guide, we entered upon an exploration of the ancient quarry beneath the city.

The entrance to this quarry is close to the Damascus gate. Our guide opened an iron door, and we each took a candle, having lighted which, we first descended a long slope; by the time we reached the bottom we began to appreciate the

THE SULTAN'S KHAN—JERUSALEM.

116

vastness of the excavations we were exploring. In some places we could reach the roof, but in many instances this was impracticable. We saw one or two prodigious blocks of stone, which had been detached from the rock, but left in the quarry, apparently on account of some discovered fault. It is believed that some of the larger stones which entered into the structure of Solomon's temple, were quarried here. We could in many instances see the long and deep chisel chases, cut in the parent rock and which, from the nature of the work, had followed a curved line, and into which, I apprehend, the wedges and levers were introduced for detaching "the great stones" (1 Kings v. 17.)

As we penetrated further into this wonderful excavation, a sense of the vastness of the labour which had formed it, and of the amount of material which it had yielded to the ancient builders, grew upon our minds. In many places where the lime-stone roof was sufficiently low to be reached, it was inscribed with names in the Arabic and European languages. These writings are made with the smoke of the candles carried by the explorers. I believe it is now about twenty years since this quarry was re-discovered, so that the writings have no connection with past generations.

When we had progressed a good distance, I noticed among them, in a well-chosen place and in well-formed characters, the words " Rob Roy," and needed no other assurance that I was on the track of John McGregor, Esq., captain and crew of the canoe of that name. Here I resolved to make my essay at writing in smoke, and applying my candle to an adjoining piece of rock, wrote the motto which is on the walls of my Sunday-school, "God is love." I was not very well satisfied with this first attempt, so before quitting the quarry, at a moment when the rest of the party were engaged in the same way, I applied my candle to a fresh surface, and re-formed the words in a less apprentice-like style.

Having penetrated to the farthest part from the entrance, we were informed we stood beneath the middle of the city, or thereabouts. Water was dropping from above into a chamber. I collected some in the little cup belonging to my palette, and found it strongly impregnated with the salts contained in the rocks above. At one time, when we were halting in one of the deepest and largest vaults of the quarry, my companion addressed me with,

" Well, brother, what shall we sing here?" and, in agreement with my rejoinder, the galleries were made to resound with the first verse of

" Rock of Ages, cleft for me."

I collected a few specimens of the stone, and in due course we retraced our subterranean way from the centre to the outside of Jerusalem.

ANCIENT QUARRY.

We next visited the British Hospital for Jews, and were greatly interested in what we saw and heard of the good work there being done for the benefit of the bodies and souls of the children of Abraham. The word of God is daily read, and the gospel preached to the inmates of the wards.

In the afternoon we went to the pool adjoining St. Stephen's gate, called by the Arabs "Birket Israil," which is reputed to be the Pool of Bethesda. It is an immense reservoir, and measures, according to Dr. Robinson, 360 feet in length, 130 feet in breadth, and 75 feet in depth, besides the rubbish which has been accumulating in it for ages. That it was once filled with water, there are believed to be sufficient evidences, but many critics are of opinion that the true pool of Bethesda was elsewhere, and the attempt to establish this one as the veritable pool rests on the assumption that St. Stephen's gate is the same as the Sheep-gate of scripture. My companion rested, while I explored the bottom of the pool, running over the heaps of rubbish which choke it. I saw fig trees and other vegetation growing there and, while in the pool, I observed a man throwing dust therein from above.

From the pool, we went to the adjoining margin of the Haram platform, upon which stands the Mosque of Omar. The true mosque is a smaller building at a remote part of the platform, but I now refer to the "Kubbab-Assakhra," or "Dome

POOL OF BETHESDA.

of the Rock," which is a large octagonal building
in the centre of the platform and covering the
sacred rock, to which Jewish, Christian, and
Mahometan traditions are attached.

I was entering the enclosure without ceremony,
when my companion cautioned me to withdraw my
foot, as we had made no compact with the keepers
of the place, and my rashness might have incurred
some of the unpleasant consequences which
Mahometan jealousy has often been known to
produce.

We had seen enough : here was the exterior of
(next to that of Mecca) the most sacred Mahometan temple. The Jewish temple, whose place it
occupies, has long since been removed. He, whose
Father's house it was, came there, but was not
received (John i. 11.) The chief priests conspired
against Him to put Him to death. Their voice
prevailed with Pilate. He was buffeted, scourged,
and spit upon, and from the judgment-hall they
led Him to Golgotha. "And with Him they crucified two malefactors, on either side one, and Jesus
in the midst." "From the sixth to the ninth
hour, there was darkness over all the earth," at
the end of which time He cried, "It is finished,"
and gave up the ghost; and the veil of the temple

was rent in twain from the top to the bottom, and the glory departed from Israel. But her alienation is not for ever. In a still future day the Lord shall suddenly come to His temple, "and he shall sit as a refiner and purifier of silver, and he shall purify the sons of Levi, and purge them as gold and silver, that they may offer unto the Lord an offering in righteousness. Then shall the offering of Judah and Jerusalem be pleasant unto the Lord, as in the days of old and as in former years." (Mal. iii.)

We now returned to the house of Mr. Azam, whom we met near the Damascus Gate riding on a white ass, and attended by the faithful Monsoul; so we together made our way home, and there I spent my last night in the vicinity of Jerusalem.

Great reason had I to be thankful for the privileges of these three days, and often, and with much pleasure, have I since remembered them and the interesting and instructive scenes I then witnessed. I have also frequently thought upon what was omitted, chiefly through lack of time. I did not go farther south than Bethlehem, or more easterly than Bethany. Fain would I have done so, but lacked the opportunity. Hebron, Gaza, Beersheba, Jericho, the Dead Sea, and the lower fords of Jordan seemed to claim a visit, the desire to accomplish which was surely pardonable, and I trust it was not without gratitude for what I had been permitted to see, that I thought of these things.

During the evening articles already purchased were delivered and others brought for selection, among which was a book of pressed wild flowers. This I purchased, and the beauty of the flowers, the skill with which they have been preserved and arranged, and the associations of the places where they were gathered have provoked the almost unlimited admiration and interest of those in England who have seen them.

Then followed the necessary arranging and packing of these things, some of them *très fragiles*, and thus my visit to Jerusalem drew near its close.

CHAPTER VII.

Thursday, 15th. (7 a.m.) Having previously sent forward some of the luggage, and taken leave of our kind entertainers, we set out on our way for Samaria and Galilee.

Getting away towards the northern side of the city, we halted at the supposed Calvary, a little hill, whose claim to be the true Golgotha rests, among other evidences, on the circumstance that excavation has brought to light many human bones from beneath.

When in Jerusalem we had visited the *Via Dolorosa*, so called from being the supposed way along which the Saviour bare His cross, and where are shewn particular traditional relics, of which, however, from little confidence in their authenticity I made no entry in my journal. The same remark applies to the Church of the Holy Sepulchre, where was pointed out to me "*le tombeau de Jésus Christ*," and where also professes to be Calvary itself, but in these instances, doubt grew into a conviction

of the impossibility of the case, and I did not even
accompany the guide to the latter shrine.

. Here, however, at the little hill outside the city,
with apparently such good claims to being Calvary,
I dismounted, and paused to think again of the one
great offering there made for sin, when the blood
of the Son of God flowed for sinners—flowed for .
me. I plucked a twig from an olive-tree growing
there, and preserved it as a sweet emblem of that
peace which Jesus made by the blood of His cross,
when "the chastisement of our peace fell upon
Him." (Isa. liii. 5.)

The first village we passed was Ramah of the
tribe of Benjamin, the birthplace of Samuel the
prophet (1 Sam. i. 19, 20), of which the prophet
Jeremiah foretold (Jer. xxxi. 15), that which was
fulfilled as we read in Matthew ii. 18: " In Ramah
was there a voice heard, lamentation, and weeping, and great mourning, Rachel weeping for her
children, and would not be comforted, because
they are not."

Hereabout I halted to scrutinize a portion of
the shaft of a prostrate column, bearing a Latin
inscription which I essayed to copy, but though
many of the characters were still distinct, the difficulty of determining what many others were, and

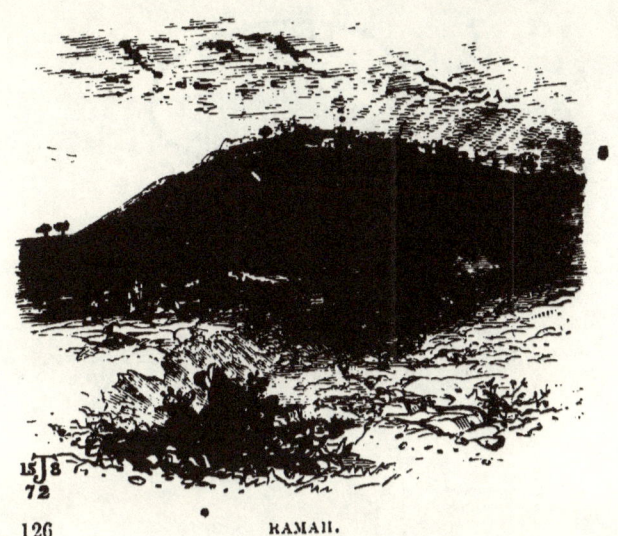

126   RAMAH.

the removal by injury of some, caused me to re-
linquish the task as scarcely likely to yield results
commensurate with the inconvenience to our party
(Mr. El Karey, myself, and a muleteer) from
delay. At Beeri, which is identified with Beer,
whither Jotham fled for fear of Abimelech his
brother (Judges ix. 21), we made a little detour to
water our horses at a fountain where some women
of the village were assembled, engaged in washing
garments.

The next spot of scripture identification we
passed was Bethel, to which Jacob gave that name,
saying, " This is none other but the house of God "
(Gen xxviii. 17), and of which frequent mention
is afterwards made in the Old Testament. As we
regarded it from the south-west, across the sterile
and stony ground, I could but reflect on the seeming impossibility, that Jacob should find here
anything else for a pillow than a stone; but when
we had passed, and came in view of the gardens
which lie to the north of the place, my impressions
of its barrenness were somewhat moderated.

To Bethel did Jacob return at the word of the
Lord, as we read in Genesis xxxv. 1. " And God
said unto Jacob, Arise, go up to Beth-el, and
dwell there : and make there an altar unto God,

that appeared unto thee when thou fleddest from
the face of Esau thy brother." Which word he
obeyed, and God appeared unto him there, "and
Jacob called the name of the place where God
spake unto him Beth-el." Here it was the Lord
confirmed unto him the word he had already
spoken. "Thy name shall be called no more
Jacob (that is, a supplanter), but Israel (that is, a
prince)." (Chap. xxxii. 28.) Times and circumstances had changed with him, but the God of
Bethel was the same, through many trials had he
been brought and made to prove that help cometh
from the Lord. And at the close of his course,
· although he spake of the days of the years of his
life as "few and evil" (Chap xlvii. 9), God and
the word of His grace were his support. "And
Israel said unto Joseph, Behold, I die; but God
shall be with you, and bring you again unto the
land of your fathers." (Chap. xlviii. 21.)

"O! blest be the goodness and love of the Lord,
For the gift of His holy, His heavenly word;
'Tis the ground of my hope, and the shield of my fait h
A lamp to my feet and a light to my path.

"How blest is the hope which the Bible supplies,
In the day when the billows of trouble arise;
How happy the soul who in Jesus believes,
When the Father of spirits the spirit receives.

15 Ja
72

128   BETHEL.

" A mother may leave the dear child of her love,
  The hills may depart, and the mountains remove ;
  But, blest be the gift ! and, adored be the Giver!
  ' The word of the Lord endureth for ever.' "

As we held our way through the lovely
valleys which form the natural highway up to
Samaria, with olive-trees growing on either side,
the doves cooing and calling to their mates, and
anon flying across the valley, and the very rocks
musical with the singing of birds, how vividly did
the thought of the company which had so often
passed this way come before the mind, till I almost ejaculated, " Ye rocks and trees have beheld
the Person and walk of the Son of God!" But
here the remembrance which faith gives came to
my relief, and I added, " But He that made you
died for me."

We stopped at a vineyard to purchase some
grapes of the owner, and having filled our water
bottle at a wayside spring, about noon we rested
under some olive-trees and opened our stores of
bread, meat, and fruit, from which and the water
we made our dinner. While we were thus bivou-
acked, a caravan of asses passed, coming from
Nablûs. We invited the leader to our repast ; so,
leaving the caravan to continue its way, he joined

K

our company, ate some of the grapes, and with a السلامه‎ مع "*Má salameh*" (Peace be with you!) turned off to overtake his own party.

MID-DAY HALT.

Having rested for about an hour, we remounted and continued our way northwards. In these rides we frequently acted literally according to the couplet,

" The way may be rough, but it cannot be long,
So we'll smooth it with hope, and cheer it with song."

Mr. El Karey having a good knowledge, and being very fond of our English hymns, we often joined in one or another that might be suggested by the circumstances around, or the turn which conversation had taken. The favourite was, most unmistakably,

"For ever with the Lord."

On the next page is printed an Arabic hymn (evidently in some sort a paraphrase of Psalm cxxxvii.), which my companion also frequently sang to the accompanying Welsh tune, and to which I have added a free translation. The latter makes it evident that the writer was not one of those who apply only the blessings of the Old Testament to the Church and believers, and restrict the interpretation and application of all else to the Jews.

On this and other occasions when, from my brown holland coat being sent forward to the wash, I was wearing my tweed at midday, I was struck with its appearing to be of a much lighter shade than that which I knew belonged to it, so that for a moment, I suspected I must have got on some one else's coat. But on a little reflection I was convinced that the lighter appearance was the result of, to me, the unusual power of the sun's rays, filling every crevice with strong light, such indeed, that I found real comfort in wearing the dark folding spectacles which I had brought with me from England. Of course the rays of heat were in proportion to those of light, but although I was provided with a small thermometer, I made no observations therewith, as I left it in one of the saddle bags the whole journey. Sufficient, then, that I could frequently feel the sun pricking my toes through the leather of my boots.

ARABIC HYMN.

U-hi bu bí at-an, Yá rab ban-al a-zím: Tilk-al-la-tí

shtara-yu-thá, Bi-da mikal karím, Bi-da mi-kal karím.

In karihat yadi,
Barakat-al banín;
Yalsaq lisáuí bifamí,
Watan sani-l-yamin.

Wa-in nasítu má,
Yaduru au yufid ;
Yaada mu qulbi farahan,
Wa huz nuhu yazíd.

Abki liájlihá,
Wa usadussalat :
Wa kullu ataábí lahá.
Má dumtu fíl hayua.

TRANSLATION.

The church, O Lord, I love,
Which Thou Thyself, hast bought,
Who purchased with Thy precious blood,
Those who were sold for nought.

If ever I seek not
Their weal, who are Thine own ;
Then let my mouth be parched with drought,
My right hand me disown.

From all that does annoy,
To all that blessing is ;
Be mine to seek Thy church's joy,
Or mine own grief increase.

For her I lift my voice,
And supplicate Thine aid;
In Thine own strength make her rejoice,
Who hast her ransom paid.

The country on the borders of Judea and Samaria we found to be less hilly than that which we had just traversed or that which lay before us. As we were crossing the hills to-day, when noticing the flinty hardness of the bare rock, which yielded a sound as from adamant, beneath the flat shoes of our sure-footed little Arab horses, my attention was diverted to a scene of activity on my right. It was a quarry, in which four or five Arabs were hewing away at the stone with heavy hammers, detaching and shaping the pieces, which brought vividly to my mind the words in Jeremiah xxiii. 29: "Is not my word like as a fire; saith the Lord; and like a hammer that breaketh the rock in pieces?"

A short distance into Samaria, we had to climb a hill higher, perhaps, than any we had crossed this day. The hill being steep, and the heat of the day still great, horses and riders wore an aspect of fatigue. When we reached the summit, I caught sight of a number of black objects moving in the valley beyond, and by the help of my pocket telescope, discovered them to be droves of cattle, goats, and sheep, with two or three Arabs attending them, either going to or returning from a gathering-point at the end of the valley, into which we descended by steep and rugged zig-zag paths, and rode to the place of assemblage. It was a well, and the herdsmen were engaged in watering the herds and flocks. "This," said my companion, " is Lebonah's well." Lebonah is only once mentioned in scripture, namely, Judges xxi. 19.

Here was a scene of the deepest interest : The well which Lebonah gave to his children and, doubtless, drank thereof himself, his children, and his cattle. In some of the rocks around the well, holes had been formed, into which the Arabs were emptying water from goatskin buckets. Having given up my horse to the care of the muleteer, my first impulse, though very thirsty, was to make a hasty sketch of the scene; and what a scene ! What a mixed company of cattle, sheep, goats, horses, mule, and men, all gathered round the well —TO DRINK.

Away down the valley lay the village of Lebonah. On the hillsides and in bye places were the pastures, but here, to the uninhabited and rocky extremity of the valley, we all came crowding, because the well was there, the well of water ; and we gathered there TO DRINK. So is it in the gospel. The Lord Jesus says (John vii.

37) "If any man thirst, let him come unto me *and drink.*"

Having finished the sketch, I found our party was remounting, and I made known, through Mr. El Karey, my wish for a draught of the water. Inmediately one of the Arabs lowered his bucket which, from having been down the well so many times before, was in several places worn into holes, from which the water was running in various directions. · I applied my hands to the water-bag (for such it was), and directed the largest stream to my mouth, so obtaining a good refreshing draught. Such was the pleasure of drinking, that it was not till afterwards that I could afford any attention to the fact, that while I was drinking from one of the holes, the water was running down my clothes from three or four others. However, this was of small moment, for in the atmosphere through which we were passing, all moisture soon evaporated. This disregard of other things brought to my mind the words, "With *joy* shall we draw water out of the wells of salvation." (Isa. xii. 3.)

All being refreshed, we left the well and passed the village, around which · some fields of millet were standing, nearly ready for the sickle, all the other crops being gathered in.

LEBONAH'S WELL.

136

At several other villages which we passed, we saw the threshing-floors, and oxen treading out the corn. If I record the whole truth, I must state, that in the majority of cases, the oxen were muzzled, contrary to the injunction in Deuteronomy xxv. 4. In some places we also saw the threshing implements, consisting of two pieces of wood joined at an obtuse angle, and one of them armed with sharp stones, which are dragged over the corn by oxen or horses, with sometimes a man standing thereon, to increase the weight Sundry scripture allusions to the threshing-floor were thus brought to my mind; amongst them Psalm i. 4, which compares the ungodly to "the chaff which the wind driveth away;" several striking examples of which scene were presented to us.

On one or two occasions, when we were passing the threshing-floors by night, we saw the owners and some of their retainers asleep "at the end of the heap of corn" with their outer garments spread over them, and the corn partly covering them, as we read of Boaz in Ruth iii. 7 ; and more than once did his prototype rouse from his slumbers to respond to our salutations, and answer our enquiries as to the direction we should follow in continuing our journey.

Soon after 4 p.m., which would be the tenth hour of the day, we met some women going out of a village to draw water, a spectacle which was to be seen from that time till a few hours later. As we were riding along a mountain path this afternoon, we heard mournful cries issuing from holes in the earth, and which were made by the young owls concealed there. There is reference to these cries in Micah i. 8: "Mourning as the daughters of the owls." (See margin.)

Our way still lay over the hills, and for a while we were riding along a mountain ridge, so that our shadows were distinctly visible in the valley below. At length, the sun declining in the heavens, and our path leading us beneath the higher slopes of the hill, we fairly entered into its shadow, and could no longer trace our own on the plain beneath, though it was easy to watch that of the hilltops, creeping along the ground, and covering one object after another. Immediately we entered the shade, I experienced the most refreshing coolness, and a pleasant breeze fanning my face ; so, doubling up to within speaking distance of my companion, I asked, "What is the name of this mountain?" "Gerizim," he replied. Truly we proved the blessing of "the shadow of a great rock in a weary land." (Isa. xxxii. 2.)

Beneath, on our right, lay the valley which was trodden by the footsteps of Jesus, as mentioned in John iv. And soon we came in sight of the low stone wall which surrounds Jacob's well, whereon being weary with His journey, He sat. Beyond lay Joseph's tomb. The muleteer filled the water bottle at a spring in the hillside, and we again slaked our thirst, this time in sight of the place where the Lord of all asked for a drink of water, which we do not read that He received; "Whose meat and drink was to do the will of him that sent him, and to finish his work."

We descended the north-east slopes of Gerizim, and with the well now behind us, and our faces toward the west, took the way of the valley between Mounts Ebal and Gerizim, along which the Samaritans of Sychar came to the well, at the words of the woman, "He told me all things that ever I did;" and found Him there who is "Christ the Saviour of the world." (John iv. 42.) In these valleys too, did Joseph, at the age of seventeen, seek his brethren, when sent of God to save life. (Gen. xlv. 7.) He befriended his *brethren*; Jesus died for His *enemies*. Joseph's coat was torn and taken back to his father's tent, stained with the blood of *another*; for the vesture of

Jesus they cast lots, and He entered again into
the glory He had laid aside, not by the blood
of goats and calves, but by *His own* blood,

NABLÛS.

"having obtained eternal redemption for us."
(Heb. ix. 12.)

We presently came to a Turkish guard-house,
with, I think, a sentry or two on duty, and three
or four soldiers playing cards, I know. This was
on our left, and a little beyond, on our right, we
passed the Mahometan cemetery. I was amused
with the abundance of lively little grey lizards

running over the rough ground, and up the trunks of trees in quest of hiding places. This cemetery was, I think, the largest I saw in Palestine. One feature common to the cemeteries, Christian and Mahometan, was the whitened exterior of the graves, which were formed of stone and plaster, the whiteness evidently being renewed from time to time, reminding me of the Saviour's comparison in Matthew xxiii. 27 : "Woe unto you, scribes and Pharisees, hypocrites! for ye are like unto whited sepulchres, which indeed appear beautiful outward, but are within full of dead men's bones, and of all uncleanness."

The ground we next passed over, there is little doubt, was the site of the ancient city, which appears to have removed westward, during successive generations, so increasing the distance between it and Jacob's well. When near the city, with a rising ground before us, we were suddenly reminded of the vicinity of a place of present importance, by the appearance of two native gentlemen, well mounted, galloping over the ridge, and, having exchanged salutes, riding on before us, over a bridge and soon disappearing from our view.

We were now passing between the gardens of

Nablûs, which is Sychar, and soon turned into its streets. Through one narrow roughly-paved street after another we passed, now on level, now on sloping ground, until riding beneath an archway, we entered a small courtyard and dismounted. Having ascended a flight of stone steps, we were met by Mrs. El Karey. In short, we had reached our resting place for the next four days.

Having exchanged greetings and inquiries, I was shewn my chamber, which seemed to possess an additional charm from being on the wall. (2 Kings iv. 10.) True, its provisions were not restricted to a bed, a table, a stool, and a candlestick; for, to begin, there were two beds. A glance within reminded one of the kindness which was now engaged for my comfort. The soiled and tumbled garments which I had sent forward, reappeared washed and smooth. I exchanged my hot clothing for the clean holland suit, getting a bath between, and soon after we were sitting at the tea-table, sharing and telling the Lord's mercies. But I am remiss, and must introduce Mrs. El Karey as an English lady. Shortly afterwards we adjourned to the housetop where mats being spread, we stretched ourselves and enjoyed the cool, though balmy, evening air.

It was a lovely scene : the gibbous moon was shining over the city and on the mountain-sides, shedding her silvery light on rocks, and walls, and domes, and minarets. The sounds and objects were so purely Eastern, and the spot so sacred in its associations, that the happiest thoughts filled my mind.

Soon after we had reclined on the rugs, our company was added to by arrivals coming up the staircase, which led direct from the court beneath to the housetop without passing through the house, after the ancient manner of the east, and illustrative of such passages as Matthew xxiv. 17. "Let him which is on the housetop not come down to take anything out of his house." Our visitors were members of the christian community with which Mr. El Karey is in fellowship, and who were assembling for the usual Thursday evening prayer meeting. The first hour was occupied with edifying conversation, after which we adjourned to a "corner of the housetop." (Prov. xxi. 9, Acts x. 9.) Two hymns were sung, a portion of scripture read, and two brethren led in prayer. Thus was another stage of my journey completed, under circumstances well fitted to raise a feeling of gratitude to Him whose loving hand had pro-

tected me from the heat by day and the cold
by night, both of which, though I had felt, I had
not suffered from either.

> Thy presence, everlasting God,
> Wide o'er all nature spreads abroad ;
> Thy watchful eyes, which cannot sleep,
> In every place Thy children keep.
>
> While near each other we remain,
> Thou dost our lives and souls sustain ;
> When absent, happy if we share
> Thy smiles, Thy counsels, and Thy care.
>
> To Thee we all our ways commit,
> And seek our comforts near Thy feet ;
> Still on our souls vouchsafe to shine,
> And guard and guide us still as Thine."

145

EBAL.

NABLÛS.
FROM THE WEST.

GERIZIM.

15|8
72

CHAPTER VIII.

As already explained, my bedroom was on the
housetop, and was reached from the yard beneath
by two flights of stone steps. In my new circumstances well might I recall the events described in
the early part of John iv. The journey had made
me weary, although I had reached Nablûs in the
cool of the evening and had rested and been
refreshed on the way. During the latter portion of
the ride I had been sheltered by Mount Gerizim
from the oblique rays of the sun. We know that
He whose journey is recorded in that chapter
travelled on foot, and was exposed to the midday
heat in the sultry valleys; Jesus "the man of
Sychar," the same yesterday, and to-day, and for
ever.

Fatigued, then, and thankful for a christian
home in the place where my Lord Himself abode
two days (John iv. 40), I retired to bed. My
bedroom window was almost level with the flat
roof outside, on which the assembly before the
prayer meeting had taken place, and, through

L

various accidents, had lost some of its glass, so that several of the frames, failing the arrival of the panes purchased in Jerusalem, were closed with paper. In the middle of the night I was awoke by sounds which convinced me that a body was being forced through one of these paper screens, which, though sleep was scarce dispelled, I discovered before its disappearance, to be a cat ; so, raising myself and making the noise which in England is found to scare away *Felis domestica*, I had the satisfaction of witnessing the precipitate retreat of the intruder, and lay down again to sleep. A second entry was made during the night and repelled in the same way; if there were any more, I was not conscious of them.

Friday 16th. I am in Nablûs, the Shechem of the Old Testament, and the Sychar of John iv. as we have seen. The present name is evidently an Arab corruption of the Greek Νεάπολις, under which name it is mentioned by Josephus. (Wars, book iv. chap. viii. 1.)

My companion having sundry engagements to fulfil this day, we did not extend our explorations beyond the city. I noticed the faggots of thorns, donkey loads of which we had passed at different times on the road, and their dry and slender character summoned to my imagination, what must be the nature of their burning as referred to in such scriptures as, " They are quenched as the fire of thorns " (Ps. cxviii. 12); "As the crackling of thorns under a pot, so is the laughter of the fool" (Eccl. vii. 6), &c.

I had the pleasure of seeing the girls of Mrs. El Karey's school assembled in an industrial class, as well as of witnessing the boys and girls in the school room, receiving instruction, the basis of which is the word of God. Here, then, was a little seminary, where the good seed was being sown, and we cannot doubt that fruit will be borne to His glory who here foretold the day when " he that soweth and he that reapeth shall rejoice together." (John iv. 36.) It was my privilege to address a few words to these interesting young hearers. Thursday being the day for the mothers' meeting, I had just missed the opportunity of witnessing their assembly.

. The principal mosque in Nablûs, of which we only surveyed the exterior, was originally a Crusaders' church, and is still a building of some pretensions. This morning, a wealthy Arab gentleman calling to see Mr. El Karey, I was introduced to him. He brought his son with him, and after a little conversation, it occurred to me to beg his acceptance of the only complete Arabic New Testament which I had with me. This he did very readily, asking if I could not give him the whole Bible, a request with which I was unable to comply. I returned to my room, however, and found some key-rings, twelve of which I had bought for a penny in London. With two of these I returned, and gave one to him and one to his son. Immediately scissors were put in requisition to cut the string, which had served hitherto to keep his keys together, and, discovering some of that pleasure with which a child receives a new toy, he put the gift to its proper use; nor was his son less backward in attaching his only key to the other ring. I noticed that after this, the Testament was again taken up and looked into with apparently fresh interest.

For these two or three days, we were inconvenienced by the difficulty of obtaining horses. My friend had restored the one he had been riding to its owner and depended upon making fresh arrangements, but met with many obstacles. Owing to the disturbed state of the country beyond Jordan, the government had found a pretext for requisitioning most of the horses in Nablûs for the use of the

troops. This caused owners of horses to be loth
to let it appear that they had any, lest theirs also
should be impressed, from which circumstance it
arose that a considerable number were in concealment. Thus, part of our time was unsuc-
cessfully occupied with efforts to obtain a mount
for my companion.

One of the places whither our business took us,
was the telegraph office, and I noticed, in a long
and animated conversation which passed (in Arabic
of course) between my companion and the manager
of the instruments, that he was describing what I
imagined to be a case of illness, as he placed his
arched hand over his right cheek, and used the
word كبير "Kabir," which I knew to be "great."
After the conversation, Mr. El Karey turned to
me and explained that the speaker had an infant
child at home, afflicted with a large and angry
swelling on the side of its head, which, instead of
being reduced by the treatment it had received,
had rather grown worse; that the infant was in
continual pain, causing great anxiety to parents
and nurse.

Happily I felt that this was a case in which I
could prescribe with some hope of success, and
recommended warm fomentations, to be followed

by the application of a cold-water compress, and
these to be alternated three or four times in the
course of the day. Upon this we repaired to the
house, where a novel scene awaited me.

There were the Mahometan grandmother and
mother, so closely veiled that only their eyes were
visible, but the anxiety and interest expressed by
these could not be mistaken. The nurse was a
negress, whose whole appearance and behaviour
justified the words of Cowper:

> " Skins may differ, but affection
> Dwells in black and white the same."

The poor little sufferer was evidently in great
pain from the abscess which, by squeezing and the
application of cataplasms of lemon leaves and white
of egg, had (no wonder!) grown worse. I again
insisted on the importance of applying the water
at such a temperature at first as would allow of an
elevation as the bathing was continued, the danger
of urging the discharge by any pressure beyond
the gentlest touch, and the necessity of covering
the cold-water rag with oil-silk, a piece of which
was happily forthcoming from Mrs. El Karey's
stores. The linen cloths, the hot and cold water
were brought forth, the old plasters discarded,
and, with English surgeon and Arabic dresser to

151   AUDIENCE WITH THE GOVERNOR.

regulate the temperature, and the African nurse to apply the fomentation, the father looking on, and mother and grandmother peeping over their veils with looks of the profoundest interest—baby (who was a fine little fellow of four months, but whom I should have judged to be at least ten months) was soon under the influence of the new treatment; in hopes of the success of which, we left him for the night.

Saturday 17th. Rose at 5 a.m., and accompanied my companion to the Turkish bath. After breakfast, although he had not obtained a fresh horse, to avoid being left altogether in the lurch by the muleteer who had accompanied us from Jerusalem and whom, under all circumstances, it seemed advisable to shut out from any opportunity of absconding, Mr. El Karey ordered him to bring my horse and the mule to the house, while we waited on the governor and explained the difficulty of our position. The governor, who had been recently appointed, received us with great urbanity and kindness, giving us coffee and promises, and instructing an officer to see our wants supplied.

We took leave of his Excellency, and were conducted by the officer to a gallery overlooking a yard, in which were pointed out three or four sore-backed animals, to place a saddle on either of which would have been simple cruelty. My companion expostulated, but was informed that these were the best that could be obtained at the time.

Upon this we set out for the Jewish quarter and made our wants known there, as it sometimes happens that such lack can be supplied by one or other of the Jewish families. We were most kindly received and inquiries had been instituted in our behalf, when two soldiers from the government house presented themselves, having been commissioned to use all lawful arguments to dissuade us from availing ourselves of Jewish, when government resources failed. It is now literally true that where of old it was said "The Jews have no dealings with the Samaritans," the rulers and the Samaritans have no dealings with the Jews. The peculiar oppression which the latter people are now under was yet more strikingly illustrated before we left Nablûs, as I shall have occasion to describe.

We next visited the quarter of the Samaritans, after the hour of their synagogue service (Saturday being their sabbath). We found the high priest at home, reading from a Hebrew manuscript, and were received very kindly. He is a man of a very handsome and venerable appearance and of an amiable expression. Having learned that I was from England, he inquired in broken English if I knew Mr. Mills?* My answer in the affirmative seemed to act as a talisman. Immediately he exceeded his former self in kindness, and presently his good wife, a worthy dame whose healthy appearance suggested that athletics are among the customs of Samaritan ladies, brought us a repast of bread, cheese, butter, water melons and water. (It will be remembered that on nearly all occasions, by bread is meant the Arab cake baked on the hearth.) This gave an opportunity for speaking about the water " which if a man drink, he shall live for ever." I proposed that he should visit England, and he expressed his willingness on condition that I should receive him, which, of course, I promised to do.

After a little while, my companion delicately introduced the matter of our desire to see the celebrated Pentateuch, the accredited oldest Biblical MS in the world. His nephew, and apparent successor to his office, conducted us to the syna-

---

* Author of " Nablûs and the Modern Samaritans " (lately deceased). *Et vide* p. 39.

gogue, and having carefully locked the door, that it might not be seen by others of the Samaritans that we were being shewn the sacred relic, placed a stand before us, on which to rest the scroll. He went behind a screen and reappeared, bearing the MS in its silver case; having opened which, and placed it on the stand, he allowed us to approach and look on the relic. It is now well-known that many European and American travellers have been put off with the sight of one of the less ancient MSS, but my companion and other esoteric informants assured me that it was none other than *Manuscriptum Antiquissimum* which I saw.

On our way home we passed by "the potter's house" and turned in to look on him at his work. He sat at the wheel which he turned with his foot, and taking a lump of clay, placed it on the wheel, then while sustaining the rotation with his feet, having previously dipped his hands into a tub of water, applied them to the revolving lump in such a way as speedily to make it assume the form of a solid cylinder. He now directed his hands to the upper portion of the clay, so as to produce a hollowness therein and to complete it to the shape of a little water-pot, having finished which, he stopped the wheel and detached it; then renewing the rotation, he repeated the operation on the rest of the clay, and so proceeded from *"the same lump"* to make two or more vessels.

I especially noticed the facility with which, by a momentary alteration of the position of one of his fingers, he produced the most radical change in the form of the vessel, which brought out very strikingly another point in the scripture comparison, "Hath not the potter *power* over the clay, of the same lump to make one vessel unto honour and another unto dishonour?" (Rom. ix. 21.)

We called to see the sick baby and were very pleased to learn that the remedies had, through the Lord's blessing, been successful, and the patient and nurses had passed a better night than for the previous week. To add to the assurance that everything was being properly done, the compress was removed, and the English pseudo-surgeon and Arabic dresser, with the help of the nurse, applied the fomentation and renewed the compress, leaving everything in a hopeful condition.

In the afternoon, having obtained another horse, we started for Mount Gerizim, passing by the spot which bears the name of Jotham's Cliff (see Judges ix. 7). Near the top of the Mount, we came to the Samaritan encampment and temple, which consist of two or three places set apart, within dry walls of broken rock, in which the Samaritans assemble for the annual keeping of the passover. On these occasions, six or seven lambs are offered, according to the house of their fathers, "A lamb for a house." (Exod. xii. 3.) Over this celebration the high priest presides, and at his bidding, the lambs are simultaneously slaughtered and the feast is kept in more or less conformity to the details which marked its first appointment. Thus "on this mountain" (John iv. 20) do the Samaritans still worship (must we not say?) "they know not what." (Ver. 22.)

My companion pointed out the rock on which, it is said, once stood the Samaritan temple, and on which the Samaritans believe that Abraham offered up Isaac. Near to it were the ruins of a crusade church, which must have been, originally, a grand structure. On the mountain, I noticed some partridges, flying away at our approach, reminding me of the words of David to Saul in 1 Samuel xxvi. 20, "As when one doth hunt a partridge on the mountains," while the eagles soared

above our heads with that vigour and dignity so
often referred to in scripture, e.g., Isaiah xl. 31,
"But they that wait upon the Lord shall renew
their strength ; they shall mount up with wings
as eagles ; they shall run, and not be weary ; and
they shall walk, and not faint."

Having come down from the mountain, my
companion pointed out to me the reputed site of
the oak, under which Jacob buried the idols. (Gen.
xxxv. 4.) We next took our places on opposite
sides of the valley, my companion on that part of
the slopes of Gerizim upon which, it is believed,
the six tribes, Simeon, Levi, Judah, Issachar, Joseph, and Benjamin stood on the occasion mentioned in Deuteronomy xxvii. 12, 13, and Joshua
viii. 33, while I rode to the corresponding part of
Ebal. Although there was a rather strong breeze
blowing along the valley, we found that at the
distance we were apart (about three quarters of a
mile), we could, without raising our voices to a very
high pitch, hear what was said by one to the
other. Thus did we put to a practical test the
conditions under which the law was here read,
and the responses made by the tribes on either
side of the valley. And be it remembered, that
in the days of Joshua, the law was read in the

valley between ; a situation still more favourable
for others, on either side, to hear. Therefore,
even upon the low ground of experiment, the
audibility of the words, under the conditions described in the word of God, instead of being simply
impossible (as some sophists have endeavoured to
say) is a simple fact. Just as we had finished
our dialogue, an Arab in the neighbourhood discharged his gun, which produced reverberations
along the mountain sides, strikingly illustrative
of the peculiar fitness of their formation to produce
these acoustic phenomena.

We next proceeded to Jacob's Well, in the im-
mediate vicinity of which we noticed a long monolith shaft of a column of polished granite, and
other indications of ruins of a church which doubtless was that mentioned by St. Jerome as standing
here, and in the same neighbourhood were two or
three frustums of columns of the same form and
material, one of which had been built into a wall.

We now arrived at the one unique spot in all
Palestine of which we felt we could say, "Jesus
came here." The well is surrounded by a ruined
wall, having entered within which, we found a
domed cover surrounding the well. We let ourselves down by the irregularities of the masonry,

and stood at the true mouth of the well. This
was stopped by a wedge-like block of stone,
through the fissures between which, and the stone-
work of the well's mouth, we dropped two small
stones, and they returned a sound which told that
they fell on a dry bottom. The time between
dropping a stone and hearing it fall (two seconds
and a half, I believe), gave some clear impression
of the depth of the well. Maundrell says the well
" is dug in a firm rock, and contains about three
yards in diameter, and thirty-five in depth; five
of which we found full of water." * That the well
is now constantly dry has been proved by the
circumstance of a traveller's pocket bible falling
down, and being recovered after lying four or five
years at the bottom in a state uninjured, or little
injured, by damp.

What memories attach to this spot, connected
as it is with the histories of Abraham and Isaac
and, more especially, of Jacob and Joseph! Many
have expressed a surprise that Jacob should have
dug this well at the entrance of a valley in which
were so many natural springs; but it has been
justly replied that, there being no cordiality in

* " A Journey from Aleppo to Jerusalem," p. 84.

the terms upon which Jacob dwelled among the men of Shechem; like his father Isaac when he dwelled in Gerah, (Gen. xxvi. 6, et seq.) it was his interest to secure an independent means of watering his flocks. From the time of Jacob who sunk the well, and drank thereof himself and his children, and his cattle, how many strangers and pilgrims had not rested and been refreshed there; who, from various considerations, eschewed a divergence to the springs in the adjoining valley. Now one comes there, on His way from Judea to Galilee and sits on the well, His disciples only going into the city to buy meat, as though He had no purpose of turning from His northward journey. Who is this weary stranger? A little time will discover; for it is made known through the coming of a Samaritan woman, that He is the Saviour of the world, (Verse 42) and, when invited, He turns in and sojourns two days in the city. Such is His grace, and not only such:

"Behold a stranger at the door !
He gently knocks—has knocked before ;
Has waited long—is waiting still,
You use no other friend so ill.
Open the door, He'll enter in
And sup with you, and you with Him."

From the well we rode a short distance to the

Mahometan *wely*, known as Joseph's tomb. It is a walled enclosure, surmounted at one end with a dome, and containing, besides the reputed tomb of Joseph, that of a wealthy Mahometan, who obtained interment here. There are two tablets bearing inscriptions, one in the Samaritan, the other in the Hebrew character, the latter of which I commenced to copy, but soon abandoned the attempt and brought away as a memento, three or four leaves from a vine growing on the spot, which I regarded as suitably associated with the name of him who is compared to "a fruitful bough," even a fruitful bough by a well, whose branches run over the wall (Gen. xlix. 22); type of Him who is the true Joseph (that is, "increase ") "who shall see of the travail of his soul and shall be satisfied, and of the *increase* of whose government and peace there shall be no end." (Isa. ix. 7.)

What instruction too there is in the conduct of Joseph, who by faith gave commandment to the children of Israel concerning his bones, and was of the number of them who "died in faith, not having received the promises, but having seen them afar off, and were persuaded of them, and embraced them, and confessed that they were

M

strangers and pilgrims on the earth." (Heb. xi. 13.)

We next wended our way westward, along the valley, and ascended the slopes of Ebal, where the mountain is terraced and planted with the prickly pear. It was the season of ripe fruit, and we ordered a basketful, which one of the owners proceeded to gather, while we contemplated the view of the city at our feet and of Mount Gerizim beyond. A part of this time I occupied in endeavouring to defend my poor horse from the attacks of innumerable flies, of which there were at least two kinds, one being protected by so hard a skin that all moderate blows fail to destroy them. They crowded to all those parts of his body where the poor animal had no power to reach them, and the gratitude with which he yielded himself to my efforts to defend him was a happy assurance that they were appreciated.

On the topic of insects I may take this opportunity to speak as exhaustively as appears desirable. Of course I did not escape my share of annoyance from those which attack *genus homo*. That they were various, was evident from the different marks which their bites produced, and among which experts pointed out those of the

mosquito. I confess I was pleasantly disappointed
in the small amount of suffering from these
causes, which, though they evidently existed, did
not give me much trouble.

On Mount Gerizim this day, while I was contemplating the herbal and entomological specimens at my feet, with the thought of collecting
some, I found that I was attended by a hornet,
which seemed disposed to put to the test the more
exquisite pleasure of stinging an Englishman, as
compared with that yielded by the same performance on an Arab; so remembering what I had
learned at school some twenty-three years before,
" *Crabrones ne irrita* " (do not irritate hornets), I
comported myself with quietness, and suspending
my researches, escaped from his attack; making
with him a schoolboy's bargain of mutual for-
bearance, as I afterwards did with other members
of his family.

I saw a few locusts, and, especially when crossing the plain of Esdraelon, was attracted by the
great variety of insect life, of which however I
did not collect any specimens.

But I must return to Mount Ebal where, the
pears we had ordered having been gathered, we
commenced the descent, attended by a boy carry-

ing the fruit, with which we returned to the house. Having taken off their prickly coverings and received payment, he left and we remained within doors for the evening.

Lord's day, 18th. In the morning a small congregation assembled in the house, when we had hymns, prayer, and the reading of the word, all of course in Arabic. The portion read, and from which Mr. El Karey addressed the assembly, was Luke vii., upon which (especially the raising of the widow's son) it was also my privilege to speak a few words, which were interpreted by my companion. I believe we all felt the occasion had been one of privilege and blessing. After the meeting the Samaritan high priest called to return our visit. I took the opportunity of presenting him with an Arabic copy of the Gospel by John, opened at chapter iv., upon which we conversed a little. Afterwards a native doctor called, to whom I gave a copy of Luke, opened at chapter v. 31, " They that are whole need not a physician, but they that are sick."

The muleteer not having shewn himself to-day, we went in search of him, and were informed at the Khan where he had kept the horses, that the previous midnight he had gone back to Jerusalem, taking with him the mule and my horse. In this state of things, the horse which my companion had engaged for himself was of no avail, but we spread the matter before our heavenly Father, and felt the proper course to take was to go direct to the governor. We did so, and the scene of the day before was re-enacted. The governor listened to the tale of our difficulties, and offered to supply the best remedy in his power. Should he send a soldier to Jerusalem to bring back the truant muleteer, horse and mule? But the certainty of losing two days, and the uncertainty as to how many more, was so far removed from our ideas of a remedy, that we urged our need of one, if not two horses and a mule, with the least possible delay. The same officer as before was summoned, and the following dialogue took place:

Governor. "These gentlemen wish to go to Kaifa, and through a breach of contract on the part of their muleteer, who ran away last night with a horse and mule, they have only one horse between them. They cannot proceed without another horse and one mule, but two horses and a mule would suit them better. Attend to this at once."

Officer. "I suppose I must mention it to the under-governor?"

Governor. "Do as you like about that; only get the horses."

Officer. "Very well, sir."

Leaving the matter in the hands of those who had thus undertaken it, we returned to the house, and in an hour a muleteer, accompanied by a Bashi-bazouk (a private of irregular cavalry) followed us, having been sent by the officer. Preliminary arrangements were soon made, the nature of which I will, however, postpone to the minutes of the next day, when they were confirmed and carried out.

This afternoon two poor Jews called, to entreat Mr. El Karey's interest in their behalf, the government having ejected them from their home, turning them and their property into the street, for the purpose of occupying their house with soldiers. They came a second time on the same business, and received the assurance of being spoken for when an opportunity should arise, as was the case in the office of the British Consul-General, Beyrout.

At 8.30 p.m. there was a prayer meeting on the house-top. Again the manifest reality of the faith and love of some of those who assembled was very refreshing to witness. This evening we could hear the sound of music and rejoicing on account of a wedding, preparations anticipatory of the cry, "Behold the bridegroom cometh." On the preceding night I was long kept awake by hearing a company of Mahometans, in the upper chamber of an adjoining house, singing for hours at a stretch, the long story of the birth of Mahomet. These sounds and the cries of the Muezzin at the hours of prayer were painful reminders of the number of the followers of the impostor of Mecca.

Monday, 19th. This morning the Bashi-bazouk and muleteer came again, the governor having put into requisition for us, a mule and two horses, belonging to a large proprietor who has a mule caravan trafficking between Nablûs and Damascus. My companion's plan had been to proceed to Kaifa by road, and thence by steamer to Beyrout, whence we might visit Damascus. One ground upon which he recommended this course was, that it would save me some expense. This, however, was clearly my consideration, and it appeared to me, that the uncertainty about the steamer (although the time spent in waiting for it, might be most profitably occupied), the risk of greater delay, and the omission of some of the interesting sites we might hope to visit in going by road, would more than countervail the advantages of such a course; so that it was with much pleasure I learned that two horses and a mule were at our service, on condition that we proceeded across country to Damascus, to which city they belonged.

The government having made this provision, the Bashi-bazouk was sent with the muleteer, it being deemed right we should have an escort of, at least, one horseman, and when it became known that one was wanted to go to Damascus, this man begged for the appointment, urging the special plea, that his wife and children, whom he had not seen for a long time, lived there. While he was sitting waiting for Mr. El Karey and scanning me with an inquisitive glance, which I thought expressed the idea, "I wonder how much I shall get out of him," I used the opportunity in making the annexed sketch of our gallant escort. The terms having been arranged, we felt greatly relieved, and did not forget to acknowledge the love of our heavenly Father in thus providing for us in our need.

I now accompanied my companion about the city where he had some arrangements to make before leaving, one of which was to lay in a stock

168   ESCORT.

of wheat; for this purpose we proceeded to the bazaar, where a corn merchant was sitting in his store, receiving and selling the corn. There were one or two asses which had arrived laden with corn, and sacks pitched with open mouths, from which samples could be taken by the buyers. The particular quality having been chosen and the price agreed to, the sack was emptied into a heap on the floor, and a man proceeded to measure it. To do this, he sat on the ground and just scooped up as much wheat into the bushel as he could, in the way usually practised in England; then with his hands he quickly shovelled up sufficient from the heap to fill it to the brim, when, instead of striking off the grains which were above the top, he proceeded to shake it lustily by torsion in alternate directions, so as to cause the grain to settle down considerably. Again he piled it up with his hands, and again shook it down by jolting it on the ground, using one edge of the base as a fulcrum upon which to raise it. Once more he piled it up, squeezing down the grain with his wrists each time of putting in a double handful; then he heaped it up into as high a cone as it would form, and, while the wheat was yet flowing over the brim in all directions, emptied the bushel into a fresh sack, and proceeded to measure up another.

Who would fail, with these things passing before him, to recall the words, " Give, and it shall be given unto you; good measure, pressed down, and shaken together, and running over, shall men give into your bosom. For with the same measure that ye mete withal, it shall be measured to you again." (Luke vi. 38.) As to the expression "into your bosom," I may mention that the bosom of the loose upper garment of the Arabs is used for carrying many things. Thus we read in Psalm cxxix. 7, " Wherewith the mower filleth not his hand, nor he that bindeth sheaves his bosom," as it is allowed to the binders of sheaves to put the broken ears into their bosom, and, when this becomes full, by pulling more of the loose robe above the girdle, they enlarge the receiving capabilities of the bosom.

We found that the horses would not be ready till the afternoon, so there was every opportunity to make all necessary preparation, and to respond to a request which reached us, that we should visit the sick baby once more before leaving Nablûs. We did so, and found his progress everything that we could expect, and with the most hearty acknowledgments on the part of his parents and grandmother, we left him. I have since learned, by a letter from Mr. El Karey, that the improvement continued unto a complete recovery.

In the afternoon, as my companion's clean shirts, and other provisions for the journey, were being laid out ready for packing, looking up from a letter which I was writing, I saw the cat jumping from a chair, and carrying off bodily a piece of mutton which had been cooked, cooled, and placed in readiness for our commissariat-bag. I happily raised an alarm in time to save the mutton, which, with hard boiled eggs and *khubbs* (Arab bread), was duly stowed.

My companion's spare things occupied the holsters at his saddle-bows, and when at 3.30 p.m. it was announced, " The horses are come," I was not long in producing my portmanteau and saddle-bags.

By 5 p.m. everything was ready, and, taking leave of our kind friends, we mounted. Let not the reader imagine that we were beyond the range of all detention. One or two who had been concerned in our obtaining the mount, now came forward, and, at the outskirts of the town, in the presence of witnesses (Ruth iv. 7-9) made a parley, which occupied some time, before my companion felt justified in acknowledging their claims, which however he at length did, to some extent.

We now took leave of Sychar, or Shechem, whither Abraham journeyed and where the Lord appeared to him and gave him the promise, " Unto thy seed will I give this land ;" and there he builded an altar unto the Lord, who appeared unto him (Gen. xii. 7) ; where Jacob bought a parcel of a field at the hands of the children of Hamor for a hundred lambs (chap. xxxiii. 18, 19, margin), on the inhabitants of which his two sons Simeon and Levi were avenged for their sister (chap. xxxiv.), which was made one of the cities of refuge (Josh. xx. 7), and inhabited by the Kohathites, of the tribe of Levi (chap. xxi. 21), and where other Old Testament scenes are laid. But, though each has its distinct importance, there remains the one greater and culminating fact, (as in the case of Israel, " to whom pertaineth the adoption, and the glory, and the covenants, and the giving of the law, and the service of God, and the promises ; whose are the fathers, and [last and chiefest of all] of whom as concerning the flesh, Christ came, who is over all, God blessed for ever : Amen "—Rom. ix. 4, 5— so) Sychar, although connected with the histories of Abraham, Jacob, Joseph, and the kings of Israel, has this pre-eminent interest on which the heart most delightedly dwells; that hither did Jesus, the Son of God, come. Here He made known His salvation and sojourned two days, while many believed on Him.

Farewell, Sychar! Though I never again see thy walls, climb thy hillsides, or wander to the well where Jesus sat; I look to see Him who is the same to-day as when He sat there, and shall be for ever.

"To Jacob's well a woman came,
   For water from a neighbouring town;
A stranger there, unknown His name,
   Had, faint and weary, sat Him down.

He meekly said, 'Give me to drink,'
   As water from the well she drew;
Ah! little did that woman think
   The tribute that to Him was due.

He asked for water; but had she
   Known that the Lord of life was there,
For His salvation, full and free,
   Had been her own, her earnest prayer.

From His own lips the truth she learn'd,
   From His own love the gift received;
And in the stranger's form discern'd
   The Lord, in whom she now believed."

CHAPTER IX.

HAVING got fairly on our way, we passed along the foot of Mount Ebal till, nearly half-an-hour from Nablûs, my companion remembered that he had left his blanket behind. The Bashi-bazouk was therefore dispatched to fetch it, while we and the muleteer advanced steadily; but we soon called a halt on account of one of my stirrups, which was suspended by a mixture of leather and cord, giving way. By dint of tying about three knots, the muleteer restored it to its former length, with what want of elegance I need scarcely add. As we were crossing the lower spurs of Ebal northward, before the valley of Nablûs was excluded from our sight, we saw the horseman hastening to overtake us, bringing the blanket.

This incident, though trivial, will serve to illustrate certain allusions in scripture to the circumstances of travel. To avoid the almost endless delay which would occur in ascertaining before setting out that nobody and nothing was left behind by a large travelling party; as of old, the caravans advance the first day only a sabbath day's journey, or about six miles, so that at the first halt, if it be found from actual test that any deficiency exists, it may be made good with only a small sacrifice of time. After this the caravans generally progress at an average pace of twenty-five or thirty miles a day.

This custom bears especially on Luke ii. 41-49. " Now his parents went to Jerusalem every year at the feast of the passover. And when he was twelve years old, they went up to Jerusalem, after the custom of the feast. And when they had fulfilled the days, as they returned, the child Jesus tarried behind in Jerusalem; and Joseph and his mother knew not of it. But they, supposing him to have been in the company, went a day's journey, and they sought him among their kinsfolk and acquaintance. And when they found him not, they turned back again to Jerusalem, seeking him. And it came to pass, that after three days they found him in the temple, sitting in the midst of the doctors, both hearing them, and asking them questions. And all that heard him were astonished at his understanding and answers. And when they saw him, they were amazed; and his mother saith unto him, Son, why hast thou thus dealt with us? Behold, thy father and I have sought thee sorrowing. And he said unto them, How is it that ye sought me? wist ye not that I must be about my Father's business?"

Reading these words in the light of the custom above mentioned, the conduct of Joseph and Mary loses that appearance of unnatural regard about the child Jesus which it would otherwise wear.

It may create a natural surprise that we did not visit Sebaste, the ruined city of Samaria. The reasons were the shortness of time and the difficulty of obtaining horses, already mentioned; the lateness, too, of the hour when we obtained a fair mount, and the restrictions under which we were placed to follow a tolerably direct course to Damascus.

But what I was disappointed of seeing, my readers need not therefore be prevented reading about; and from the descriptions of others who have visited this place of remarkable interest to the traveller and Bible student, I select that given by the Rev. George Fisk.

"Samaria was visible for full an hour before we reached it; and perhaps there is not a more

177   SAMARIA.

lovely scene in Palestine than that which presents itself when its commanding position first
meets the eye. I cannot well imagine a more
noble site for a royal city. Israel was indeed
magnificently enthroned there. It is a bold and
stately mountain, belted about with guardian
hills, as if to afford a natural fortification to the
royal habitation. The mountain itself is of an
oval form, and richly clothed, almost to its summit,
with stately olive groves. We quitted the heights
from which we first gazed upon Samaria by a
winding path, through thick plantations which
led us to green and fertile plains, extending
around the spreading base of the mountain.
Surely these must have been among 'the fat
valleys of them that are overcome with wine.'
(Isaiah xxviii. 1.)

"The prophecy concerning Samaria is most
distinct, and its fulfilment has been exact. I
wish an infidel could have stood with me and
compared the present state of Samaria—even in
the minute particulars—with the prophecy of
Micah, which I read on the spot, Micah i. 1-6.
'The word of the Lord that came to Micah the
Morasthite in the days of Jotham, Ahaz, and
Hezekiah, kings of Judah, which he saw con-

cerning Samaria and Jerusalem. Hear ye, all
people; hearken, O earth, and all that therein is:
and let the Lord God be witness against you, the
Lord from his holy temple. For behold, the
Lord cometh forth out of his place, and will come
down and tread upon the high places of the
earth. And the mountains shall be molten under
him, and the valleys shall be cleft, as wax before
the fire, and as the waters that are poured down
a steep place. For the transgression of Jacob is
all this, and for the sins of the house of Israel.
What is the transgression of Jacob? Is it not
Samaria? And what are the high places of
Judah? Are they not Jerusalem? Therefore I
will make Samaria as an heap of the field, and as
plantings of a vineyard; and I will pour down
the stones thereof into the valley, and I will
discover the foundations thereof.'

"Though Israel's monarchs have swayed the
sceptre—though there Herod reigned and revelled
—though pomp, splendour, and the glory of the
world there shone and dazzled the thousands of
Israel—yet, Samaria is a desolation. The sceptres
are broken—the revel is hushed—the splendour
has faded—Samaria is an heap of the field, and as
plantings of a vineyard; her stones have been

literally poured down into the valley—her foundations have been indeed discovered—and there
they now lie; while from every heap and from
every fragment there goes forth as it were a
testimony, which cannot be silenced, to the
righteous severity of an angry God.

" We ascended the heights for the purpose of
exploring the remains, and in our way met many
of the Samaritan women coming down with their
water jars, gracefully borne upon their heads, to
a fountain which flows below. They are coarse
and masculine, and contrast strongly with the
men, who both in countenance and figure are
extremely handsome. Their complexion is florid
and clear, and slightly bronzed by their native
sun.

" The ascent is by a steep narrow pass which
leads up to a small village—poor and insig-
nificant; and to the left, on the eastern brow of
the hill, are the bold and prominent ruins of a
Greek church, said to have been built over the
bones of John the Baptist—the victim of the
heartless Herod and Herodias, his adulterous
paramour. A small enclosed part of the church
is now used as a mosque, the door of which was
closed against us as soon as we arrived. On

either side of the ascent immense masses of stone
are piled and huddled together, and have the
appearance of ancient foundations. On the summit there is a considerable extent of table-land
thickly planted with fig and olive-trees, among
which are to be found a great many shafts of
Corinthian columns deprived of their capitals—
some of them erect, and others thrown down and
partly buried in the soil.

" No one can survey these ruins without being
sensible of the splendour with which this remarkable spot was once graced ; all which is increased
by glancing down into the valleys—particularly
on the north-east, south and west, where the remains of bold and stately colonnades are still
visible, amidst the heaps of piled-up stones. Such
are the remnants of Samaria, ' the crown of
pride.'

" Was it here that Ahab built his house in
honour of Baal ? And here that Jezebel bore her
cruel sway ? And here, too, that those men of
God—Elijah and Elisha, wrought wonders in the
strength of the Lord of hosts ? Even so. And
what do we now find instead ? A few Syrian
boors—a poor rude cultivation—spiritual dearth
—the light of Christianity not merely dimmed,

but extinguished; a monument—a memorial—
the traces of Jehovah's presence in wrath and
retribution.

" The surrounding scenery, as beheld from the
heights, is very charming; and it was beautifully
garnished by the declining sun, as we gazed upon
the grassy and olive-clothed valleys and 'mountains of Samaria.' We did not fail to notice the
terraced sides of the hills, on which the vine and
the olive once grew in cultivated profusion (compared with which the present is but barrenness),
when the Ephraimites thence traded with Egypt,
in oil (Hos. xii. 1)—the rich produce of the olive
tree. Shall the poor and scanty cultivation which
now marks the desolation of the land continue ?
Is there no promise on which to ground a hope of
better things ? O yes; Israel—the beloved—the
redeemed of the Lord shall return. He who foretold the desolation, and who brought it, hath
given promise—hath said to banished Israel, ' I
have loved thee with an everlasting love ; therefore with loving kindness have I drawn thee.'
Again, ' I will build thee and thou shalt be built,
O virgin of Israel; thou shalt again be adorned
with thy tabrets, and thou shalt go forth in the
dances of them that make merry. Thou shalt yet

plant vines upon the mountains of Samaria; the planters shall plant, and eat them as common things.' (Jeremiah xxxi. 5.)"*

We now entered once more on the plain of Sharon, passing occasionally a village, and once and again my companion drew my attention to a landmark beyond which lay some place of scripture association, e.g., "Tirzah." (Solomon's Song vi. 4.)

As I write, there returns to my mind with peculiar vividness the recollection of this ride, with the solitary Arab crossing our path, the eagle and the owl that contributed to the scene, the spirit, though not the *ipsissima verba* of our conversation, the places of thrilling interest we had left, and the prospect of others of which we had formed anticipations more or less defined. These and other things combined to make it a most happy season.

At 8.15 the moon rose, and soon after, we reached Jebba. The soldier, who was now the guide of the party, led the way along an ascending path, being himself conducted by a guide, whom he impressed into the service in a most

* "A Pastor's Memorial of the Holy Land," pp. 364— 367.

unceremonious way, such as I could neither admire nor prevent, but which brought to my mind the words of John the Baptist when "the soldiers likewise demanded of him, saying, And what shall we do? And he said unto them, Do violence to no man." (Luke iii. 14.)

At the place where we dismounted, we found a company of the villagers assembled in friendly confab. They bade us welcome to their company, and we shared their coffee. My companion preached, and it was my part to distribute three or four copies of the gospels among them.

After resting awhile, Mr. El Karey and I, accompanied by two of the villagers, set out to visit Lieutenant Conder and Mr. Tyrwhitt Drake, who were engaged on the Palestine Exploration Fund Survey of the country. We found their tent a short distance from the village, and on being announced, were requested to enter. Having performed a heavy day's work they had retired to bed, but their lamp was burning. The whistle was blown, and the servant requested to bring in water, to some of which a little brandy from their stores being added, we accepted the Christians' hospitality, as freely as we had just done that of the Mahometans. The survey was progressing northwards, and they told us that they expected very shortly to move their base line on to the plain of Esdraelon.

After spending, probably, three-quarters of an hour in the tent, we returned to the Arabs, some of whom we found endeavouring to read the books we had given them, by the fire light. At one of the usual hours, we heard the call to prayer, the Muezzin on this occasion crying from an adjacent roof, and instantly the mats and upper garments were spread on the ground, the shoes slipped off, and simultaneously with one who led in a higher voice than the rest, they went through their prostrations, and the repetition of prayers, with their faces toward Mecca.

We now prepared to rest for the night in the open air, on the roof of an old house. The Bashi-bazouk considerately spread his cloak for my companion and myself to lie on. We availed ourselves of his kindness, and turned in about 10.30 p.m., with blanket and scarf spread over us. We managed to sleep awhile, but disturbing influences prevented my doing so for long. The lowing of the herd in the yard just beneath us, the barking of the dogs who were prowling and sniffing about, and chiefly, I think, a third occupant of the horseman's cloak disturbed my slumbers, and I turned out again at 12.30 a.m. My companion and the rest were sleeping on, and by 1.15 a.m. I felt urged to make a fresh attempt, in which I succeeded till 2.30 a.m.

Tuesday 20th, when we had the horses saddled, the mule laden, and with one of the villagers for a guide, we got once more upon the road.

Passing the village of Sinoor, we heard several

JACKAL.

jackals barking in the gardens close to us, and, in order to scare them away, our escort unslung his gun. This gun had impressed me with its wrecked condition when I first saw it in Nablûs, giving one the idea, that the man who could make it go off, must be decidedly clever. It having an old flint lock, he cocked the trigger, uncovered the pan, and presented in the direction whence the jackals' howls proceeded. Quite up to my expectations, he produced a flash, and this was the grandest performance he made therewith, the whole way to Damascus.

We passed very near the village of Kabati and, just before sunrise, reached Jenin, to the judge at which place we were bearers of an introduction from the doctor in Nablûs, who had called on us the preceding Lord's day. Jenin is accredited to be the same as En-gannim of Joshua xix. 21, and presents a fine aspect in the midst of the level on which it stands—the plain of Jezreel. As we drew near, we passed some well-mounted riders leaving the place, with whom we exchanged salutes, and with the cooing of a welcome from the doves still in our ears, we rode up to the judge's house, sent in our letter, and having left the horses in charge of the escort and muleteer, awaited the arrival of our host on the roof of his house.

Having witnessed the sun-rising, we were not indifferent to the sound of pounding the coffee, which proceeded from within-doors, and a little more than half-an-hour from our arrival, the judge joined our company, and bade us welcome, while the servants spread a breakfast of the choicest fruits of the land, with butter and honey, newly baked bread, &c. At this meal we were joined by the Governor, whom the judge had done us the honour of inviting to meet us.

This repast on the house-top brought specially to my mind the words of the Lord Jesus in Luke xvii. 7, 8, "But which of you having a servant plowing, or feeding cattle, will say unto him by-and-by, when he has come from the field, Go and sit down to meat? And will not rather say unto him, Make ready wherewith I may sup, and gird thyself, and serve me till I have eaten and drunken; and afterward thou shalt eat and drink?" During breakfast, the judge's servants, assisted by our escort and muleteer, were zealous in attending to our wants, bringing coffee, water, and, after the repast, a towel wet at one end and dry at the other, for use as a napkin; but our rising from the table was a signal for them to gather round it, and make their breakfast from what was left.

We retired to the divans, where conversation was carried on for about an hour, Mr. El Karey preaching (I presume that by preaching, I shall not be understood to mean a set address, according to the conventional use of that word), and copies of two of the gospels were presented.

It could not have been that our fame as baby doctors had preceded us, but rather from the general supposition that a Frank is also a *Hakeem* (physician), that a neighbour brought a poor little sick infant for us to look at. The child was suffering from a number of blind swellings, with which its head was covered, and its unceasing crying was most distressing to hear, but we were both obliged to confess that we had no knowledge of the nature of its disorder, or what remedy might be used even at a venture. Besides this, one of the principal inhabitants of the place made a similar application on behalf of his wife; so, having taken leave of our kind entertainers, we accompanied him on foot to his house, followed by the soldier and muleteer leading the horses.

After waiting a short time, we were shown into an ante-chamber where the patient, ready seated, was evidently suffering extra exhaustion from the effects of leaving her own room. She was completely covered over with a garment, according to Mahometan notions of propriety, and only produced one

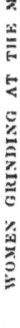

WOMEN GRINDING AT THE MILL.

189

hand, that examination might be made. My friend applied his fingers to the pulse, but I need hardly say, that a diagnosis made under such restrictions, and by one unqualified to perform it, had no better result than to elicit expressions of sympathy and regret that we could do nothing. It is not so with the Great Physician. In our poor measure we were willing, though quite unable, to relieve. To Him belongs *all* power as well as perfect willingness. Even the leper who had misgiving about the latter, "Lord, *if* thou wilt, thou canst make me clean," was answered by the touch, and "I will, be thou clean," and immediately the leprosy departed from him." (Luke v. 12, 13.)

As we rode away from Jenin, I noticed at one of the house-doors, two women sitting and grinding at the mill, preparing meal for the day. Of course the sight and sound of the mill at this hour, was a common one. (See Matt. xxiv. 41.)

This was an almost cloudless and especially hot day, and the plains of Jezreel and Esdraelon lay before us. When crossing the former, which is for the most part uncultivated, we started a coney, which on seeing us, ran for concealment into its hole beneath a rock ; this circumstance led our conversation into a train suggested by Proverbs

xxx. 24-28. "There be four things which are little upon the earth, but they are exceeding wise: The ants are a people not strong, yet they prepare their meat in the summer; the conies are but a feeble folk, yet make their houses in the rocks; the locusts have no king, yet go they forth all of them by bands; the spider taketh hold with her hands, and is in kings' palaces."

In these four children of wisdom, we have, *first* the ants, whose example teaches like that of Noah, "who being moved by fear, prepared the ark for the saving of his house," that in the day of salvation we should flee to Christ. (Matt. vii. 24, 25.)

Secondly, the coneys, resembling the Christian who, knowing his own weakness, finds the place of dependence to be the place of strength.

In connection with this my companion drew my attention to the many examples which exist of the selection of high rocks, as offering a natural defence, for the purpose of erecting forts thereon, whereby are illustrated the words so often used by David, "The Lord is my rock, and my fortress." (Ps. xviii. 2; *et alt.*)

Thirdly, the locusts, which suggest the assembling together of the Lord's people, to which we are exhorted in Hebrews x. 25.

Fourthly, the spider shows the final place of the believer, in the mansions which Jesus has gone to prepare. (John xiv. 2.)

Our road led us close to the small village of Jelameh.

The mountains of Gilboa (1 Sam. xxxi., 2 Sam. i.) were pointed out on our right, and now the plains lay before us which have been the scenes of so many scripture battles : those of Jezreel and Esdraelon, called also the plain of Megiddo, the theatre of the overthrow of Sisera's host (Judges iv.) ; the battle with Pharaoh-necho, and the death of Josiah. (2 Chron. xxxv. 20-27.) Here, also, were the prophets of Baal slain at the brook Kishon. (1 Kings xviii. 40.)

As we approached Jezreel we passed a mixed flock of sheep and goats which could not fail to bring to my mind the words of the Lord Jesus in Matthew xxv. 31-46. " When the Son of Man shall come in his glory, and all the angels with him, then shall he sit upon the throne of his glory. And before him shall be gathered all nations : and he shall separate them one from another, as a shepherd divideth his sheep from the goats : and he shall set the sheep on his right hand, but the goats on the left. Then shall the King say unto them on his right hand, Come, ye blessed of my Father, inherit the kingdom prepared for you from the foundation of the world : for I was an hungered, and ye gave me meat : I was thirsty, and ye gave me drink : I was a stranger, and ye took me in : naked, and ye clothed me : I was sick, and ye visited me : I was in prison, and ye came unto me. Then shall the righteous answer him, saying, Lord, when saw we thee an hungered, and fed thee ? or thirsty and gave thee drink? When saw we thee a stranger, and took thee in ? or naked, and clothed thee ? Or when saw we thee sick, or in prison, and came unto thee ? And the King shall answer and say unto them, Verily I say unto you, Inasmuch as ye have done it unto one of the least of these my brethren, ye have done it unto me. Then shall he say also unto them on the left hand, Depart from me, ye cursed, into everlasting fire, prepared for the devil and his angels : for I was an hungered, and ye gave me no meat : I was thirsty, and ye gave me no drink: I was a stranger, and ye took me not in : naked, and ye clothed me not : sick, and in pri- son, and ye visited me not. Then shall they also answer him, saying, Lord, when saw we thee an

hungered, or a thirst, or a stranger, or naked, or
sick, or in prison, and did not minister unto thee?
Then shall he answer them, saying, Verily I say
unto you, Inasmuch as ye did it not to one of the
least of these, ye did it not to me. And these
shall go away into everlasting punishment: but
the righteous into life eternal."

On our reaching the village, some children,
incited by a young ringleader, commenced as-
sailing us with roots of Indian corn to which the
earth was still clinging, one of which struck me;
but scarcely had we begun to expostulate, when
the escort coming into view sent them flying into
the town, while he turned it into an opportunity
of displaying his prowess, and handled his horse
so as to drive one of the men of the place who
happened to be near, before him, when with an
angry parley the matter ended. This was the
only insult we received during the whole journey.
The stubble with the earth clinging to the roots,
illustrates the custom of gathering some of the
corn crops by plucking up, as referred to in
Ecclesiastes iii. 2, " A time to plant, and a time
to pluck up that which is planted." And, assuredly, between us and the children of the village

o

our brief stay at Jezreel witnessed both "a time of war, and a time of peace." (Ver. 8.)

We visited a spring which is pointed out as the water to which, at the command of the Lord, Gideon brought down the people, and set aside the three hundred that lapped, to go against the Midianites. (Judges vii.)

We now continued our way across the plain of Esdraelon, passing a few camels, and now and then seeing some bleached bones of that animal, calculated to remind us that where we were travelling other pilgrims had journeyed before us, and the place which once knew them shall know them no more.

> " Soon will *our* pilgrimage end here below,
> Soon to the presence of God we shall go ;
> Then if to Jesus our souls have been given,
> Joyfully, joyfully rest we in heaven.
> Joyfully, joyfully onward we move,
> Bound to the land of bright spirits above."

The plain of Esdraelon is, to a great extent, cultivated, but all the crops had been gathered in, except the millet, several fields of which were standing ready for the sickle. It was in the corn-fields on this plain, that the Shunammite's son went out to his father's to the reapers, in the

days of Elisha (2 Kings iv.), when (no doubt
from a sunstroke) he was cut down.

Then, like Abraham, the father of the faithful,
did the Shunammite undergo the trial of her faith,
and like him she was found to endure.

> " For faith within the mother's breast
>   Shall calm her agony,
>   'The God who gave,
>   Is the God who shall save,
>   And give back my boy to me.'

> " Though sad be her heart, the bright lamp of hope
>   Shall light up its innermost cell,
>   The son lies dead
>   On the prophet's bed,
>   But the mother can say ' IT IS WELL.' "

Shunem was pointed out to us as we passed by.
Just as we reached the end of the plain, seeing
my companion, who was a little in advance of me,
regarding something on the ground with intent-
ness, on coming to the spot I looked too, and
found that it was the wing of an eagle, lying
beside the path at the edge of a cornfield.
The bird had probably been shot, and eluded
capture by the sportsman only to fall a prey to
the jackals, and they finding nothing tempting in
the wing, had gnawed it off from the body, which

was not to be seen. Although not sufficiently pleasant to be carried away as it was, the wing was fit to be handled, so I contented myself with

BEARDED EAGLE.

plucking four of the best feathers, that they might adorn the caps of my four boys. And here let me pay a tribute to the memory of the youngest who, although on my return I found him in as good health as his brothers and sisters, has since succumbed to a weakness engendered by dentition.

He did not wear the eagle's feather, but, far better, we know that he will have a golden crown and a victor's palm, to cast at His feet whose head is adorned with many crowns.

' How sweetly their voices shall pra'se Him there,
     For the blessings His hand has bestowed,
         They shall shine there bright,
         In their robes of white,
     For they all have been washed in His blood.

" And crowns they shall wear of the purest gold,
     And a wonderful song they shall sing,
         And each shall cast down,
         His glittering crown,
     At the feet of the heavenly King."

As we passed through these fields, before striking upon the mountain path leading to Nazareth, and afterwards as I contemplated them from the hill-tops, the mind was filled with thoughts of Him, whose childhood and youth were spent here, of whom we read that "He went down with Joseph and his mother to Nazareth and was subject unto them." As I looked on the labourers in the field, or passed the townspeople on the road, I was irresistibly led to picture Him whose delights were with the sons of men (Prov. viii. 31), anon easing some weary one of his burden; carrying water to the thirsty reaper, or assisting the gleaner to bind and carry home the results of her industry. And not only so, but, as we find Him in the temple at the age of twelve, reasoning with the doctors, doing His Father's business, may we not believe that to these things were added words which they who hid them in their hearts would find yielded rest to the soul, as the acts ministered comfort to the body. I am aware that scripture is almost silent about these things, but the scenes I looked on this day, seemed to be eloquent with them, and this we do know, "Jesus increased in wisdom and stature, and in favour with God and man." (Luke ii. 52.)

At length, an increase of number in the people on the road indicated the vicinity of a town, and Nazareth came into view. With whatever inattention to the description given in Luke iv. as to its situation on a hill (ver. 29), Nazareth might have been otherwise pictured, such disregard of that which is written was effectually rebuked by the toils of nearly two hours' hill-climbing, and the view of the place, at an elevation of three hundred and fifty feet above the plain beneath.

Here then was Nazareth, the early dwelling-place of Jesus who was called a Nazarene (Matt. ii. 23), as the prophet had foretold.

NAZARETH.

The spot was pointed out to us which is reputed to be that from which, after reading the word in their synagogue and expounding it to them that sat by, He was led to the brow of the hill whereon their city was built, that they might cast

Him down headlong, and well did it appear to fulfil the conditions required for that scene.

We repaired at once to the Latin Hospice, where, after knocking three or four times and waiting awhile, we were joined by a priest from the adjoining monastery, who gave us an entry. Our arrival being without notice, we were regaled with bread (not too new), cheese (not too soft), and water, qualified with wine (*de Chypre*). We next paid a visit to Dr. Vartan, labouring here as a medical missionary, with whom and Mrs. Vartan, we spent an agreeable and profitable hour, being refreshed with tidings of the Lord's work in Nazareth. On our return to the Hospice, we stopped by the roadside to purchase a pair of horse-shoes (which I wished to bring to England as specimens), and while they were being finished by the smith, to whom and other bystanders my companion preached, I was occupied in observing the scene around.

At a gunsmith's shop near by, a Bedouin was waiting for his gun which he had left to be repaired with a new stock, and to have the lock fettled. A group of men were playing some game of skill, priests from the monastery, and Arabs of various ages and appearance were passing

by. While making a little sketch of some houses,
I was accosted by a young man to whom we had
given a copy of one of the Gospels, and who

HOUSES IN NAZARETH.

brought a newly baked cake of bread, begging
me to eat with him. We made a covenant of
bread, and I would fain remember the circumstance as an exhortation to be always ready to
break the Bread of Life to those of my poor
fellow creatures who are "without God and without hope in the world," "who know him not and
have not obeyed the gospel of his Son."

It is by many doubted if anything beyond the

smallness or isolation of Nazareth was referred to in the words of Nathanael, " Can there any good thing come out of Nazareth?" But it is reasonable to suppose that the facilities which the recesses of the neighbouring hills afford for the hiding of dishonest and violent men, would involve the whole town in an ill repute. I confess that, though I said nothing to the Bedouin at the gunsmith's, nor he to me, the manner in which he eyed me started the conjecture that he might be reasoning within himself as to the possibility of making his gun pay for its own repair and the loss of his time, by means of an ambush prepared against our morrow's journey. Perhaps I do him a wrong, not knowing the peaceableness of his heart; sure, however, we are that from Nazareth came Him who is the Prince of Peace." (Isa. ix. 6.) The hearts of others we cannot search, but Jesus has laid His bare—

"Our misery reached His heavenly mind,
    And pity brought Him down."

Can there any good thing come out of Nazareth? Come and see.

For our supper the priest provided us with some soup, and three or four dishes of meat and fowl, which, with the wholesome bread and wine and water, furnished an excellent meal. Moreover we lay down upon beds with clean sheets, and had jugs of water, and wash-hand basins, all *en règle*.

Before closing this chapter, I feel constrained to refer again to one who is named therein, but who has passed away since the appearance of the first edition of this book. I mean Mr. C. F. Tyrwhitt Drake, who died at Jerusalem on Tuesday, the 23rd June, 1874, at the age of twenty-eight years. His renown as a scholar and worker in the field of biblical archæology, and the extent of the labours of his short life have been and, no doubt, will yet be told by other pens. It is my sad pleasure to speak of his kindness and geniality.

> "Here we meet to part again,
> In Heaven we part no more."

CHAPTER X.

WEDNESDAY 21st. Having settled with the priest at the customary tariff (ten francs each for a night's rest and meals) we left Nazareth at 5.30 a.m., directing our way across the plain to Mount Tabor, the top of which we were anxious to reach before the mid-day heat.

At the outskirts of the town, we stopped to water the horses and mule at a way-side fountain, and descended the hills into the plain, having traversed which we crossed a region bearing many trees—the number of which increased as we drew near to the lower spurs of Tabor. Having discovered the old Roman road, we started up the mountain, the number of the trees still increasing, and conspicuous among them being many oaks. The toil of the ascent was, no doubt, considerable, but not so excessive as I had been led to anticipate, great invigoration being imparted by inhaling the mountain air.

On the top of Tabor there is a Greek Church monastery which was founded by a Russian of the

205   MONASTERY ON MOUNT TABOR.

name of Ilinariko, who lived and died here, and is buried within the precincts. At the time of our visit the monks and their assistants were busily employed erecting boundary walls, about which I shall have occasion to speak hereafter.

We fell in with a company of them, who were assembled at a spot commanding an extensive view of the country beyond. They pointed out to us several places of scripture association, after which we rode on to the monastery. The muleteer and the escort took charge of our horses, and we seated ourselves in the shade of one of the buildings, facing a row of dwellings for the monks, one of whom lowered a bucket into the well belonging to the monastery, and fetched us a draught of most delicious water.

Although on the top of a mountain, it did not appear to be from a very considerable depth that the water was drawn, and, whatever might have been my ideas of monastic institutions, I must acknowledge I found reasons to be thankful that the well had been dug, and that the means of drawing water were attached.

Having surveyed the country around from various points, contemplated Safed, which is believed to be the place referred to by the Saviour

as " a city set on an hill which cannot be hid "
(Matt. v. 14), and taken sketches of the convent,
and the plain in the direction of the Sea of
Galilee, I joined my companion, who informed
me he had learned that the boundary walls
which we had noticed as in the course of construction were the occasion of a dispute between
the Greek Church monks and a Romish priest
who was holding services in an adjoining grotto,
prior to the erection of a Latin Monastery ; that
a general boundary line had been agreed upon,
but a dispute had arisen as to the plan in detail.

Under a tree near the monastery, we dined off
a fowl which we had brought, ready cooked, from
Nazareth, in the midst of discussing which, we
were joined by a French officer, travelling with
his dragoman, who differed from us, among other
things, by each carrying a pair of pistols. They
spread their dinner opposite to ours, and it proved
that they belonged to a larger party travelling
with tents, the rest of whom had forborne to encounter the fatigue of climbing Mount Tabor.

The officer being newly arrived, and interested
in such facts concerning the locality as I had
already gleaned, placed himself under my guidance for a general survey of the exterior and pre-

206 PLAIN OF ESDRAELON FROM MOUNT TABOR.

cincts of the monastery. He seemed particularly
interested in what I told him of the feud between the Greek and Latin priests (whose ever-
recurring jealousies are associated with nearly all
the sacred places) ; and we undertook to visit the
adjoining property together.

We found the Latin priest ensconced in a part
of the ruins of the Crusaders' church, with his attendants making their dinner of pottage. He
mixed us a cooling draught of pomegranate (or
some other) juice and water, and entered fully
into the dispute between himself and his neigh-
bours, producing a general plan of the approaches
and the lines upon which the Greek priests were
intending to erect the walls, which, if adhered to,
would conduct all travellers arriving by the principal entrance to the Greek monastery only ; in
opposition to which, he proposed that this principal way of approach should lead to an open
piazza, from which travellers could visit either
monastery at their own discretion. He led us
to a grotto beneath part of the ruins, which had
been, I suppose, the crypt of the church, and
where he told us he conducted service. As we
examined the dark chamber, the appearance of
a bat which was fluttering about within, struck

me as being truly in harmony with a system
which adheres with so much tendency to human
traditions, and avoids the free circulation of that
word in its purity, the entrance of which giveth
light. (Ps. cxix. 130.)

We took leave of him and rejoined Mr. El
Karey. An interesting diversion was afforded us
in the agile gambols of a beautiful gazelle which
seemed to be a great favourite with the monks.
I noticed one of them digging about and dunging
a young tree, which naturally reminded me of
the parable in Luke xiii. 6—9. The monks
brought us relics of beads, and carvings in wood,
expecting us to make purchases. I selected a
wooden spoon, which I found useful before the
completion of my journey and, since returning
home, have valued it as an ornament and a relic.

At 1 p.m. we commenced the descent, accompanied by the French officer about half the way
down the mountain, when he and his dragoman
turned off into the path leading to Nazareth, by
which we had arrived in the morning, and we followed another leading to Tiberias. The country
we now traversed was very level, and the ruins of
a Saracen castle and of a Crusade church formed
striking features at one place on the road. The

208   MOUNT TABOR.

former, my companion told me, is used as a market-place where the corn growers and merchants assemble periodically.

During this ride, on an occasion when we halted, and the rest of the party drank from the water-bottle which the muleteer carried; not feeling very thirsty at the time I forbore to do so, thinking to defer to another opportunity when I should feel my need the more, and was confirmed in my decision by the fact that the angle at which the last drinker inclined the bottle, justified the conclusion that there still remained sufficient for me when I might require it. An hour or two later, feeling thirst rather strongly, I looked behind me for the muleteer, but the pace of the horses had been such that he was a long way behind (the impression, as I write, is that he was not in sight), so in the hope that he would soon double up, I held on for another half-hour, by which time, though in sight, he was so far behind that I thought it prudent to wait for the lessening of the distance between us before turning back.

In about another half-hour, with perhaps three-quarters of a mile between us, I turned back. Seeing me coming, he made the mule improve his pace, and soon we met, when to my application,

اسغني *Iskeeni!* (give me to) "drink," he replied, ما فيش *Ma fish*, (there is) "none." But such an answer my thirst, and the recollection of the unexhausted state of the bottle the last time I saw it used, forbade me to receive; so, with a still clearer voice, and in an entreating tone, I repeated "*Iskeeni!*" and was answered with a still more decisive and emphatic "*Ma fish.*" No doubt the poor fellow, counting that we should require no more till we reached Tiberias, had quenched his own thirst with what was left; so, accepting the situation which it was too late to prevent, I faced about to overtake my companion and the escort.

What an illustration was this of the consequence of neglecting the gospel! (Heb. ii. 3.) I needed the water at a time when I might have had it freely, but I neglected the opportunity through a misplaced reliance on another and better; then when I would have had it, and even entreated, I was too late. The only answer I could by any means obtain was "*Ma fish.*" The Arabs have two ways of emphasizing this expression; one is by wiping the hands alternately one with the other while uttering it; but a still more emphatic way is to strike the teeth with the thumb-nail, springing it with a fillip from the doubled forefinger, at the same time uttering "*Ma fish.*"

210   MA FISH.

Having ridden to the top of a ridge which stretched across our road, we obtained a view of Tiberias, while some broken columns and other ruins in the neighbourhood, told of the importance of the place 'during the Roman period. We now traversed a volcanic district, with a black calcareous ground and sulphurous odour, which reminded me afresh of my folly in despising the water when I might have had it. Moreover, the ground was so broken and inclined, that it became necessary to dismount and lead the horses, so that when we reached Tiberias and found our way to the Latin monastery, we were by no means fresh in condition.

We applied for accommodation, but were told by the monks (whom we found busy in decorating the ceilings of their rooms), that it was not their custom to provide it, but that we should find no difficulty in obtaining what we wanted in the town. I had yet a request to prefer, which was " *Un verre d'eau au nom de Jésus*," and, in response, the monk to whom I made it, ordered an attendant to supply my wants, which he did with a glass of delicious water and a little *vin de Chypre* added thereto.

We now sallied forth in quest of a sleeping-room, which we obtained in the house of a Jew (nearly all the inhabitants of Tiberias are Jews). Having deposited our packages and dismissed the escort and muleteer, who made independent arrangements for themselves and the horses, we purchased two fowls after the manner of the country. Three or four live birds are brought, and the selection is made by feeling the breast for plumpness, when, the price having been agreed to, the birds are killed to order. In the present instance we ordered both to be cooked, one for our supper, the other to be carried in our provision-bag for the morrow's need.

These arrangements being made, we took our towels and went down to the Sea of Galilee, "which is the Sea of Tiberias." (John vi. 1.)

In the accompanying woodcut, from a sketch by Miss Barfield, may be noticed the inclination of the tower and the extra ruinous condition of the walls, which are in great measure the result of the earthquake of A.D. 1837, many other traces of which are noticeable in the town.

On this the south side of Tiberias we stripped for a bath, laying stones on our clothes to prevent the wind from removing them whilst we were in the sea. The beach here consists of large boulders,

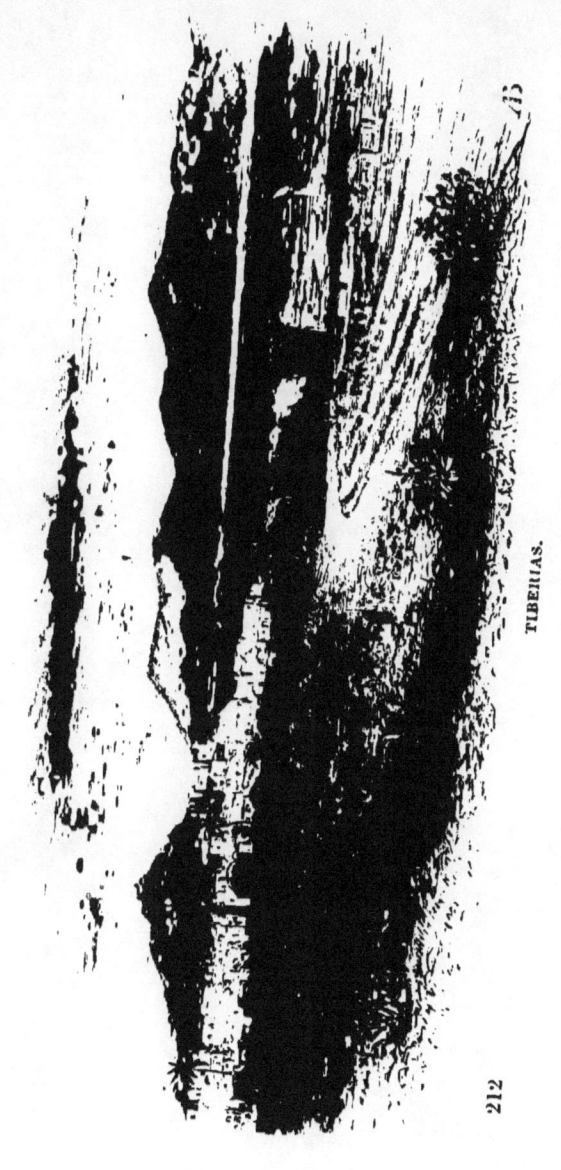

TIBERIAS.

212

and walking barefoot cannot be done in an easy or graceful way. Not being a swimmer, I took my bath by walking out to a big stone, seated upon which, I could duck and wash to contentment. Moreover, the balmy temperature of the air and the evening breeze left little for the towel to do.

In inquiring our way to the bathing place, I noticed that when my companion said كثر خيرك *Katar khairak* (thank you) to a woman who had directed us, she rejoined, شو صار *Sho saar?* (what is done?) which struck me as being even yet a happier form than "Do not mention it."

Across the lake, where was the country of the Gadarenes, I thought I recognized a spot which could fulfil the conditions described in Luke viii. 33, where the herd of swine, into which the legion of devils had entered, rushed violently down a steep place into the lake and were choked. But on this point J. Mc Gregor, Esq., is no doubt the paramount authority, having surveyed the entire coast of the sea from his canoe, the "Rob Roy."

Our bath, I need not say, proved an immense refreshment after the ride from Mount Tabor. We returned to our lodgings and were soon after waited on by an inhabitant, who brought some, apparently, valuable Roman coins and other relics which he offered for sale. I proposed a price which, as he refused it and did not return to accept, I conclude that they were, as they appeared to be, genuine *antiqua*.

Although in the city celebrated for its fleas, we spent a quiet night. Degradation, however, is the great feature of this Jewish town. The zeal of the Jew, " but not according to knowledge " (Rom. x. 2), was exhibited in a little tin tube containing, I presume, the Decalogue or some words of the law, nailed to the door-post of the house (Deut. vi. 9), and further by mutterings of prayer and reading in the Hebrew tongue which we could overhear proceeding from the chamber of our host each time we awoke in the night.

CHAPTER XI.

THURSDAY 22nd, 4 a.m. The horses were brought and, being ready dressed, we mounted to continue our journey. Having cleared the town, we rode by the shore, witnessing the breaking of day over the Sea of Galilee, and the lovely surrounding country.

Many scenes now crowded together, now succeeded one another in my mind, as we held our way along the western shore of the Sea of Galilee in the grey morning twilight. Two or three row-boats moored to the shore of Tiberias naturally suggested the worldly occupation of those whom Jesus, walking beside this lake, called to follow Him, saying, "I will make you fishers of men." (Matt. iv. 19.) But the sea itself, with its waves swelling and rippling on the shore, and the country on every side, seemed to be so full of memories of Him who chose Capernaum for His own city (Matt. iv. 13, 16; ix. 1; and Mark ii. 1), who here spake out of Simon's boat to the people who stood on the shore (Luke v. 3), at whose word the fisher-

men letting down their nets enclosed great multi-
tudes of fishes (Luke v. 6, John xxi. 6), the tribute
money was brought forth from its depths (Matt.
xvii. 27), the waves were made to support the Maker
of all things walking thereon (Matt. xiv. 25), and
the wind and the sea ceased their raging. (Mark
iv. 39.)

On the right was the sea which furnished the
subject of the parable of the net (Matt. xiii. 47, 50),
and on the left, the hills and fields whence were
drawn the comparisons of the kingdom of heaven
to the sower, the good seed and the tares, the
mustard seed, the leaven, the hidden treasure, and
the pearl of great price, where the lilies grow and
the ravens feed which the Lord bids us to consider.
(Luke xii. 24-28.)

About 5.30 a.m. we reached Magdala, with its
one palm-tree waving in the morning breeze and
its well-furnished threshing-floor (shewn on the
left of the illustration).

Leaving my horse with the muleteer, I climbed
to a rock on the adjoining hillside in order to take
a sketch of this truly interesting scene. It was a
spot fragrant with the memory of Him who found
here one who, being much forgiven, loved much ;
for out of her, " Mary of Magdala," He cast seven

MAGDALA.

216

devils ; and we were near to the positions of Chorazin, Bethsaida, and Capernaum, which not receiving Him, the word is already literally fulfilled,
which He spake concerning them, " Woe unto
thee." " And thou Capernaum which art exalted
unto heaven shalt be thrust down in hell." (Matt.
xi. 23.) Their very sites are uncertain, their names
are no longer preserved in the district where once
they stood, while Magdala, where she lived who
loved her Lord with a love that took her to the
foot of the cross and detained her at the sepulchre
when the diciples had gone away to their own
home (John xx. 10, 11), still flourjshes : like
Bethany where they lived of whom we read,
" Now Jesus loved Martha, and her sister, and
Lazarus." (John xi. 5.) What cannot the love
of Jesus do ?

> " His love's a refuge ever nigh,
> His watchfulness, a mountain high ;
> His name's a rock, which winds above
> Nor waves below can ever move."

Having finished the sketch, I quitted my elevated
position in such haste that I forgot to bring away
some specimens of leaves and fruit of trees which
I had gathered on Mount Tabor ; my precipitation
being, I think, superinduced by the menacings of

a hornet, examples of which insect so continually finding me out, I felt inclined to give it the name of " the irrepressible uhlan."

A little before reaching Magdala, I had noticed what appeared to be a sailing boat, and the fuller light of day confirmed the impression. I observed that at intervals of about five or six minutes, she put up and took in her sail, from which I inferred she was shifting ground and taking up the nets. How many incidents in the life and ministry of the Lord did not this spectacle bring to mind ! It set me singing the Sunday-school hymn,

> " A little ship was on the sea,
>   It was a pretty sight."

My companions were as glad for me to rejoin them, as I was hasty in doing so ; for the number of flies (which are no doubt greatly attributable to the sedgy character of the place,) proved very irritating to the horses. As we rode away, I plucked a handful of beautiful oleanders which where growing close to the shore.

A short distance beyond Magdala, south of the district of ruins among which the sites of Chorazin, Bethsaida and Capernaum are suspected to be, we quitted the sea-coast near to some ruinous

walls bearing the name of *Khan-el-minyeh*. Here
we dismounted to get breakfast, and the mule
and my horse, being left free for a minute, bolted
off to seek shelter from the sun and flies, in the
interior of the *Khan*. Obeying an impulse I
followed them, and was just in time to witness
the astonishment of an Arab who had been
awakened by their scampering close to his ears
and who, having sprung to his feet, seemed at as
great a loss to account for the presence of the
quadrupeds and " Frank," as I was to offer an
apology for them and myself in his vernacular.

We kept to the old Roman road across the
hills to the Jordan, which we struck at an angle
of 45°, a few miles below Lake Huleh. Almost
involuntarily I turned myself in the saddle again
and again, until the view was cut off, to take
another look at the lake of which M'Cheyne so
sweetly wrote :

THE SEA OF GALILEE.

" How pleasant to me thy deep blue wave,
  O Sea of Galilee !
For the glorious One who came to save
  Hath often stood by thee.

Fair are the lakes in the land I love,
  Where pine and heather grow,

But thou hast loveliness far above
What nature can bestow.

It is not that the wild gazelle
Comes down to drink thy tide,
But He that was pierced to save from hell,
Oft wandered at thy side.

It is not that the fig-tree grows
And palms in thy soft air,
But that Sharon's fair and bleeding Rose
Once spread its fragrance there.

Graceful around thee the mountains meet,
Thou calm, reposing sea :
But oh, far more ! the beautiful feet
Of Jesus, walked o'er thee.

Those days are past—Bethsaida, Where ?
Chorazin, Where art thou ?
His tent the wild Arab pitches there,
The wild reeds shade thy brow.

Tell me, ye mouldering fragments, tell
Was the Saviour's city here ?
Lifted to heaven, has it sunk to hell,
With none to shed a tear ?

Ah ! would my flock from thee might learn,
How days of grace will flee ;
How all an offered Christ who spurn,
Shall mourn at last like thee.

And was it beside this very sea,
The new-risen Saviour said,
Three times to Simon, 'Lovest thou me ?'
My lambs and sheep then feed.

O Saviour ! gone to God's right hand !
Yet the same Saviour still,
Graved on thy heart is this lovely strand,
And every fragrant hill.

Oh ! give me, Lord, by this sacred wave,
Three-fold, thy love divine,
That I may feed, till I find my grave,
Thy flock—both thine and mine."

In this ride across the hills, we came upon the skeleton of a camel which, to all appearance, was devoid of even a shred of flesh or sinew ; nevertheless, a vulture was industriously plying it with his beak, and as we drew near, he rose heavily and flew to an adjacent rock, where he sat awaiting our departure in order to return to his quarry.

As elsewhere, we found millet standing in the fields, and at my request, the muleteer gathered a head which I brought to England, to place in the collection of a friend who is curious in these matters. I have since regretted that I did not do the same with the camel's skull, which would have proved still more interesting and scarcely more difficult to secure.

When we had crossed the higher ridges of the hills, Jordan came into view, adding life and beauty to the scene. We were on the Canaan side of the river, with the prospect of crossing to the other, which, however, was contrary to the usual allusions in scripture, where the people who were redeemed out of the house of bondage, having traversed the wilderness, are mentioned as being led to the eastern bank of Jordan, over against Jericho; nevertheless, there was Jordan, whose waters were divided for the passage of the children of Israel, when the priests, bearing the ark, stood firm on dry ground in the midst of Jordan, and all the Israelites passed over on dry ground, until all the people were passed clean over Jordan. (Josh. iii. 17.) Where Naaman, the valiant, yet leprous, captain of the host of the king of Syria, dipped seven times and his flesh came to him again as the flesh of a little child. (2 Kings v.) Where Jesus was baptized of John (Matt. iii.); and, with desire to reach its banks, we kept on our way, again outstripping the slower-paced mule with his heavier burden.

When within about half-an-hour of the river, my poor old stirrup gave another lurch, and on examination, was found to have fairly broken away from its supports which, though still holding together, were an elongated wreck of leather and cord, such as no ordinary skill could repair; so taking things as they were, I threw the dis-

223   JACOB'S BRIDGE.

abled stirrup across the front of my saddle, which was of the most uncomfortable Arab pattern. It was so thickly padded in front that, to relieve the muscles of my thigh from the distress resulting from long sitting in the distended form which the shape of the saddle compelled me to assume, I had many times since leaving Nablûs (including of course the ride up and down Tabor) been glad to throw myself on the chisel-pointed wooden back for a little relief; but now, with the power to ease myself reduced almost to a minimum, by the carrying away of my starboard stay, a little extra jolting from the broken and sloping ground we were crossing, and the discomfort from perspiration and numerous flies, it was entirely without regret, that I reached the halting-place, beneath some trees, close to جسر بنات يعقوب *Jisr benât Yakub* ("the bridge of Jacob's daughters").*

If any asked why I did not secure a better mount, at least as to the saddle, I would remind them that through the muleteer who had accom-

---

* Some people in the East assert that the above Arabic name must be written in the following manner :

جسر بنأة يعقوب *Jisr benáat Yakub*, "The bridge of the building of Jacob."

panied us from Jerusalem to Nablûs returning
to the former place without notice, taking away
my horse, and saddle (of European make), and
through the dearth of horses which existed at
the time, we were restricted to the most limited
choice, and had reason to be thankful that we
could obtain any mount at all.

At the foot of the bridge is a watch-tower occupied by a few Arabs. We went down to Jordan
and drank of its water, with which I also filled
two little bottles, in accordance with the requests
of some friends in England.

We now gathered under the shade of a tree and
opened our provision-bag, but were not tempted
by the appearance of the fowl, which had been
cooked in Tiberias and carried in the bag during
the heat of the morning ride ; so, having made a
refreshing draught of pomegranate juice, sugar,
and water, we set about preparing "a dinner of
herbs." From the Arabs we obtained some toma-
toes and an onion, which, with our pocket knives,
we peeled and shredded into a dish, sprinkling a
little salt to make the juices flow and mingle. To
this we added the juice of two sour pomegranates,
and the whole being well stirred, we dipped our
khubbs ("bread") therein, and this was a "dinner

of herbs " which, having the scriptural accompani-
ment of " love therewith " (Prov. xv. 17), we felt
that we fared sumptuously. To a similar dish
allusion is made in Ruth ii. 14.

The mule, by his idiosyncrasies was continually
doing something maladroit, which caused both
inconvenience and amusement to our party,
and on this occasion added his share to the scene
in a truly characteristic way. To windward of
where we were sitting was a heap of litter and
dust, and having slaked his thirst at the Jordan,
the animal found out this dust mound, and commenced pawing and disturbing it so effectively,
that the wind carried a large amount of litter and
grit into our dish, which was by no means improved by such a condiment.

As we were thus engaged, one of the Arabs put
his hand into my pocket and abstracted the telescope, which he had seen me directing towards
Mount Hermon ; so, letting him see that I was
aware of what he had done, I waited till he and
one or two others had made a trial of its power,
and received it back again.

CHAPTER XII.

ACROSS JORDAN.

HAVING made a sketch of the bridge and tower from where we dined, and of the Jordan from the bridge, I rejoined my companions, who were preparing to leave the place, the muleteer having made a jury-rig of my starboard stay.

We crossed the bridge and passed over some hills from which we could see Lake Huleh very distinctly. Beyond the hills we entered upon the wilderness-country with our faces towards Damascus. From this point there are three roads to Damascus ; the lower, which is the principal and practicable for carriages is, no doubt, the ancient highway along which Naaman the Syrian came to the land of Israel with chariots and horsemen (2 Kings v.) ; and in after days Saul of Tarsus, having received letters from the high priest, went from Jerusalem to Damascus. (Acts ix.)

How various are the ways of God, and yet how uniform His purposes of mercy and blessing ! To effect the same result in these two men, bringing them to brokenness of heart and the knowledge of

226   THE JORDAN FROM JACOB'S BRIDGE.

Himself, He led one from Damascus to the land of
Israel, and the other from Jerusalem to Damascus.
The first having reached the land whither he was
sent for a cure, and having heard the words of the
prophet, turned away in a rage; the other in a
rage set out "breathing out threatenings and
slaughter against the disciples of the Lord."
Quietly to dip himself seven times in Jordan was
the first brought in the obedience of faith ; by
the majestic display of a light brighter than the
sun at noon, and with a voice from heaven, was
the latter smitten down, that unto each the Lord
might be revealed.

> " God moves in a mysterious way
> His wonders to perform ;
> He plants His footsteps in the sea,
> And rides upon the storm.
>
> Deep in unfathomable mines
> Of never-failing skill,
> He treasures up His bright designs,
> And works His sovereign will."

Besides this lower road there are two others, the
middle and the upper : the latter, which is a mere
camel-path scarcely traceable in many places, was
chosen by us, and, according to what afterwards
transpired, I feel bound here to acknowledge the
Lord's mercy in guiding us to the choice.

We were fairly now in the wilderness-country,

" Where grass, nor herb, nor shrub takes root,
Save poisonous thorns that pierce the foot."

Even the latter were wanting. There were of
course patches of pasture in various places, but
the general aspect was that of a stony wilderness.

At 1.30 p.m. we reached a Bedouin camp and
applied for shelter, which was freely granted.
The existence of a spring of splendid water near
by had, no doubt, determined the selection of this
spot for the camp, as other springs in the same
neighbourhood had also procured the forming of
other camps which were in sight from the one
where we rested.

At the moment of our arrival the Sheikh was
not at home, but some of his family made us
truly welcome, and spread their best rugs in the
most eligible part of the tent for our use.

The Sheikh's tent was easily distinguished from
the rest by its greater length, being divided into
three parts by curtains of goat-hair, of which
material the whole of the tents were made. We
were received into the first section, as is the
custom. (Gen. xviii. 1, *et seq.*) This, then, we
will call Abraham's tent, seated wherein we could

IN THE BEDOUIN'S TENT.

229

overhear the women's voices in the adjoining
section, but were not, of course, invited thither,
it being the women's or family tent. (Vers 12-15 ;
chap. xxiv. 67 ; Judges iv. 18.) The third is, I believe, occupied by the fowls and kids of the flock.
(Gen. xxvii. 9.)

Our arrival was the signal for preparations
being made for our refreshment. A piece or two
of camel dung were put into a fireplace of stones,
and being kindled, an iron pan was placed over,
and raw coffee put therein, and stirred with a
metal rod until roasted to an even shade of colour,
then pounded in a wooden mortar while still hot,
and cast into the simmering pot, from which, in
a few minutes, we were served with little cups of
the beverage. So I tasted Bedouin coffee, the
perfection of that drink. Soon afterwards they
sent us in from Sarah's tent, bread newly baken
on the hearth, with *lebn* (curdled milk), olive oil,
goat-milk cheese, and other good things.

In the same tent was another visitor, an officer
of irregular cavalry; and here my companion
was informed of the state of the country through
which we had to pass. The Hanazi tribe of
Bedouins, who spend every winter in the vicinity
of Aleppo, and summer near Damascus, and

are amongst the most lawless of the sons of
Ishmael, with their hands against every man,
and every man's hand against them (Gen. xvi.),
had, the week before we passed, been in collision
with the villagers, and the soldiers coming to the
assistance of the latter, a Turkish officer had
been killed. This circumstance had led the
Governor of Damascus to send out Hamid Said
Pasha, of which captain of the Syrians are said
the same things as of Naaman who held the same
office of old—a great man with his master, and
honourable, by whom victories had been won, a
mighty man of valour. He led two thousand
cavalry against the Bedouins for their punishment, and although the combatants were suspected to be in the vicinity of the lower road, it
was uncertain in what direction, through the
fortunes of war, they would move.

· *His rebus cognitis* (these things being known),
the officer offered to accompany us as an addition
to our escort, which kindness was, however,
declined by Mr. El Karey who, thinking to spare
me anxiety, did not disclose these facts to me at
the time.

While conscious of his kind intention, I cannot
commend the course he adopted, believing that
fellow-pilgrims should share *all* the joys and

231   BEDOUIN CAMP.

sorrows, hopes and fears, pleasures and distresses of the way.

Not far from the camp, a caravan of mules belonging to the proprietor of our mount, also bound for Damascus, had halted, intending to start again by moonlight, and we agreed to go in their company, especially when we were told they expected to be joined by some horsemen as an escort.

As we were sitting in friendly chat in the tent, I noticed that the arrival of an elderly Arab of noble aspect produced risings and salutations on the part of others; but, failing an introduction, I kept my seat, and it was not until he had taken his that I learned he was the Sheikh. I confess I felt somewhat perplexed: the chief, whose hospitality I had already so largely received, had come and I had made him no recognition. To rise now would put him to the trouble of rising too; therefore, waiting till he turned his countenance towards me, I saluted him from my seat, placing my right hand to my breast and forehead, and received a most ready response from him.

During the afternoon, my companion and I slept awhile and at one time, leaving him in his cosy quarters, I wandered beyond the precincts of

the camp to take a sketch. This done, as I was
leisurely returning to the tent (at the door of
which, after the Sheikh's arrival, the spear of
about twelve feet in length was planted), close to
the margin of the camp, a big watch-dog, whose
presence I had not heeded, sprang to his feet
and menaced me with the most savage barks and
growls, presenting an aspect of rage almost
exceeding anything I had ever before seen de-
picted in dog or wolf. However, observing the
rule to keep my eye on the threatener, I continued my way into the camp, and a woman in
one of the tents came to my support, ordered the
dog to lie down and, in turn, threatened him with
a stone half as large as my head.

Later in the afternoon, when my companion
was still asleep, noticing that the muleteer had
gone down to the spring to water my horse and
the mule, I motioned to the soldier to follow me,
intending to attempt conversation by signs. My
companion being the pay-master, I had parted
with nearly all my silver money to provide him
with funds, and having a not unnatural desire to
give these poor fellows a small present *med
manu*, additional to any which Mr. El Karey
might think well to add to their stipulated pay,

¹²**T**³
₇₂

233   BEDOUIN.

I called upon them for attention as we stood at the spring, concealed from the inmates of the tent.

Placing a ten-franc piece between my teeth and pointing to it, I held up my ten fingers as expressing its value, then uttering the words *fi Damascus* (in Damascus), I directed one hand towards the soldier, and the other towards the muleteer, and, to make my meaning still clearer, I picked up a piece of grass, and, having pointed to it and the ten-franc piece, I broke it in two parts, giving one to each. They motioned to me that they perfectly understood my wish, so holding the piece on my open hand between them, I left it for them to decide who should take charge of it. They exchanged a few words, and with agreement on their part, the soldier took the half *Napoleon*. Placing my finger on my lips to suggest that they need not tell anyone what had taken place, I returned to the tent, when being noticed engaged with my pencil, I was requested to sketch the Sheikh's nephew who, thereupon, stood up for the purpose and I secured the annexed representation.

About sunset the scene was enlivened by the arrival of a considerable herd of cattle brought home from the pastures and tethered to a number of large stones in the centre of the camp. The Sheikh's splendid chestnut mare, too, tied at the tent door and receiving the caresses of her master, was an attractive object.

This Bedouin family declined the copies of Arabic Gospels which we offered them, because being Turkish by extraction, and having adopted the Bedouin life only a few years, they were still Turkish as to language. They listened, however, to the gospel message delivered by my companion, and accepted our little presents of knives, scissors, &c. Late in the evening they sent in from the family tent, a lordly dish of rice stuck with parts of fowls beautifully dressed and accompanied with little bowls of gravy, the mode of taking which is to hold the poultry by the bone and bite it off in mouthfuls, and pinching the rice into balls, to dip them in the gravy and convey to the mouth with the fingers. This diet, with the delicious water from the spring, proved the most suitable preparation for the journey which lay before us. It also afforded me an illustration, by the help of which and my companion's interpretation, to speak to these friendly people about the Saviour. I told them that I had often heard the excellence and freeness of Bedouin hospitality extolled; but

now I had done much more, for I had received
and proved it ; and so would they, who had heard
from my companion of the love of God and the
grace of the Lord Jesus Christ, *taste* and *know*
that the Lord is gracious if they put their hearts'
trust in Him who died and rose again.

About 10 p.m. the moon rose, and the Sheikh
and I who had become quite sociable, looked at
her through my telescope and endeavoured to
teach her name and those of a few other objects
to one another, in English and Arabic. He was
also amused by the burning of some magnesium
wire which I had with me. Twice during the
evening, in the midst of conversation, he broke
away from his company, spread his upper garment
on the ground, slipped his shoes from his feet,
and went through the usual Mahometan prayers,
with his face towards Mecca.

Moon-rising being the only condition upon
which, I had understood, depended the putting
the caravan of mules in motion, I was in a state of
expectation from about 11 p.m., but though wake-
ful and alert, refastening the bundles which had
been opened and strolling about to counteract the
influence of the cold night air, I was careful, after
my experience in the afternoon, to keep within

the camp, remembering that "without are dogs."
(Rev. xxii. 15.)

But for this consideration, I should doubtless
have wandered away again to experience the soli-
tude of the wilderness, and to drink in with an
increased appreciation the sentiments expressed in
the words:

> "And here, while the night-winds around me sigh,
> And the stars burn bright in the midnight sky,
> As I sit apart by the desert stone, -
> Like Elijah at Horeb's cave alone,
> 'A still small voice' comes through the wild
> (Like a father consoling his fretful child),
> Which banishes bitterness, wrath, and fear—
> Saying, MAN IS DISTANT, BUT GOD IS NEAR!"

Yet, although foregoing this pleasure, I had
good opportunity for musing upon the wilderness
and a tent life, with their teachings. The forty
years' journeyings of the children of Israel " when
the cloud was taken up from the tabernacle, then
after that the children of Israel journeyed: and in
the place where the cloud abode, there the children of Israel pitched their tents. At the commandment of the Lord the children of Israel
journeyed, and at the commandment of the Lord
they pitched: as long as the cloud abode upon the

tabernacle they rested in their tents." (Num. ix.
17, 18.) Then, if we may so say, Jehovah was their
Sheikh; His presence was marked, not by a spear,
but by the Shekinah. Their tents were pitched
in sight of His; "and it came to pass, when the
ark set forward, that Moses said, Rise up, Lord,
and let thine enemies be scattered, and let them
that hate thee flee before thee. And when it
rested, he said, Return, O Lord, unto the many
thousands of Israel." (Chap. x. 35, 36.)

" DRINK AND AWAY."

" There's a well in the land of the date-tree and palm,
Where the Arab pursues his wild war of alarm,
Where the Bedouin wanders in search of his prey ;
And the name of that fountain is ' drink and away.'

On, weary-foot traveller, onward in haste,
Nor stay by the brink of that well, but to taste ;
To rest thee awhile ? nay, one moment's delay
May be death to the pilgrim, then ' drink and away.'

'Tis a spot like an island of verdure and bloom ;
A rose in the desert; a light in the gloom ;
He bends at the front, and its waves seem to say,
In musical murmurs, ' haste, drink and away.'

The horizon is clear, the sun mounts on high ;
No foe can the traveller around him descry ;
But he thinks of the Arab, nor dares here to stay,
But stoops at the fountain to ' drink and away.'

There's a well in the country of suffering and grief,
To the parched and the weary its waves bring relief:
Unceasingly flows its pure crystalline tide,
And the name of this fountain is 'drink and abide.

O wanderer o'er mountain, o'er valley, o'er moor,
Neglected and friendless, unhappy and poor,
Here's elixir indeed ! then turn thee aside,
And drink of this fountain—yea, 'drink and abide.'

Think not to exhaust this perennial spring,
Think not as a payment your treasures to bring ;
For the King who has spoken His words ne'er belied,
' Freely' drink at this fountain—yea, 'drink and abide.'

'Round the fountains of earth there is danger and death,
Their sources may fail, like thine own fleeting breath ;
But exhaustless this water, whate'er may betide—
Ye may drink of this fountain—yea, 'drink and abide.'"

DRINK AND AWAY.

My companion informed me that it still frequently happens, at a time of continued hostility

between two tribes of Bedouins, with the usual concommitant surprises and reprisals on either side without any decisive advantage being gained which would lead to the submission of one tribe to the other, that appeal is made to the combat of champions, as was done by the Philistines and the men of Israel in the days of Saul (1 Sam. xvii.), when David, the stripling of Bethlehem, fought and overcame the giant of Gath, thereby securing victory to the Israelites; type of Him who "was manifested, that he might destroy the works of the devil." (1 John iii. 8.)

Did the women out of all the cities of Israel celebrate David's victory? Then,

> "Awake, my soul, in joyful lays,
>   To sing thy great Redeemer's praise;
>   He justly claims a song from thee :
>   His loving-kindness, O how free !
>
> He saw thee ruined in the fall,
>   Yet loved thee notwithstanding all ;
>   He saved thee from thy lost estate :
>   His loving-kindness, O how great !
>
> Though numerous hosts of mighty foes,
>   Though earth and hell thy way oppose ;
>   He safely leads His saints along :
>   His loving-kindness, O how strong !"

My friend also furnished me with the following war song, the general purport of which is the same as in the words with which Goliath defied his enemy. (1 Sam. xvii. 43, 44.) The bold style of the original will be best reproduced by singing the words to the air, without any reference to the accompaniments.

BEDOUIN WAR SONG.

Tayabtih men niged elaca'a Tooness,
Badez el gana walmerafat el sagäel ;
Wa-amack Handle fee emagal gataltoo,
Wazahran chalatoo min elserj mile.
Abock ramatooand ma ra'a sawaghu,
Wachalate damoo aleckabäne sael.
Gada mooltacka el medan beenie wabenack,
Henack yebaen behe redie el faäel ;
Aatenie Harba wachoodlack badalha,
Waamran dana ma yawadooloo wasael.

CHAPTER XIII.

ABOUT midnight I found the escort and muleteer making their preparations, saddling the horses and arranging the luggage for loading the mule, and a little before 1 a.m. on

Friday, 23rd, the order to march reached us in a very musical way. Borne upon the wind was the sound of numerous bells, which the initiated knew to come from the caravan of mules. In a minute or two our mule was loaded, and we in our saddles. Farewell was taken of such of our hospitable friends in the tent as were awake and, just as the caravan was passing the camp, we rode out and fell into the rear.

There were about thirty mules with packsaddles; several of them laden, and the rest carrying empty crates. Every mule had a collar decorated with several double bells, that is, one bell within another and a tongue within it. There were also two mules carrying a litter between them which, having borne an invalid from Damascus to Nablûs, was returning empty.

R

The caravan was accompanied by the owner's son riding on an ass and about six muleteers. The fewness of men is accounted for by the fact that it is generally sufficient to guide the leading mule, and the music of the bells serves to keep them together, whether by day or night. And should it happen (as I noticed it sometimes did), that irregularities of the road should divert one or other of the mules from the track followed by the majority, and that its deviations should compel it to wander to some distance from the path, yet the attractiveness of the bells would soon prevail to urge it to an effort to return. Thus the bells assist the wanderer to recover the track and would enable the muleteers to trace a truant mule.

Two of the party carried guns, and one of them discharged his piece as an announcement to whoever might be near, that we were armed; so, with those carried by our escort and muleteer, we had four guns, all told. It had been said that four armed horsemen were to join our party, and such was the intention when the caravan left Nablûs, but owing to the disturbed state of the country, from the causes already named, it had been deemed prudent to keep back four mules (which were to have been sent, laden with specie: the revenue from Nablûs to the government head-quarters in Damascus), and the horsemen who were to have escorted the treasure.

There was much entertainment in the novel spectacle of the string of mules (which it should be understood, are much finer animals than the examples we occasionally meet with in England), and in the merry sound of their bells, as they went jogging over the rather uneven ground.

Thus the night wore on; and, keeping to the upper road for Damascus, about two hours before sunrise we were crossing the lower spurs of Mount Hermon, passing through a thick cold mist. Indeed we had experience of the "dews of Hermon" which, however refreshing and fertilizing to the country around, are trying enough to the traveller exposed to their influence. Riding in this saturated atmosphere, a sense of exhaustion as of one ready to perish came over me, and I cast in my mind the desirableness of making terms for passing the succeeding two or three hours in the mule litter. But this I was reluctant to do, and hope of the sunrising cheered me on. Still the coldness of the air produced an irresistible drowsiness, so that although we were riding along a hillside path where a false step would certainly have been serious, I was so overcome as to be every minute or two in dream-land, and only shaken out of it to relapse almost as quickly. This lasted for about an hour, when, though still suffering from cold, the nearer hope of seeing the sun seemed to give me fresh energy.

At length, although his disc was not visible, I could see through the mist on the left above me, the top of Hermon with his white snow-patches shining in the light of the sun which had risen upon him, and managed to sing a verse or two :

" O Saviour ! whom absent we love,
　　Whom not having seen we adore,
　Whose name is exalted above
　　All glory, dominion, and power.

O come and display us as Thine,
　　And leave us no longer to roam ;
　Let the light of Thy presence, Lord, shine,
　　Let the trumpet soon summon us home.

When that happy morning begins,
　　When we in Thy glories shall shine,
　Nor grieve any more by our sins,
　　The bosom on which we recline.

O then shall the mists be removed,
　　And round us Thy brightness be pour'd
　We shall meet Him, whom absent, we lov'd,
　　We shall see, whom unseen we adored."

I was drawn in contemplation to the glorious scene on my left until, above a small hill in front towards my right, the sun himself appeared in all his splendour, chasing away the mists and increasing in power every minute. The effect was wonderful : in about half-an-hour I was fully restored from my previous state of distress, and could well understand that it is not a hyper-figurative use of words which we find in Malachi iv. 2 : " Unto you that fear my name shall the Sun of Righteousness arise with *healing* in his wings."

When the mists were quite dispelled, and Mount Hermon stood out in his true majestic boldness with the shining snow on his summit, the muleteer directed my attention, as if with a feeling of national pride, to جبل الشيخ *Djebel-es-Sheikh* (the Arabic name).

Soon after this, finding that the pace of the caravan was slower than that to which we had been accustomed ; from no unwillingness to share their fortunes, but a desire to hasten our arrival in Damascus, we determined to push on at our own pace, and did so, but not before we had noticed that, in passing through some fields of ripe millet, which the villagers had left unreaped through dread of the Bedouins, the muleteers ran among the corn and gathered a quantity which they stowed in the crates on the mules' backs.

In a little time we were out of sight of the caravan and of the sound of the bells, and the muleteer
having traversed the country more frequently than
the escort, was appointed guide at his own request;
but we had not proceeded very far before a dispute
arose between him and the soldier, who was of
opinion that we were getting too far to the right;
but, the muleteer insisting on his fuller knowledge,
we continued until we found the track was leading
us to the wrong side of a hill which is one of the
well-known landmarks of the road.

This discovery led to some altercation between
these two men, who appear to have had other
grounds of jealousy; the escort seeking to magnify
his office to the full, and the muleteer probably
counting that religiously, as a professed Christian
(he belonged to the Greek church), he stood in a
place of greater favour than the Mahometan
soldier.

The error being admitted, we struck across
country to recover the proper road, and on doing
so were just in time to fall in again with the mules,
when, noticing our approach, the owner's son came
to meet us, and, bringing us to a halt, delivered
himself of such an eloquent rebuke, that I was
fully carried away with admiration of the lad of

fourteen. The canvas only could convey any just idea of the scene which ensued.

Here were four self-reliant men who, left for two or three hours to themselves, had committed a great error, and were now confronted by a mere lad, whose zeal in the interest of his father, to whom the horses and mule belonged, was such that, though a mere stripling, like the shepherd boy of Bethlehem who slew the lion, the bear, and the giant of Gath (1 Sam. xvii.), now, with his ruddy cheeks, swarthy bare legs, and loosely shod feet, he stood before us and with all the eloquence of earnestness, delivered his rebukes.

My impulse was to ride up and applaud, patting him on the back, but I was restrained by a sense that I was in an erring and inferior position and should be offering praise, in circumstances unfavourable to its being accepted, to my own superior.

After this, it will not be astonishing that the jealousy between our muleteer and escort gathered strength and, although our ears were not annoyed with so many Kurdish songs from the latter as before, they were continually over-hearing the uncomfortable dispute which was proceeding. It now came out that another contention existed, of which I had been the unintending cause by giving the half *Napoleon* beside the desert spring, as my companion inquired of me if I had not given them ten francs to divide between them.

J "Yes; but I wished them to have it independently of any gratuity you might think right to add to their stipulated wages, so please not to take any notice of it."

El K. "But the soldier says you meant it all for him."

J "Then I shall thank you to tell him that I did not, and quite believe that they both understood my wish, and if you will be so good as to pay him five francs short, and the muleteer five francs over, when settling in Damascus, I shall be much obliged."

With these principal drawbacks, we traversed the bold and rocky district in the vicinity of Hermon, the commencement of the Lebanon range contributing to the splendour of the landscape,

> " Where every prospect pleases,
> And only man is vile."

During this and the following day we passed two or three caravans one or two of which appeared to be of considerable size. In one I counted sixty

CAMELS AT REST.

camels, though this is, we know, as nothing compared with some of the annual caravans. It produced a very peculiar impression to be riding along
the narrow path, through an atmosphere so heated
that a shimmering effect was produced before the
eyes, making every object appear to quiver; to
pass the long string of camels and men, the
leisurely strides of the former, and the swaying
motions of the latter adding drollery to the scene,
beside the utterances they made as they passed,
which, charitably assuming to be salutations, I
endeavoured to imitate, but withal felt too wearied
to use much effort in the attempt.

This morning we crossed two brooks of snow-
water (Job ix. 30), having their source on the
heights of Hermon, from which the horses, as well
as ourselves, drank with much delight. They
were, I believe, feeders of the Pharpar. As my
horse was stooping at the second, the slight strain
broke the bridle; so I waited for the muleteer to
repair it, which he did with his needle and string,
quilting it for strength, during which operation
my companion and the escort got considerably in
advance.

Having re-mounted, I overtook them at *Kefr
Houwara*, our halting place, and we rode to some

trees which the escort had selected for our shelter; but scarcely had we tied our horses to the boughs, when the shouts of the muleteer announced that he had found a place where we might rest more comfortably.

My companion gave heed to his assurances and we re-mounted to join him, and found him near a threshingfloor which we had passed a few minutes previously. He told us he had made arrangements with one of the villagers for us to rest in an adjoining garden ; but jealousy could endure no longer : the escort, finding that his competitor had succeeded better than he, renewed the old quarrel and, being answered impertinently in the hearing of the villagers, the hot-blooded Kurd dismounted and commenced to belabour the muleteer with the barrel of his gun, which the latter, being stronger than he, soon wrenched from his grasp. The soldier then succeeded in drawing the ramrod and commenced flogging with it. The effect was more serious to the ramrod than to the receiver of its blows, as it soon buckled up into a shape very unpromising to its again being serviceable as a ramrod. Upon this my companion, whose commands for them to desist were disregarded, rode up and began to address them with cuts from the tethering line attached to his bridle, and he being supported by a villager who carried a gun, the combatants drew off.

This is, perhaps, a fit occasion for reviewing the state of our outward defences in passing so near to the Hanasi Bedouins and some others about whose good will we might not be fully assured. It is true that my companion's saddle was fitted with two pretentious pistol holsters, but they contained only socks, nightshirt, &c. I had neither firearms nor the appearance of carrying them; the other two carried guns, but here, in broad daylight, they were seen to be at enmity among themselves, and when the escort proper essayed to discharge his piece, he produced only a flash, and now, his ramrod was so crippled as to render the operation of loading almost hopeless.

With so small an appearance of united strength we drew rein within eight hours of Damascus; it was enough to recall the words of Joseph to his brethren, " See that we fall not out by the way." (Gen. xlv. 24.) Into the merits of the case, it is, perhaps, not my place to enter. Doubtless the muleteer was wrong in speaking before the villagers reproachfully to the escort, who was held responsible for our safe conduct, while a little less assertion of his own importance would at least have made the soldier more agreeable. But he was a Kurd.

"A heathen ? teach him then thy better creed,
Christian, if thou deserv'st the name indeed."

The muleteer led us to our new quarters, which we entered by a small gate, leaving the horses outside with our servants. The proprietor, who was an aged and infirm man of more than seventy years, bade us welcome, and we sat down beneath a walnut tree, for we were now on the table-land on which Damascus stands, and had entered into a region supporting a vegetation more strictly typical of the temperate zone than that of the country through which we had passed.

I was greatly interested in our aged benefactor, who told us the story of his life. He had brought up a family of two sons and several daughters; both the sons were dead, and of the daughters, only two or three had been married, while of them I think two were widows. We saw one or two of them, the husband of one, and a grandchild.

The old man depended for an income chiefly upon his garden and, being no longer able to culti-vate it himself, and having no sons to do so, with several of his family dependent on him, the cares and sorrows of life seemed to bear heavily. He, and others who visited us, freely accepted copies of the Gospel, as well as knives, &c., which we distributed.

We prepared a dinner of herbs as on the day before, the old man furnishing the salt from a supply which he carried tied in the corner of his garment, according to the custom of the country. I also noticed the same practice with respect to money; in the bazaars of the cities the purchasers untying a corner of an upper garment to take out money from thence; suggesting the allusion in the parable of the pounds: "Lord, behold, here is thy pound, which I have kept laid up in a napkin." (Luke xix. 20.)

The fatigues of our ride since 1 a.m. induced sleep, from which we awoke much refreshed to find our host still sitting near us, smoking his pipe, the Arab's solace; also when I opened my eyes I was saluted by one of the men of the place who had found out the strangers in their retreat, and who, taking from his bosom some cucumbers, offered them to us and received a pocket knife in return. Here also we were visited by a young man of good position and education, who held a long conversation with my companion, and accepted a copy of one of the Gospels.

As evening drew near, Mr. El Karey opened negociations for obtaining sleeping quarters, which were provided in a watch-tower over the threshingfloor, close to the scene of the mid-day scuffle. This watch-tower was such an one as is referred to in Isaiah i. 8, in the comparison of the daughter of Zion to "a lodge in a garden of cucumbers." We saw other examples of the same thing in the vineyards which we passed. It was a stage, supported twelve or fourteen feet above the ground on four poles, the floor being laid with fragrant herbs and the top and three sides-thatched with boughs of the walnut tree.

Taught by the experience of the early morning, I placed my brandy flask in my pocket, and having left our baggage in charge of the servants (under which comprehensive name I have ventured, without apology, to include the escort), we retired to our sleeping quarters, being quickly followed by one of the villagers who brought us a bowl of boiled rice, a basin of excellent goat's milk and the water-bottle. Thus did the Lord provide us food and shelter in the wilderness and, asking His blessing, we ate our supper, I trust with thankfulness as well as gladness.

The friendly villager having taken away the empty basin, we settled ourselves for the night, which performance required a little care that we should not both stand up or move at the same time, for fear of bringing down the entire fabric of our bedroom, but by dint of a little management, we were soon comfortably settled on pillows improvised from small bundles of our things. There was just room for us to lie full length, head to feet, on our bed of herbs, covered with blanket and plaid, nor do I remember ever to have had a better sleep or more comfortable bedroom.

Saturday, 24th, 12.30 a.m. We arose and prepared to renew our journey with only one more horseback-stage before us. Having descended form our elevated bedroom, a sense of the special mercies of which we had been the receivers prompted us to unite in lifting up our voices in the well-known glorious doxology:

" Praise God from whom all blessings flow,
Praise Him, all creatures here below,
Praise Him above, ye heavenly host,
Praise Father, Son, and Holy Ghost."

We kept our way along the camel path, until it united with the other two roads already referred to.

24⁵⁄₇₂ 8

256   OUR BEDROOM AT KEFR HOUWARA.

A little before sunrise we were passing through
the vineyards south-west of Damascus, into one of
which the watcher came down from his lodge,
which was similar to the one where we had spent
the previous night, and gave us several bunches
of the most delicious grapes. They were of four
varieties, and seemed to corroborate the reputation
of the grapes of Damascus as the best in the
world, and the dew being still upon them, they
were in their finest condition.

Our journey next led us beside the "rivers of
Damascus," the Fiji and Balada, branches of the
Abana, and the entire aspect of the country was
that of luxuriance, with vineyards, gardens and
trees, comprising even the poplar, and good roads
well kept, while the bleachers, washing cloth ·in
the Balada and laying it out on the banks,
brought to my mind representations of Indian
scenery.

At a branch in the road the muleteer left us to
enter Damascus by another than the highway, so
as to avoid the heavy tolls levied on goods at the
barrier. We met several well-mounted Syrian
gentlemen, one of whom entered courteously and
fully into our inquiries, and crossing the Balada
by a stone bridge, rode into Damascus, the most

BALADA.

ancient city in the world, still flourishing, num-
bering, as it does, a population of a hundred and
eighty thousand. We soon reached Sook-ul-
Khail (the horse market), where was our hotel, of
which Mr. Demitri-Cara is the proprietor.

CHAPTER XIV.

DAMASCUS.

THE muleteer having joined us and the baggage being stowed in our room, we obtained the luxury of a good wash and change of clothes, and realized that we had left the wilderness for the city.

The hotel is built about the four sides of a quadrangle, the centre of which is occupied by a tank of gold and silver fish into which several almost perennial fountains discharge themselves.*

The level of the streets of Damascus being somewhat lower than that of the river, a constant supply of water exists for these fountains without the intervention of pumping appliances. All that I had opportunity to notice of the waters of Syria during my brief stay impressed me that it would be most natural for any of the inhabitants to hold in high esteem "Abana and Pharpar, rivers of Damascus." (2 Kings v. 12.)

About 9 a.m. we were taking our roll and

---

* This is the tank in which John McGregor, Esq., placed his canoe "Rob Roy" at the time of his visit to Damascus. *Vide* "The Rob Roy on the Jordan," p. 127.

coffee beside the fountain, under orange, lemon, and *mishmish* (Damascus apricot) trees, loaded with ripe fruit, after which we sallied forth into the city.

Our first business was at the Telegraph Office, whence we sent messages to Nablûs and to Brading in the Isle of Wight, at which latter place my family spent the period of my absence. This telegram, which informed my wife that she might consider me homeward bound and in good health, reached her before my letter posted in Jerusalem, to say that I had arrived in the Holy Land.

We were here joined by the muleteer and escort who, having received payment for their services, took our hands, kissed them, placed them to their breasts and foreheads, and left.

The rest of the day we spent at the hotel, and in rambles through the city. Three or four diplomatic representatives of other countries and one young English traveller were among the inmates of the hotel, and our host, who is, if I remember rightly, of Greek nationality, made every provision for our comfort and was always ready to expatiate on the doings of the British fleet at St. Jean d'Acre and the valour of Sir Charles Napier, of which he was an eye-witness.

The water we drank here was cooled with snow from Mount Hermon, for fetching which several mules are constantly employed during the summer, and to a similar practice reference is no doubt made in the words "As the cold of snow in the time of harvest, so is a faithful messenger to them that send him, for he refresheth the soul of his masters." (Prov. xxv. 13.)

As a whole, Damascus impressed me with ideas of past and present magnificence, and the moving spectacles in its streets and bazaars seemed to bring back in one heterogeneous living crowd, all that I had ever heard or read in Eastern tale or fable about princes, merchants, fortune-tellers, asses, Cadis, camels, and beggars.

Lord's Day 25th. This morning, contrary to arrangements made the night before, we found the young Englishman still in the hotel; such are the delays continually happening to travellers in the East. A misunderstanding existed between his dragoman and the proprietor of horses from whom they had hired a mount to take them to Baalbec. Then, when a compromise had been agreed to and the animals produced, one could but notice the amount of opinion and advice gratis which was given with all imaginable volubility by the Easterns upon the quality of the horses, and the entire unfitness of the ass to carry the luggage, the young fellow all the time waiting for matters to be settled somehow, with an expression which, if I mistook not, meant "I should prefer half the talk and twice the performance." *

At length they started, with the understanding that we should probably meet them again in Beyrout, which, however, did not take place, although when there we heard of their safe arrival.

We left the hotel, passing by the Grand Mosque, which is an adaptation to their own purposes by the Mahometans, of the structure known to be the Crusaders' church of St. John the Baptist; and made our way to the christian quarter, which

---

* A copy of the first edition of this work having come into the hands of this gentleman, he has written to me : " Your guess at the meaning of my 'expression' during the confab we had about the horses and ass was a shrewd one, and hit the mark. Notwithstanding the doubts expressed as to the capabilities of the latter to perform his part of the work, he proved himself the most effective and least troublesome of the party. The lad who accompanied us was as cheerful and merry as a cricket, and sang all the way like a lark ; even when we were suffering most acutely from thirst and 'thinking' most longingly many a time ' of the water we once threw away.' "

still bears evident marks of the massacre of 1860, when about twelve hundred of the inhabitants of the city were put to death. I noticed many new houses occupying the sites of those which had been destroyed, and many others, their blackened basements still exhibiting the effect of the fires, which appearance is the more striking in contrast with the superstructures of new masonry.

At the American Mission we listened to an address by the missionary based on the words in Titus ii. 11—15, "For the grace of God that bringeth salvation hath appeared to all men, teaching us that, denying ungodliness and worldly lusts, we should live soberly, righteously, and godly, in this present world; looking for that blessed hope, and the glorious appearing of the great God and our Saviour Jesus Christ; who gave himself for us, that he might redeem us from all iniquity, and purify unto himself a peculiar people, zealous of good works. These things speak, and exhort, and rebuke with all authority. Let no man despise thee."

The marked attention and evident interest of the hearers greatly delighted me. In order to meet the native prejudices, a curtain divides the men from the women in the mission chapel. After the meeting we repaired to the house of Dr. Meshakah, whose own deeply interesting narrative of what happened to his family during the massacre is given in Appendix B to that well-known book, Porter's " Giant Cities of Bashan."

We found him sitting in his room, his right hand nearly paralysed from the effects of the cruelties he underwent in 1860, but himself rejoicing in the Lord who redeemed him, has preserved him so many years, and enabled him so long to testify the grace of God.

In order to prevent the paralysis from being completely established, though no longer able to use a pen with his right hand, he had exercised himself in the handling of other instruments and had constructed a psaltery which he proceeded to tune and, applying his left hand to the finger-board and using the bow with his right, he sang a verse or two of a psalm accompanied by the instrument, presenting a most striking illustration of the spirit of the words, " While I live I will praise the Lord." (Ps. cxlvi. 2.) He had also, for about a year, been accustoming his left hand to the use of the pen, but, as I understood, with very partial success. He was then in the eightieth year of his age.

Before dinner I was invited to join in a walk with two or three of the other visitors at the hotel. To this I consented, but finding they were bent on exploring a mosque, I left them to enter without me, and awaited their return in an adjoining field near the banks of a branch of the Balada. As I wandered near the stream, reading a chapter from my pocket Bible, I noticed that with almost every footfall, I startled one or two frogs which leapt into the stream and swam to a hiding-place. The vicinity of the mosque, and the city of mosques (for such Damascus deserves to be called), with the incident of the frogs, was enough to bring to my mind Revelation xvi. 13—not that I apprehend Mahomet to be *the* false prophet there referred to.

Having been rejoined by my companions, we returned to the hotel where, from time to time, with one or another of the visitors and sometimes several together, Mr. El Karey found opportunity for preaching the gospel.

This night a son was born to our worthy host who, having been previously bereaved of all his children, the next day was one, not only of great but special congratulation.

Monday 26th. We rose early and went to the

Turkish bath which, according to promise, I will
briefly describe. Our landlord directed us to one
of the best in Damascus. On entering we were
led into a large domed building with chambers
around and passages leading to various depart-
ments of the institution. The floor was of marble;
in the centre a fountain was playing, while light
entered through various coloured glasses in the
dome and through windows in the courses beneath.
We were conducted to a comfortable room with
a window opening on to a flower garden. The
description which follows combines the recollection of this and other baths which I took in the
East.

Having undressed and fastened a towel about
the loins, and another of large dimensions being
thrown over your shoulders by an attendant,
you descend from your room, place your feet in a
pair of clogs, and are conducted to one of the hot
chambers, an Arab supporting you lest you should
slip upon the wet marble. You probably pass
through two or three chambers, in each of which
are bathers in various stages of their bath, till
you have reached one which you consider hot
enough, and the upper towel having been removed, you are seated on the floor close to a

marble trough, through which a fountain of hot
water is running. With a copper dish you throw
a little of this water on your head, and wait until
a good perspiration has been instituted and sustained for probably three-quarters of an hour,
after which time the shampooer comes to you.

As you are sitting in Turkish fashion, your
limbs feel the confined position perhaps enough as
it is, but this is as nothing compared with what
follows, when the lusty Arab, spreading his hands
over your shoulders, bears you down, pressing as
he advances from shoulder to ribs.

After a few of these manipulations, he pro-
ceeds to your arms and legs, then you lie on
face and back, while every part is well sham-
pooed with horse-hair gloves; at frequent intervals hot water from the fountain being thrown
over you by dishfuls. Your persecutor (as you
may have been tempted to consider the shampooer)
now withdraws, but in a minute returns with
fresh instruments, namely a large copper bowl,
some soap, and a double handful of tow. He
quickly prepares an emulsion of soap-suds, and
then with the tow for a vehicle applies it in the
shape of a good scrub from head to foot. (N.B.
If your eyes are not used to much soap, keep them

shut during this portion of the bath.) Having
poured more hot water over you, before you have
had time to clear your eyes or to recover breath
for an answer, he interrogates you with طيب
Tayib? (" good ?"), and in a manner which almost
carries its own contradiction you gasp " *bono.*"
You are next led to an adjoining chamber and
instructed by signs to plunge into a tank of still
hotter water. If you prefer it you can have
water of the same temperature poured over you
instead. You are now ready for your cold
plunge which, though perhaps it takes the breath
a little, is most refreshing, and afterwards, with
clean towels put about and over you, you are
conducted back to your room ; but before entering,
you are requested to sit on a bench and stretch out
your feet that they may be rinsed from whatever
may have adhered to them during your passage
from the other chambers. "He that is bathed
[Ὁ λελουμένος] needeth not save to wash [νίψασθαι]
his feet, but is clean every whit." (John xiii. 10.)

After this you re-enter your room, fresh towels
are put about you, and you recline on a divan
beside a' window opening into the garden, from
which the scent of flowers and the hum of bees is
borne to where you are lying ; while a pleasing

sense comes over you that the toils of a Turkish
bath are finished and nothing remains to you but
the delightful consequences. These impressions,
however, are quickly dispelled by the opening of
the door and the appearance of another operator,
who bids you sit up, puts your arms in some
novel position, not unlike that in which a cook
arranges the wings of a fowl trussed for roasting,
and kneeling behind, hugs you, perhaps placing
his knee to your back and bending your body in
various directions, produces cracks in your bones,
in some places where you had scarcely suspected
the existence of a bony articulation.

He next bends your knees, making them crack
by levering one leg with the other; each toe and
finger is made to contribute a crack to the treble
portion of the gamut and, having once more
changed your towels, you are motioned to lie down
again. But scarcely has your reverie recommenced,
before another attendant appears, wearing a pouch,
from which he produces scissors and razor, to the
action of which he invites you to submit the ex-
tremities of your anterior and posterior digits.
The disappearance of this operator is the imme-
diate prelude to the entry of another, who offers
you a *narghile* (hubble-bubble pipe), coffee and

sherbet, of which you make your own choice and
while to his predecessor's *tayib ?* your conscience
may have allowed you to reply *tayib,* the same
mentor requires, at least, some distinction, and
you return the coffee-cup or sherbet glass with a
كتير طيب *tayib katir* ("very good").

Once more you relapse into a reverie, coloured
by the scent of the flowers and the hum of the
bees, but if your " companion of the bath " be a
dragoman like Adam, you must be prepared for
sundry questions such as " Why you do not shave
more ?" so that whatever the bees are saying to
each other, your heart does not follow their hum
with :

اگر بر زمین فردوس است

همین جا است همین جا است همین جا است

" Agarbar zamín firdús ast,
Hamín já'ast, hamín já'ast, hamín já'ast."

" If Paradise be upon earth,
It is here, it is here, it is here." *

Having thoroughly dried, cooled and dressed,
you leave the room in borrowed slippers, which

* From the palace of Shah Jehan, Delhi.

having exchanged for your own boots, you proceed
to the place of payment, on your way thither
passing all the manipulators and attendants who
have taken any part in your bathing, and whose
looks, if not words, say as distinctly as ever you
heard it, " *bakhsheesh.*" Having settled all claims
according to your conscience, means, or humour,
you leave the building feeling all the better for
your bath.

Having taken coffee at the hotel, we hired donkeys in order to explore Damascus ; visiting the
bazaars, and climbing to the top of a minaret,
from which we obtained a splendid bird's-eye view
of the city. There lay beneath us, and spread out
as in a panorama, the most ancient city in the
world ; from which place came Eliezer, the steward
of Abraham's house (Gen. xv. 2), over which
David gained a victory, slaying 22,000 of the
Syrians of Damascus (2 Sam. viii. 5), and whither
in the days of Ahaz, king of Judah, many of the
men of Judah were carried captive (2 Chron.
xxviii. 5); of which the prophets have written (Isa.
vii. 8; viii. 4; xvii. 1—3; Jer. xlix. 23—27, &c.);
whither Saul of Tarsus went, having authority
from the high priest to take thence all that called
on the name of the Lord Jesus, and bring them

T

bound to Jerusalem; before whose gates he was
struck down, and beheld a light brighter than the
sun at midday, and heard from heaven the voice of
Him whom before he had persecuted, but who
became from that time the one controlling aim and
object of his life. (Phil. iii.) The "street called
Straight" (Acts ix. 11) was pointed out to us, a
part of which we also visited.

Passing through one of the gates, we surveyed
the ancient walls and one or two of the cemeteries.
The annexed sketch I took of that portion of the
outer wall which is the reputed spot where St.
Paul, through a window, in a basket, escaped the
hands of the governor, under Aretas the king, who
sought to take him. (2 Cor. xi. 32, 33.) The walls
on either side of the path are built of mud blocks,
and I noticed some labourers mixing clay with
chopped straw for the making of such blocks,
which circumstance reminded me of the bondage of
the children of Israel in Egypt, and the command
of Pharaoh that the "task-masters should with-
hold the straw." (Ex. v. 6, 7.) A part of this
day was occupied in purchasing relics for friends
in England.

In the afternoon as we were walking in the outskirts, we witnessed the spectacle of the head-

26J8
72

274   ANCIENT OUTER WALL OF DAMASCUS.

governor with his sons and attendants riding out. In addition to the military display, I was particularly struck with the easy motion, as well as good speed, of the little trotting camel or dromedary which was ridden by the youngest of the sons.

Tuesday 27th. This day was partly occupied in completing purchases, and getting everything which I was not likely to need on the voyage home, packed in a case for shipment from Beyrout; we also called to take leave of Dr. Meshakah.

Having previously booked our seats in the night-diligence to Beyrout, we repaired to the office, where a brush and a colour-pot being put into my hands, I addressed the case to my agents in London. The horses were put to and we were settling to our seats, when our attention was called to an interesting spectacle. A picket from the seat of war passed by with a drove of camels, which we were informed had been taken by the cavalry under Hamid Said Pasha from the Hanazi Bedouins. Further information was to the effect that the government troops had obtained a decided advantage over the latter; but the Bedouins having fled, baffled their pursuers by mingling themselves with the men of another tribe; that

this state of things would make it exceedingly
difficult for Hamid Said Pasha to follow up his
victory, and as to the spoils of war which we had
seen, they would probably be bought at the government sale for a nominal price by the neutral
Bedouins, and speedily find their way back to
their original owners.

We were thus reminded of the Lord's goodness
to us, in preserving us amid the perils of the
wilderness.

CHAPTER XV.

At 6 p.m. we started in the little two-horse diligence along the road constructed by the French engineers across the Anti-Lebanon and Lebanon ranges, to Beyrout. Outside the city we passed several fine buildings, the residences of the wealthy, and as we got upon the hills we noticed numerous springs, feeders of the Barrada, running down to the valley beneath.

Gradually we ascended the Anti-Lebanon, stopping now and then to change horses. My friend occupied the only outside passenger's seat, and, being within, when night had fairly commenced, I slipped off my boots and arranged myself for sleep, from which I was occasionally awakened, once by feeling something pulling at my toes, which proved, on seizing it, to be the hand of my companion which he had thrust through the window in quest of his blanket.

About midnight, at one of the villages where the horses were changed, we obtained supper. The first course was cold boiled fresh-water fish (I

suppose from the Hashbany, which runs here).
Here, too, I think it was we found a little circle
of villagers engaged in friendly chat, conspicuous
among whom was a hearty-looking Romish priest.
Thus we traversed Anti-Lebanon, Cœle-Syria,
and the Lebanon, with its grand features of rocks
and springs, commanding, too, the finest land-
scapes (山 川 *shan chuen*, "hills and streams," as
the Chinese would say). As the day broke, we
could appreciate these things the more: we passed
a string of tilted waggons, belonging to the mule
caravans which convey the goods traffic on this
road, and one or two small caravans of loaded
camels. In some parts, the mountain sides were
terraced for the cultivation of vines.

Crossing the Lebanon at this part, we did not
obtain a view of the cedars, of which, however,
there are still some notable clumps further to the
north-east. I noticed that we changed horses nine
times, thus making ten relays between Damascus
and Beyrout.

On retaking my seat, I found I had a new companion, who proved to be a member of the French
engineer staff of the Suez Canal, returning from
a short furlough to Baalbec, and who told me that
about thirty English vessels pass through the

CEDARS OF LEBANON.

canal every month, and that this number repre-
sents seventy per cent. at least of the whole
traffic.

Within a few miles of Beyrout we were joined
by a British merchant going to the city from his
suburban villa. I found him sceptical of the
wisdom of the numerous efforts for the christian
education of the children of Syria, which are now
happily being made ; but I suspected his lack of
zeal in this direction to proceed from a disregard
of the salvation of their souls, which is precious.
(Ps. xlix. 8.)

On being told about my journey, he did not
hesitate to congratulate me on having escaped
those evils which, I have already explained, were
presaged by others as likely to befall me. We
chose the Hôtel d'Europe, with which we were
every way satisfied.

Wednesday 28th. We learned that the next
steamer for Alexandria was to leave on Friday.
Having breakfasted, we set out in quest of my
letters, but, although we applied at both the
French and Austrian offices, there were none
forthcoming. This surprised me, as, according
to arrangements made in England, some should
have been there.

We next called on a merchant to consign the package from Damascus to my agents in London, through his in Liverpool, which was duly carried out and the contents have long since been nearly all distributed. We also called at the office of the British Consul-General to leave my passport for a *visa*, before quitting the territory of the Sultan, and next repaired to the Bible warehouse, where we met a Mr. Mackintosh who is labouring as an evangelist in the villages of Mount Lebanon, and had ridden into Beyrout the same morning. My companion and he, being mutually anxious for an interview, were the more glad of this well-ordered occurrence, and we returned to the hotel together.

After dinner, at which we met many of the principal merchants and other European residents, we hired horses and accompanied Mr. Mackintosh to the village of Sook el Gharb, where his quarters were fixed for the time.

On our way we first called on Dr. Bistani, whose Arabic and other works are known to the learned in Europe. He received us very kindly, and would fain have detained us longer than one at least of our number thought our time would allow.

A short distance further along the road, we fell in with one of the native assistants belonging to the British Syrian schools, founded by the late Mrs. Lowen Thompson, and now superintended by her sister, Mrs. Mott. On hearing my name, he enquired its orthography and stated that three letters so addressed had been forwarded from the post-office to the school, on the assumption that, whoever I was, I should be calling there. Not having seen or heard of me, they had, an hour or two before, sent the letters back. Thus was my morning's disappointment accounted for.

It being the vacation, and the principals away in Europe, we could not visit the schools, which otherwise I should have much desired to do.

Having cleared the gardens of Beyrout, we crossed a sandy flat which, in the time of Ibrahim Pasha, and after various attempts with other trees, had been planted with fir. The trees have flourished well, and impart comfort and adornment to what was a desert waste before.

Near the outer limits of this place, we met a young man with a horse, well loaded with bed and other personal luggage, and himself on the top, who proved to be the new teacher whom Mr. El Karey had engaged for a school then about to be

SCHOOL HOUSE—SOOK EL GHARB.

283

opened in Gaza ; in which place, on the occasion
of one of his missionary tours, a great interest
had been evinced in the gospel message on the
part of many of the inhabitants. The opportunity
was taken to give the young man some fresh instructions and to appoint the time and place for
meeting him next day, and we continued our way
to the Lebanon.

About an hour from Beyrout, we witnessed a
most lovely sunset, and in another hour the hill-
climbing had fairly begun. In some places, the
road was cut into steps, to provide foothold for
the horses and mules. At length we could see
before us the lights of the village, and in due
course we rode into Sook el Gharb, and tied our
horses to the trees, shewn in the annexed illustration of the Boys' Training School. Mr. Mackintosh having made arrangements for their care
and feeding, we withdrew to the house of Dr. P.,
where my bed was provided.

Dr. P. (a clergyman), his wife and family, have
resided here a few years, but at the time of our
visit the Doctor was in England.*

One of the dishes on the supper table contained

* Since the first edition was published, Mrs. P. has gone
to rest, and the Dr. returned to England with his family.

Dipse, which is a thick syrup made from raisins, and into which we dipped our bread in the usual manner of the country. Mr. Buckingham, quoting from the learned Dr. Vincent, says that "this article, under the name *Dipse*, formed one of the exports of the ancients, from Diospolis in Egypt to Arabia and India. It is mentioned as frequently by early writers as by modern travellers."*

Thursday, 29th. I visited the boys' school at the hour of opening. They sang a hymn, and read Isaiah xlix., after which the native teacher led them in prayer. Having still a little time to spare, I asked permission to address a few words to the boys, most of whom had some knowledge of English. By the help of a blackboard, I endeavoured to illustrate the allusion made to the chapter they had been reading in 2 Corinthians vi. 2: "Behold *now* is the accepted time; behold *now* is the day of salvation."

After the address, the way in which some of them gathered round the board, and began to rehearse what had been said, and in other ways to express their interest, made me feel that here the

* "Travels among the Arab Tribes inhabiting the countries east of Syria and Palestine," page 52.

word of God is indeed taking root in the hearts of the youth of the hill country of Syria.

" The Lebanon schools are entirely of native origin. No foreign society or church can claim the merit of having planted them. A foreign Mahometan was the first who brought the knowledge of the alphabet to the small village of B'Howarah. From this incident—often already detailed—may be traced the whole history of these schools.

"A native youth was taught by that Mahometan, whilst hiding from the pursuer in this sequestered district. The youth, in turn, first taught his younger brother to read, and they went to a distant school of the American mission at Abeih, and, after years of approved study, was recognized as qualified to be the teacher of a school. In the meantime an aged English gentleman, Mr. Lowthian, had arrived at B'Howarah. He was commissioned by no society, nor was any missionary or educational enterprise his object. His intention was simply to sojourn for a time, perhaps to the end of his days, in Syria ; and he was providentially directed to this Lebanon village. This incident formed an important step in the process of events in which the Lebanon schools originated,

for it introduced the younger brother to the knowledge of the English language, and brought him
into acquaintance with England and Scotland, and
with christian friends in both countries. When
accompanying Mr. Lowthian on a visit to Europe
in 1852, the sight of the English sabbath, and contact with English Christianity, produced a deep
impression on his mind. Having himself been
raised out of the darkness of superstition in which
the Greek church keeps its people throughout
Syria, and felt somewhat of the power of Bible
truth, he became desirous of imparting to the
children of his native Lebanon the same things
which he had received; and when, with this desire
formed within his own heart, he applied to Christians
in England to help him in accomplishing it, then
for the first time did British Christianity and be-
nevolence interfere. And when he made an appeal
on behalf of his country—told of the moral and
intellectual degradation of its people, and of his
desire to obtain teachers for villages where any
teacher, however imperfectly qualified, had never
before been seen—what could, what should, the
christian people in England and Scotland have
answered? Ought they to have advised him to
care nothing for the spiritual welfare of his country-

men, but to look after his own interests in some
secular employment, in which the little education
which he had obtained would soon give him advantages over most of his countrymen? Ought
they to have told him that it was much better for
his countrymen to have no education at all, than to
receive it from one so imperfectly qualified as he
then was? At all events they did not do so; and
British Christians are responsible for this, that,
hearing his account of the moral destitution of his
native country, perceiving the force of his character, and confiding, as all who have *personally*
known him subsequently, have continued to con-
fide, in his integrity and simplicity of purpose,
they, in this first instance, gave him £80, with
which to carry on the object upon which his heart
was set. On returning to Lebanon with this gift,
he offered the sum to the American missionaries at
Beyrout, for the promotion of education in the
district. They declined to accept it, and encouraged him and his brother, who had now been
recognised by the American mission as a qualified
teacher, to do what good they could with the money
themselves. They accordingly expended it in the
erection of a small school at B'Howarah, which cost
£20, and themselves undertook the charge of the

school. The two brothers overcame by degrees
the prejudices of an ignorant and superstitious
people against allowing their children to be edu-
cated. They formed openings for schools in some
of the neighbouring villages. The slender fund
acquired in England (in Carlisle and neighbourhood), though carefully economised, was soon ex-
hausted, and all the addition made to it in the
district was insufficient to supply the growing
demand. Urged by a stronger sense than ever
of the spiritual wants of his countrymen, and
encouraged by the success which had been already
realized, the younger brother returned to England
in 1855, to make a fresh appeal for renewed and
more adequate assistance. Though he was alone,
almost an entire stranger (for he knew only a few
individuals in and around Carlisle), and able to
speak very little English, yet, with true moral
courage, he set himself to the work which he had
purposed, held meeting after meeting, cast himself,
with his broken English, on the sympathy of his
audience, and as he told his tale, and made his
earnest appeals, awakened confidence in himself
and interest in the mission, and acquired friends
throughout all Scotland, as well as in the north of
England—friends, of whom it is not too much to

say, that the longer they have known him, the greater their confidence and regard toward him have become."*

(Having had the pleasure of two interviews with Mr. Elijah Saleeby in this country, since my return from Palestine, I can most heartily speak of him as the above extract concludes.—'J'.)

But time began to press, and it was necessary that we should complete our business with the British Consul General before noon, the hour at which his office closes.

We mounted and set out on our return to Beyrout, retracing our way over the mountain path, with its steps cut in the hard rock, and obtaining a view, by daylight, of the Lebanon range still more glorious than that which we had in the brief twilight of the previous evening.

What abundant allusions there are in scripture to the majestic grandeur of Lebanon! and how did not these scenes bring them to mind!

Between Sook el Gharb and Beyrout we passed one or two villages, and were supplied by the inhabitants with the travellers' luxury—a draught of cold water. Travellers in Syria become expert

* Report of the Committee on the Lebanon Schools, for 1866.

U

in pouring the water from a cruse through a little spout on to the tongue, and swallowing the water without closing the lips; no easy task to the untrained, and though I several times saw it done, I did not attain to the performance. The object of so drinking is to avoid touching the bottle with one's lips where all-comers place theirs.

This ride combined several elements of a diverse character. There was the lovely scenery which supplies material for disquisition in more than one of the poetical books of the Bible; the fresh recollection of the christian intercourse we had had with several inhabitants of the village we were leaving, and withal the fact that it would be our last ride together during the present visit. But to all this was added the necessity, for cogent reasons, of hastening to the city, the nearer sight of which, and the lessening of the mountain views, produced in the mind a dissolving of the sublimer into less ethereal thoughts.

My horse was, by several degrees, superior to either that I had ridden before, and, being supplied with a European saddle, I found the whole state of things greatly improved. Although I had not forgotten the discomforts of the Arab saddle in which I travelled from Nablûs to Da-

mascus, I was quite sound and able to enjoy to
the full my new mount; and in crossing the
sandy flat both the previous night and this morning, I outstripped my companion and realised all,
or almost all, but the last condition of

> "Oh! then there is freedom, and joy, and pride,
> Afar in the desert alone to ride!
> There is rapture to vault on the champing steed,
> And to bound away with the eagle's speed,
> With the death-fraught firelock in my hand—
> The only law of the desert land!"

Under opposite conditions, then, than those in
which he gave it, I cordially endorse the advice
which De Saulcy offers when he says:

"Luckily we have brought with us our own
saddles; the Turkish saddle would soon have dis-
abled us. I expressly recommend to any traveller going out to Syria to bring with him this
most necessary article in his equipment."

On our return to Beyrout, which we reached in
good time, I found my passport waiting, with the
visa duly added. We, moreover, had an interview
with the Consul-General, to whom Mr. El Karey
communicated the complaint of oppression pre-

ferred by the two poor Jews in Nablûs, and begged such interposition on their behalf as he might deem it expedient to make. We next applied again for my letters, which, after some delay, we obtained, and spent the rest of the day in revisiting the Bible Depôt (the agent of which procured for me seven fine palm branches, which I added to my luggage). We also spent some time with another christian friend who is actively engaged in mission work, and gave the Gaza schoolmaster his final instructions prior to going on board the steamer next morning.

The annexed sketch I took from the hotel window, beneath which many young, and some older, Arabs were gambolling in the sea, diving and chasing each other with a truly amphibious aptitude. They make gain by fetching from the bottom money which is thrown in by travellers and others. The Austrian Lloyd's steamer "Ceres," for Alexandria, was now moored in the harbour, and, with the prospect of going on board in the morning, we retired early.

Friday 30th, 6 a.m. We rose, and prepared to leave. The Gaza schoolmaster met us on the quay, and his luggage being added to ours, he went in our boat to the steamer. As we pulled away from

292   BEYROUT.

shore, and the separation widened between me and
the land of Syria, although not unwilling to return
to England, I did not set my gaze so eagerly seaward as not to

"Cast one longing, lingering, look behind." •

SOOK-EL-GHARB.

CHAPTER XVI.

In a few minutes we were on board and our things in the cabin, and about 7.30 a.m. the steamer got under weigh. She carried many first-class passengers, one of them a young English physician, returning to his work in Egypt, after spending two or three months in the Lebanon for health's sake. There was also a Romish archbishop who, for an aspect of superior intelligence com- bined with the most thorough suavity of manners, came as near to my ideal of a gentleman as any one I remember ever to have met. Both on the after-deck and in the saloon we had, therefore, a tolerably full company.

I ought not to omit particularizing two French gentlemen, residents, I believe, in Egypt (who had reached Demitri's hotel, Damascus, the day of our leaving, and were now our *compagnons de voyage*), as I shall have to quote the senior (a marquis) when we reach Alexandria. Among such various companions, we steamed down the coast. The two school teachers, though holding only second-class tickets, were, by the rules of the steamer already explained (p. 30), allowed to mingle with the first-class passengers on the after-deck. Of this I was glad, as it afforded us much opportunity for conversation about the land we were visiting, the land where we hoped to meet again, and—better still—the Lord of that country.

We passed Sidon, "the mother of Tyre," as she is still called (Isa. xxiii. 12), the ancient city of merchants and mariners (Isa. xxiii. 2; Ezek. xxvii. 8.) We were also promised a view of Sarepta, the scene of the widow's ministry to the prophet Elijah out of her poverty, and of the Lord's blessing on her store, in that the barrel of meal wasted not, neither did the cruse of oil fail, according to the word of the Lord which He spake by Elijah; also of the raising again of her son from the dead. (1 Kings xvii.)

As the time drew near when I had been told the place would come into view, I industriously scanned the coast with my telescope, and was partly convinced that I could make out the little village; but as my companions were asleep, I forbore to obtain from them the confirmation or correction of my impression. However, the elder schoolmaster awaking, I applied to him, and he pointed to the same spot (now some distance astern

of us) which I had conjectured to be the site of
Sarepta. Nor is it surprising that her position was
not more evident, as I find that De Saulcy who
visited the place, describes it thus:

" Soon after, we leave on the height to our left
the modern village of Sarfent; to the right the
promontory of Ras-Sarfent overhangs the sea, and
we arrive at the ruins of Sarepta, the Zarephath
of the holy scriptures, called by the Arabs Kherbet-
e-Sarfent. Here resided the poor widow who
sheltered the prophet Elijah. At present nothing
remains of Sarepta but some shapeless rubbish
covering a good deal of ground." *

Next in order we sighted Tyre, whose king
furnished cedar, stones, and workmen, to David
and Solomon, as a contribution towards the erection of the palace and temple in Jerusalem.
(2 Sam. v. 11; 1 Kings v. 6.) The magnificence
and riches of Tyre are also referred to in Psalm
xlv. 12, and other scriptures, and her overthrow
foretold in Ezekiel xxvi. 1, et seq. "The word of the
Lord came unto me, saying, Son of man, because
that Tyrus hath said against Jerusalem, ' Aha, she
is broken that was the gates of the people; she is

° "Narrative of a Journey round the Dead Sea and in
the Bible Lands in 1850-51," page 34.

TYRE.

'n me; I shall be replenished, now she is ιαια waste:' Therefore, thus saith the Lord God, Behold, I am against thee, O Tyrus, and will cause many nations to come up against thee, as the sea causeth his waves to come up. And they shall destroy the walls of Tyrus, and break down her towers: I will also scrape her dust from her, and make her like the top of a rock. It shall be a place for the spreading of nets in the midst of the sea; for I have spoken it, saith the Lord God, and it shall become a spoil to the nations."

As we passed by the once great metropolis, I clearly discerned, by the aid of my telescope, her broken sea wall, and there were some dark patches on the rock, which I took to be fishers' nets. Travellers who visit the spot find these marks of the present minute fulfilment of the word of the Lord by the prophet; that word which shall in nowise fail till all be fulfilled. (Matt. v. 18.)

> "Dim is her glory, gone her fame,
>   Her boasted wealth has fled;
> On her proud rock (alas, her shame!)
>   The fishers' net is spread.
>
> The Tyrian harp has slumbered long,
>   And Tyria's mirth is low;
> The timbrel, dulcimer, and song,
>   Are hushed, or wake in woe."

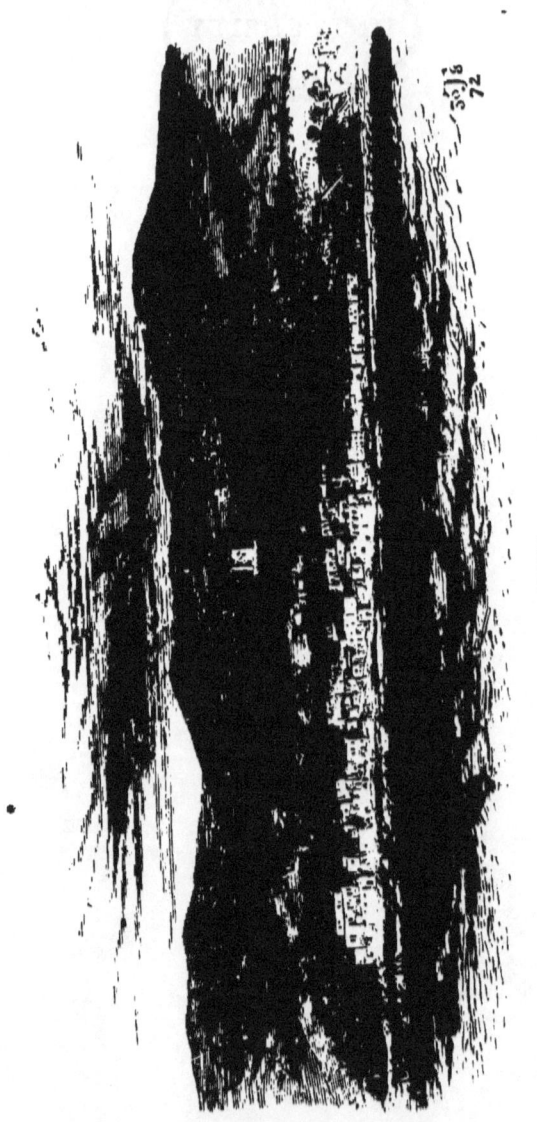

KAIFA.

In the afternoon we dropped anchor at Kaifa, and though there was ample opportunity for landing and climbing to the top of Carmel as we

CARMEL.

had proposed, my companion dissuaded me from doing so, explaining that he had found the Arab boatmen were plotting to make enormous profit out of us, if they could once get us on shore. I therefore acted on his advice not to place myself in their hands, and endeavoured to content myself with the excellent view obtained from the steamer's deck, where we could read and meditate on the

scenes described in 1 Kings xviii., when the prophets of Baal were tried by the challenge of
Elijah, the prophet of the Lord, who at the time
of the evening sacrifice, repaired the altar of the
Lord which was broken down, prepared the sacrifice,
and had water poured thereon, and the Lord
answered him by fire. " Then the fire of the Lord
fell and consumed the burnt sacrifice and the
wood, and the stones and the dust, and licked up
the water that was in the trench."

We again got under weigh at 5 p.m., and
on Saturday 31st, when we turned out, the
steamer was lying off Jaffa. About 6.30 a.m.
I landed with my companion, the two school-
masters, and the little boy. From the landing-
place we proceeded to the house of Mr. Rolla
Floyd.

After recounting the events which had happened
to us since we last received his hospitality, we
opened the word of God, reading together 1 John v.,
and in the same chamber where, twenty days before, we sought His protection, we together ac-
knowledged the goodness and mercy of the Lord
which had followed us, and besought Him for that
grace, by which we should all meet to dwell for
ever in the house of the Lord. (Psalm xxiii. 6.)

soJB
72

300   CARMEL FROM THE NORTH.

We now returned to the town, and entered the telegraph office to send messages again to Nablûs and Brading, Isle of Wight; after which we repaired to the quay. My companion having made terms for me with a boatman, we parted where at the first we had met, he thinking to accomplish a missionary visit to Gaza, and assist the new teacher in beginning his work; I to continue my homeward journey.

An account of the visit to Gaza having appeared in a published letter of my companion to Dr. Landels, the following extract will, I think, be read with interest :

" We parted from our brother Mr. Jenner in prayer. He left for England the same day that we arrived at Jaffa, 1st September.* In the night the teacher and I hired horses and left for Gaza ; the muleteer said he knew the road, but the night was dark, so we lost our way. In the morning instead of reaching Gaza, we were ten hours still further from it ; no sooner the sun rose than myriads of flies appeared, because of the heat which we had tried to avoid by travelling during the night : the horses were in such a state, unable

---

° This should be 31st August.—J.

to go on, and now and then falling on the sand,
until we reached Ashdod : near the town we
found a tent towards which I advanced; on being
asked who I was, I answered, ' I am a teacher for
Jesus Christ; ' I was kindly welcomed, and they
brought us something to eat—then the people assembled to whom I read and expounded God's word.
We afterwards mounted and went to Mijdel,
where we entered a house, and spoke and made
Christ known to its inmates. After an hour and
a half's rest, we proceeded to Gaza, on the way
meeting with a Sheikh, to whom I spoke of Jesus
and His love to poor sinners : he seemed amazed
at what he heard of the christian religion, he
seemed also much impressed by the character of
Jesus Christ. About an hour and a half's ride
from Gaza, I heard the scream of a woman with
whom was a man and a donkey ; I galloped my
horse, and reaching the woman, inquired from the
man why he beat her, I was actually going to
bind the man's hands and take him with me to
Gaza, when the woman told me the man was her
son, and that he was striking their only donkey,
by which they earned their living, and her cry
was to stop her son striking the donkey ; of
course I found I had made a shameful mistake

and stole away quickly. We reached Gaza about
an hour before sunset; finding the schoolroom
filled with soldiers, we put up with my kind
friend Mr. Nimmo. In a few days the school
was emptied, and two or three days after, was
opened; I employed my time in visiting houses
and shops. The day after my arrival I went to
a shop, reading and expounding, while doing this
a man called me to his shop, and I spoke to him
of the death of Jesus. I then visited a third shop
and did the same; thence I visited a house: the
people were much pleased to see us, with the ex-
ception of the priests.

" Mid-day in Gaza was exceedingly hot: the
heat here is greater than in any part of Palestine,
so I was indoors until 4 p.m., then Mr. Nimmo
and I went to the seashore to visit Mr. Pickard,
where he and his family are spending the summer;
we spent about five hours there talking about the
school, and the grace and glory of the Lord. Next
day I spent in visiting those whom I had conversed
with some months ago—I was glad to see the impression made on them by God's word, and that
they tried to live consistently. As I was returning
a young man told me that a young man who used
to hear me speak of Christ was ill; I told him I

would like to see him—he took me with him and I found his *Hackim* (doctor) there. I then began to lead his mind to God's word, to seek his salvation through Christ and His blood. The young man's feelings were much impressed.

"The next day I visited several shops and houses, reading and expounding God's word. In the afternoon I visited the sick young man; I found the place full; he and his family begged of me to pray for him. I read and expounded John xi., then prayed, the young man thanked me very much; then I spoke to him of death, of eternity, and preparation for it, and of the joy that awaits those who put their trust in Christ. His illness is consumption. One of those present asked me why we do not believe in the Virgin Mary, I told him that we do believe that she was the mother of our Lord, but that she can do us no good as she was as dependent for salvation in Him as we are. In the evening Mr. Nimmo and I went to visit Mr. Pickard and dined with him; and I left the oversight of the school to them both. The priest was much offended at our opening the school, so Monday morning I visited him, and explained to him the object of the school.

"About 3 p.m. I left Gaza in the company of a

soldier to Ramleh. Sunset found us at a village called Beit Jurjia, the people asked who I was; when they were told they kindly welcomed us and surrounded us. I began to speak of Jesus and His work, but I was often interrupted by a foolish man, whom the people considered to be the Sheikh, and were afraid to stop his foolish talk, which was always—'Won't you plough? won't you sow?' Then at last I looked at him in such a way, and threatened him that if he will not sit quiet, I will no doubt mesmerise him. When he heard these words he was at once hushed, and he uttered not a word again, so I spent two hours speaking to them about Jesus and His love. I travelled by moonlight, and at midnight arrived at a village called Jules. The people were watching by the crops, sitting around a great fire. I then told them who I was, and in whose service I am, for they thought that I was in the service of the Government; and I showed them the order of my Master, and began to read that holy book to them. One of them I knew fifteen years ago; we stayed two hours conversing. The fire was shining like a lamp. Several other watchers of the crops came, and to all I spoke the holy story. We then mounted our horses, and by sunrise

x

reached Ramleh, where I spent that day sleeping.
In the afternoon I visited the streets; and next
morning started for Nablûs, passing a very strong
river called Elenir. Then the flies rose in abundance, which prevented my horse hastening.
Having passed the Plain of Sharon, ascended the
mountain, and reached Nablûs at sunset, finding
our child very ill: my wife told me she had been
so ill that she thought many times that I would
not have seen her alive. She is now better. I
have been absent nearly six weeks, finding on
my return the school, congregation, in fact, all
well. A lady in England had been good enough
to send £2 worth of calicoes, so we have begun
to cut frocks for the poor school children. May
God incline the hearts of others of His people to
help us in this good work! There is a village
about three hours' ride from Nablûs, the inhabitants of which begged me to have a school. It
will cost about £30 a-year. May God incline the
hearts of His people to contribute towards opening this school in the above place! My work
here is, as usual, preaching on the sabbath and
in the week, and visiting houses and shops. We
earnestly request that we and our work may be
remembered before the throne of grace by all

JAFFA.

our friends, as we commend them all in our prayers." *

I had now (at least so far as this journey was concerned) finally quitted Palestine, the last memento of which I held in my hand, in the form of a child's water-bottle, bought of a dealer in pottery by the road-side, in Jaffa.

By 10.15 a.m. I was again on board the "Ceres." My berth was now shared by the young English doctor, who had made arrangements with the steward to be transferred thither from a less airy position in which he had been placed at the first. He had with him a Syrian servant, whom he had brought from Mount Lebanon. We being thus thrown more closely together, a friendship, already commenced, naturally improved a little.

By this time our steamer carried a large complement of deck passengers, as well as those of the first and second-class, and there was much to occupy attention in the types and nationalities which her decks presented to view. Among the second-class was a fat Mahometan, attended by his servant, who was in continual requisition to bring water, remove the chair, or in some way

* From a "Report of the Palestine Mission to the Arabs," 1872—1873, pages 4—6.

minister to his master's comfort, who sat fanning himself with a goose-feather punkah—now and then stepping into the saloon, to regard, if not admire, himself in the glass.

In addition to the human freight, we carried about a hundred and eighty horses and mules, and five hundred sheep and goats; as a consequence the odour from the hold was far from agreeable when the hatches were opened, on our touching at any of the ports. Moreover, some deaths from suffocation and accident, occurred among the sheep during the short voyage. In the afternoon we left Jaffa, and on

Lord's day, 1st September, at 9.30 a.m., dropped anchor at Port Saïd.

When the steamer had swung to her moorings, I took up my berth in a deck-chair, directly facing the union-jack, which was waving among the flags of many nations having official representation at the port. So, with my pocket Bible in hand, I could, by a glance of the eye, look at the emblem of the country to which, by birth, I belong, and again to the witness of the heavenly citizenship, which is ours who believe in the Son of God. (Phil. iii. 20, 21.)

My companion (by whom I, of course, now

mean the young doctor) landed, to visit a friend in
the port, and in a short time returned, saying that
he had not found him, but that one, holding
office under the Khedive, as well as the rank of
commander in H.B.M.'s navy, would be joining us
for the rest of the voyage. Later in the day he
did so, accompanied by some friends, including
him whom my companion at the first went to
seek. Our gallant friend (as I propose to desig-
nate the commander, R.N.) alone remained on
board after non-passengers had been requested to
leave the steamer.

We had the usual Port Saïd entertainment of
watching the big porpoises rolling about (sometimes very near the steamer) and the vessels entering and leaving the canal, with tugs and
lighters conveying cargo and coal between ship
and shore. One of the native passengers sere-
naded his fair companions on a dulcimer, which
he accompanied with his voice in the plaintive
Syrian style.

The band from the Turkish *Guardo* also landed,
in the ship's launch, playing as they were rowed,
and afterwards marching through the streets to a
piazza, where they planted themselves, and we
could overhear the music from our moorings.

At 2.20 p.m. a large homeward-bound English steamer came out of the canal. As she approached, comments were freely made upon her unfurnished appearance, and when she had passed us and anchored, and we could read the name on her stern, we ascertained the cause of her sad condition. Having encountered the S.W. monsoon in the Indian Ocean, in order to work her engines to Aden, where she obtained fresh stocks of coal, she had burned her spare-booms, top-yards, deckhouses, awningboom, boats, two thousand bags of rice, and fifty boxes of tea. As soon as she had anchored, she commenced taking in a further supply of coal.

Among the additions to our fellow-passengers were a French gentleman, his little son, and a young negro servant, whose devoted attention to his young master called forth general admiration. But the doings of the little French boy and his young negro Friday were subjects rather for the pencil than the pen, as also was the incident of one of the Arab children being allowed on the after-deck for some diversion with one of the little Frank's toys.

This afternoon the Italian *"postale"* steamship "Arabia" entered the canal, and in the evening

we left the port, and for some hours could discern
the revolving light of the Port Saïd lighthouse.
Two or three of the passengers preferred to sleep
on deck, among whom were the French marquis
and his companion. My new friend and I passed
the night in our cabin, and on

Monday 2nd, we turned out about 6 a.m. I
had mentioned to several my anxiety to catch the
weekly homeward-bound P. and O. steamer, fear-
ing that if I failed in doing so, I might not reach
London within the six weeks' limits I had pre-
scribed for myself. About 11 a.m., as we were
nearing Alexandria, having fallen asleep in a
deck-chair, I was awakened by the voice of the
French marquis calling to me, " Can you swim
well ?" · Waking up, 'I answered, " No." To
which he rejoined, " Because, if you can swim
well, zere goes your boat !" (pointing to the P.
and O. steamer, about ten miles out at sea).

Thus disappointed of the means on which I had
fully depended, I was the more prepared to hail
the departure next day of the French Messageries
boat "Saïd," for Marseilles. About 12.30 p.m.
we dropped anchor in Alexandria harbour, and my
companion, his servant, and I landed together. It
had been agreed that we should keep together, and

this we endeavoured to do, but the passport carried
by the servant appearing to be irregular in form,
we had to witness the young fellow being treated
as a prisoner and led away in custody, the expos-
tulations of his master notwithstanding. I confess
I felt resentment at such treatment, but it would
have been clearly wrong and only complicating
matters for me to interfere; so, at my companion's
request, I left them, and was met at the Custom-
house gate by Adam, whose guidance I once more
willingly accepted.

We drove, as before, to the British hotel, Adam
assuring me of the fidelity with which he had
watched for my return, commenting on the reduced number of my packages, which I had the
satisfaction of informing him was not due to any
pillage by the Bedouins, but to my having shipped
all that I could dispense with in Beyrout. I took
this opportunity of telling him that I had no intention of making my present stay in Alexandria
so expensive as the preceding. "No," said he,
fully equal to the occasion, "then, you just come,
not cost you so much this time; I go with you
everywhere to-day and to-morrow; see you on the
steamer; you pay me one pound." To these terms
I could not demur, and the agreement was made.

We visited the bazaars, making a few purchases, especially in the silk bazaar, at the shop of a Syrian Christian, whose manner of dealing, and quality of goods, seemed to be both good, and in conducting me thither, as well as in cheapening what I purchased elsewhere, I felt that Adam more than saved me his own fees, especially if we throw the time into the account. I called again on my Alexandrian friends, as well as at the American mission school, and retired early.

Tuesday 3rd, 6.15 a.m. Adam accompanied me to the bath, after which we made two or three more purchases, including some calico for packing my bundle of palm-branches more securely.

Before issuing a ticket for Marseilles, the Messageries Company required me to procure the addition of a French *visa* to my passport, which cost me ten francs. To this (having been previously made to understand that nothing more would be required) I demurred, in common with other English travellers, and we exercised our national privilege of paying and grumbling, with a talk of writing to the *Times*.

Having returned to the hotel, and put my things together, Adam and I were soon once more driving through the bazaars to the quay, where we were taken on board the "Saïd." Here he and the boatmen having received a trifle over the stipulated amount, wished me "*bon voyage*," and about 2 p.m. we got under weigh.

CHAPTER XVII.

RETURN HOME.

STEAMING out of the harbour, we followed in the wake of an Austrian Lloyd's boat, the rolling of which and the stern wave resulting from the alternate immersions and liftings of her screw were truly noteworthy.

We had not cleared the harbour when I was accosted by the Italian corn-merchant who had been my fellow-passenger on each of the other steamers, and who now pointed to the white-crested billows ahead of us, saying, "We shall have rough weather, I think." "*Tant mieux,*" I said, feeling at the time inspirited from having fairly entered upon the Mediterranean section of my homeward journey, with still the prospect of keeping my engagement.

Outside the harbour, we began to experience the swelling of the billows. It was calculated to bring to my mind the words of Psalm cvii. 23-31: "They that go down to the sea in ships, that do business in great waters; these see the works of the Lord, and his wonders in the deep. For he commandeth, and raiseth the stormy wind, which lifteth up the waves thereof. They mount up to the heaven, they go down again to the depths: their soul is melted because of trouble. They reel to and fro, and stagger like a drunken man, and are at their wit's end. Then they cry unto the Lord in their trouble, and he bringeth them out of their distresses. He maketh the storm a calm, so that the waves thereof are still. Then are they glad because they be quiet; so he bringeth them unto their desired haven. Oh that men would praise the Lord for his goodness, and for his wonderful works to the children of men!" With such majestic swellings did the waves rise, and dash, and re-form, in a way that no words can describe, or canvas portray.

I was experimenting upon walking the deck, but found that it was unsafe to take any but the most deliberate steps; otherwise, the lurches of the ship were likely, not merely to cause my feet to come down on some unsuspected part, but to give rise to the cry, "A man overboard!"

Dinner having passed off well, with a good general muster, I repaired to the deck for a while, and turned into my berth at an early hour. Here I made all snug, and obtained three or four good sleeps during the night, while the sea gradually settled down, but not into an improved state in one important respect; for, turning out on

Wednesday, 4th, and attempting to dress, I found that the fidgety motion, which had ensued on the previous night's tossing, was far more trying to the system.

To make an unpleasant story short, I lay all day on my beam-ends on the sofa. As to the sickness, it transpired that several passengers *ex Tigre* (a Messageries steamer which had broken down in the Suez Canal), who had crossed the China seas and Indian Ocean free from any attack, were made ill by the uncomfortable motion of the steamer this day. My steward was most attentive and as sympathetic as any nurse, announcing as he brought it, "*De l'eau fraîche,*" in a way that seemed to compel one to feel better.

Thursday, 5th, I showed on deck about 7 a.m., and found that we were in sight of Crete. At 8 a.m. we passed one of the Messageries steamers, outward bound to China. On board the "Saïd" there were several homeward bound passengers from China and India, who had been transferred from the "Tigre," which, as already mentioned, had broken down in the canal. This company was composed of a Dutch gentleman from Batavia, his wife and family, an English lady from Shanghai, her children and servants, two nuns, and several young Englishmen and Germans from various places.

At table I sat near to my gallant friend, an English merchant, and a French gentleman, wear ing the red ribbon of the *Légion d'honneur*. Though convalescent, I was not yet quite brave, and consequently thankful for the advice of those of longer experience in the choice of suitable dishes.

To-day the sea was rough again, there being a " white squall " at the entrance of the Adriatic. During the morning, as the English lady, her family and one of the nuns were seated on shawls and rugs spread on deck, some of their gentlemen fellow-passengers from China being seated on chairs near them, my chair being also next the group, a sideway lurch of the steamer sent us all sliding towards the port bulwarks, in a fashion which led me to fear some injury must be done ; happily, however, none was received, and we acted on the warning to seek safer moorings, the result of which was that in a short time very few of us were left on deck.

Friday 6th, a smooth sea, and fore and aft sails put up, which are not only auxiliary to speed, but give us an agreeable steadiness. Now the *malades* are convalescent, and conversation becomes more general.

One of the second-class passengers, who spent most of the day on the after-deck, was a Capuchin friar returning from India. I found him very genial and willing for me to inspect his missal; he also endeavoured to read a verse or two from my pocket Bible, but, like most strangers, found English a very difficult language.

Much entertainment was yielded by the children: English, French, Dutch, and African, making stalking-horses of the deck-chairs, and racing each other by sitting in the middle and working them scissor-fashion; so making them progress. The variety of style in which this was done struck me as exhibiting the national types of the actors. There was the giggling little African, the impetuous little Frenchman, the sturdy little Dutchman, and the manly English boy.

About sunset Etna was visible, ninety-three miles distant; the evening was truly serene, and we walked the deck with those whose companionship we had chosen, talking of the lands we came from *et præterea multa.* As the darkness increased, the phenomenon of phosphorescence of the sea became beautifully discernible over the ship's side or stern. There is plenty to entice one to linger on deck, but

> "Now is the season of rest,
> And I to my cabin repair."

Saturday 7th, 6 a.m., I turned out, and found the steamer anchored in the Straits of Messina, and the Sicilian mariners paddling alongside. One of them made fast the "painter" of his boat to the handle of my open cabin-light. Having dressed, I went on deck and gave my steward his gratuity in advance, asking him to keep my berth free from any addition to its inmates during the small remainder of the voyage; for, so far as my cabin was concerned, having been monarch of all I surveyed since leaving Alexandria, I was not prompted to exclaim

> " O solitude, where are the charms
> Which ages have seen in thy face?"

From deck, an enchanting view was obtained of the Sicilian and Italian shores, the city of Messina with its rich background of mountains terraced to

the top with vines, and the clouds floating at about
two-thirds the height. On deck, the sellers of
fruit, carvings in coral and lunettes were displaying
their wares. I contented myself with buying a
few coral beads for my two little daughters.

The Capuchin monk was now to be seen standing in the gangway, wearing the broad-brimmed
hat of his order, instead of a skull-cap in which
he had appeared before, receiving the recognitions
of many of the traders, some of whom took his
hand and kissed it.

At length the stewards were ordered to clear
the decks of strangers, and we shortly got again
under weigh. Every moment some fresh beauties
of scenery were presented as we threaded the
Straits. Just as we were clearing the passage, I
asked the second officer " Where are Scylla and
Charybdis ?" but he only answered, " *Ils n'existent
que dans l'imagination des poètes,*" but from the
writings of others I conceive this statement to be
scarcely the exact truth.

An hour or more after leaving Messina, looking
forward, my gallant friend drew my attention to
some commotion on board, and immediately after
he discovered that the unusual interest had been
awakened by the appearance of a shark.

Looking over the bulwarks, I saw another still nearer, making for the steamer. As we approached, he appeared to dive. "Cannot you see him?" said my friend. "No!" I replied. "Look out," said he, and so I did, as actively as I could, but was obliged to repeat "I cannot see him." "Jump overboard, and he'll come," said my gallant friend. In a minute or two we saw them both rise again to the surface, about a quarter of a mile astern of us, while the initiated pronouced them to be large specimens.

A little later on we obtained a good view of Etna, with its cloud of smoke gently rising. Next Stromboli loomed in view, on our starboard, and the Liparis on the larboard bows. I was struck with the appearance of a light cloud hanging over each of these picturesque rocky islands, while all the rest of the sky was clear.

In the afternoon, I noticed a shoal of flying fish shining with a glitter as they leaped and took their darting flights above the wave.

The steamer's run was now a matter of increasing interest to the passengers; and, having a copy of the previous month's special edition of Bradshaw, I was frequently applied to by one or another, who was desirous of consulting the map

322   ETNA.

or the time-table. We were making a pretty regular ten knots, and it transpired that as our engines had been recently refitted, it would be unsafe to increase the number of their revolutions, there being already as much heat in the plummer-blocks as would be safe.

Sunday 8th. This morning I read the Epistle to the Ephesians. We had still the most lovely weather and calm sea. We fell in with two or three shoals of porpoises of a much smaller species than those we had noticed at Port Saïd. Some of them attempted to accompany the steamer. One especially I noticed just under her quarter, making the strongest efforts with its fins, swimming and leaping several times alternately, and at last getting so far astern as to be convinced the race was hopeless.

We had now sighted the coast of Sardinia and, in due time, entered the Straits of Bonifaccio. In the afternoon, passing Caprera, we saw Garibaldi's house which, when it was pointed out to the Capuchin friar, appeared to start in his mind some good humoured pity for the General's views of religion. In the Straits we passed the Messageries steamer " Taje," bound for Stamboul, and with her we exchanged farewells by dipping our flags.

Monday 9th. When doing my forty paces before breakfast this morning, I saw a " black fish," the Mediterranean species of whale, diving, spouting, and rolling, a sight well worth witnessing. With this we had another sight which was still more generally appreciated—the coast of France.

As the morning wore on, one after another of the passengers appeared in fresh attire, the garments used on the voyage disappearing into portmanteaus, and those in which it was intended to land taking their place.

I was happy at being included in a little company of four with my gallant friend, the English merchant, and the French member of the legion of honour. Having put into Marseilles, ours was the first passenger-party to land. We proceeded under the guidance of our native friend, who made all arrangements in an excellent way. Having obtained our passports, booked the luggage at the railway, and ordered dinner at the hotel *(des Colonies)*, we each went our separate ways for two or three hours. In due course we entered the night-train, and on Tuesday, 10th, about 6 a.m., reached Lyons, and availed ourselves of its admirable lavatories and provisions for breakfast.

From Lyons we passed through the lovely valley
of the Rhone and the Burgundy district, with its
well kept vineyards in full fruit, and standing
crops of Indian corn and flax. Our next half-
hour's stay was at Dijon, where we were supplied
with an excellent "table d'hôte" for four and
a half francs. At Tonnerre a few drops of rain
fell, the first I had seen since passing through
Italy (August 2nd).

We now traversed a more strictly arable country which lasted until we reached Paris at 6 p.m.
and parted from our French companion.

Although we had counted upon having time in
Paris for ablutions and dinner, I had, happily
for my comfort, purchased the use of a washhand
basin at one of the stations where we stayed ten
minutes. The merchant, being the best French
scholar, now kindly took the initiative in all our
arrangements.

As soon as our things were cleared from the
custom house, we stowed them and ourselves in an
omnibus, requesting to be driven to the *Chemin de
fer du Nord*. But various hindrances arose which
tried our composure a little, considering the shortness of our time, and when we reached the station
of departure, so many fresh delays occurred that

we utterly failed of obtaining the refreshments we had counted on. In Amiens, however, we made our supper about 10 p.m., and in due course reached Calais. The steamer being a small one, liable to the influence of every wave, and the night rather rough, most of the inconveniences of the Channel passage, which have lately been so much dwelt upon, were experienced.

Landed in Dover, we left almost immediately

for London by the South Eastern Railway. As day broke, the change to English scenery after the many varieties I had so recently looked upon, seemed, I think, more strange than even that to Egyptian or any other had been ; and as the fields, woods, houses and cottages passed rapidly in review, there was noticeable such an aspect of good-keeping, solidity and practical utility, as to bring to my mind the following dialogue which took place in my cabin in the P. & O. steamer "Massilia," the night I went on board at Brindisi.

When the steward had lit my lamp and blown out the match, hearing a companion passing the cabin door, he addressed him :

S. "Jack, d'ye want a match that's just gone out ? "

J. " What d'ye say ?"

S. " D'ye want a match that's just gone out ?"

J. " A match ! I haven't seen one lately." And I felt that, as countries and customs go, I could say the same for old England.

About 6.30 a.m. we ran into Cannon Street Station, one day within the stipulated six weeks from my leaving there ; having travelled

by Rail,	about	2,300 miles,
„ Boat,	„	3,280 „
„ Diligence,	„	40 „
in the Saddle,	„	200 „

Total, 5,820

I took leave of my gallant friend and the merchant, and was soon on my way to announce my own return. Having called at home, breakfasted, and changed my attire; after a brief interview with friends in town I started for the Isle of Wight, to join my family, whom I had previously apprised by telegram of the hour at which I hoped to see them.

Between 2 and 3 p.m., as the train approached Brading station, I perceived them all on the platform; looking the better for their holiday, as I for mine.

Reader! all journeys have an end, and we have reached the end of ours to that Goodly Mountain and Lebanon. If I have succeeded in enabling you to hear the mosquito hum, to feel the heat and thirst of Syrian travel, to witness the sun setting behind Jerusalem, to dismount with me at the banks of Jordan and share a dinner of herbs, to rest in the Bedouins' tent, to listen to the music of the mule-bells, or din and clatter of the bazaars of Damascus; now that we have returned, before unpacking the saddle-bags, let me take your hand.

We are still fellow-travellers: eternity lies

before us and we shall soon be landed on it shores. Shall we spend it together? I trust so. Provision is made, the redemption price of our souls was paid on Calvary and Jesus, who died and rose again, is now at the right hand of God exalted a Prince and a Saviour, the Author of eternal salvation unto all them that obey Him (Heb. v. 9), and His commands are not grievous: "Come unto me all ye that labour, and are heavy laden, and I will give you rest." If of the blessed number of them that obey, then, although we may have together trodden the streets of the earthly only in thought, in reality we shall meet in the heavenly Jerusalem, and see the King in His beauty: Then

> " To wave the palm, and wear the crown,
> And at His feet to cast them down."

APPENDIX No. 1.

ARABIC PHRASES.

THE ARABIC ALPHABET.

NAME.	FINAL CONNECTED.	FINAL UNCON.	MEDIAL	INITIAL
Alif				
Ba				
Ta				
Sa				
Jeem				
Ha				
Kha				
Dal				
Zal				
Ra				
Za				
Seen				
Sheen				
Sad				

NAME.	FINAL CONNECTED.	FINAL UNCON.	MEDIAL	INITIAL
Dad				
Ta				
Za				
Aine				
Ghine				
Fa				
Kaf				
Kaf				
Lam				
Meem				
Noon				
Waw				
Ha				
Ya				

Arabic is written from right to left.

TRAVELLING. السفر ALSEFR.

ENGLISH.	ARABIC.	PRONUNCIATION.
Put these six things into the boat.	حط هذه الستة اشياء في القلوكة	Hat hazi assitat ashir fil filooka.
We will go ashore.	نروح الى البر	Narooa ila al bur.
The sea is very rough.	البحر كبير كثير	Al bahr kabir katir.
Give me bakhsheesh.	اعطيني بكشيش	Ateeni bakhsheesh.
Take this for a cup of coffee.	خذ هذا حق فنجان قهوة	Hoz haza hak finjan kahawa.
Here are the horses and the mule.	هنا الخيل والبغال	Hona al khail wal boghal.
Load the mule.	حمل البغال	Hamil al boghal.
I do not like this horse.	انا ما اريد هذا الحصان	Ana ma wreed haza al husan.
The road is bad.	الطريق ما هو طيب	Al tarik ma hoo tayib.
How many hours to the khan?	كم ساعة للخان	Kam saár lilkham?
Two hours.	ساعتين	Saártan.
Where is this caravan going?	الى اين هذا القفل رايح	Ila ain haza al kofl rayeh?
To Damascus.	الى الشام	Ila esh Sham.

SALUTATIONS. السلام ASSALAAM.

ENGLISH.	ARABIC.	PRONUNCIATION.
Good morning.	نهارك سعيد	Nehair-ak saäid
(Ans.) Good morning to you.	نهارك سعيد ومبارك	Nehair-ak saäid wa moobairak.
How are you?	كيف حالك؟	Kaf halak?
Praise be to God! I am very well.	الحمد لله طيب بنظرك	Alhamdoo lillahee! Tayib benazaruk.
How is your father?	كيف حال ابيك؟	Kaf halabeek?
„ „ mother?	امك؟ „ „	„ „ umbak?
„ „ wife?	ابنة عمك „ „	„ „ ebnat amak?
„ „ family?	اهل البيت „ „	„ „ ahlalbeit?
How are the camels, the ewes, and the cows?	الجمل والعنزات، والبقرات „ „	„ „ al jimel, wal anazat, wal bakarat?
They are all well.	الكل طيبين بخير	Alkool tayibeen behair.
Good bye!	خاطرك	Khatrak.
(Ans.) Go in peace.	مع السلامة	Ma-l-salameh.

336

THE TABLE. المائدة ALMEIDA.

ENGLISH.	ARABIC.	PRONUNCIATION.
Pray sit down.	تفضل اجلس	Tufuldal ijlus.
What will you take?	ماذا تريد تاكل	Maza tarid takol?
Rice, meat, and curdled milk.	رز ولحم ولبن	Riz wa-lahm wa-lebn.
Take some lamb.	اضرب من لحم الخاروف	Udrub min lahm alkaroof.
Mix tomatoes with the rice and eat.	حط بنادورة على الرز وكل	Hat banadora ala al riz, wakol.
Boy, bring the bread.	يا ولد جيب الخبز	Yawalad, jeeb al khubbs.
Praise God! I am satisfied.	الحمد لله شبعت	Alhamd lillah! shbot.
Wash your hands.	اغسل يدك	Aghsil yedek.
Bring the basin and ewer.	جيب الطشت والابريق	Jeeb altasht wal abreek.
Pour the coffee.	اسكب القهوة	Eskob al kahwa.
Add some sugar.	حط سكر	Hut sukkar.
May your coffee last for ever.	قهوة دايمة	Kahwa dayma.
Health (to you!)	صحة	Sahha.

THE BAZAAR. السوق ASSOOK.

ENGLISH.	ARABIC.	PRONUNCIATION.
Where is the silk bazaar?	من اين الدرب الى السوق	Min ain alderb ila assook?
From here (pointing.)	من هنا .	Min hona.
Have you tarbush and keffieh? (for the head.)	هل عندك طربوش وكفية	Hal andak tarbush wa keffieh?
I have the best quality.	عندي مال عال	Aindi mal hal.
What is the price?	ماهو ثمن هذا	Mahoo saman haza?
Twenty piastres	عشرين غرش	Ashrin gorsh.
(It is) Very dear.	غالي كتير	Ghali katir.
(I will) Take ten.	خذ عشرة	Haud ashra.
I will give you eight.	انا اعطيك ثمانية	Ana aartik tamania.
It cost me more, but for your sake	تهندني اكثر من هذا لكن لاجل خاطرك لزو بلاش	Samanho aktar min haza, lakin lehajil khatrak luzo belash.
I give it to you gratis.		
Thank you (pays the eight piastres.)	كثر خيرك	Katar kkairak.

THE SCHOOL. المكتب ALMAKTAB.

ENGLISH.	ARABIC.	PRONUNCIATION.
How old are you?	ما هو عمرك	Ma how amrak?
Eight years.	ثمانية سنين	Tamanyat senecn.
Can you count ten?	هل تقدر تعد عشرة	Hal tukdir taåd ashra?
O yes! One, two, three, four, five, six, seven, eight, nine, ten.	اي نعم واحد اثنين ثلاثة اربعة خمسة ستة سبعة ثمانية تسعة عشرة	Ai nam! Wahad, atnein, teleita, arba, kamsa, sitta, saba, tamaniah, tissa, ashra.
Very good! Do you know a text?	طيب كثير هل تعرف كلام من الكتاب المقدس	Tuyib katir! Hal tarif kalam min al kitab al mokudas?
Yes: God so loved the world that He gave His only begotten Son, that whosoever believeth in Him should not perish but have everlasting life.	اي نعم الله هكذا احب العالم حتى بذل ابنه الوحيد لكي لا يهلك كل من يؤمن به بل تكون له الحياة الابدية	Ai nam. Lianahoo hakaza ahab allah al ahalum hautta buzala ibnahoo al vahid lakayi la yuhlak kalman yumin b:hi bel takoon lahoo al hiat al abahiyat.

APPENDIX No. 2.

LINES BY THE AUTHOR.

The reader must not here expect to find,
In every stanza, rhyme and sense combined.
Of each there may appear a little measure ;
If that's enough to please you—take your pleasure.

"GOD IS LOVE."

1 John iv. 8, 16.

EVERY day from morn till even,
Every night of all the seven,
Everything on earth, in heaven,
 Tells us " God is love."
Every tree and shrub that's growing,
Every fragrant flower that's blowing,
Every pleasant fruit is shewing
 Plainly, " God is love."
Every lofty mountain, each refreshing fountain,
Fish that sleep in ocean deep,
 And things on earth that move;
Lions o'er the desert roaming,
Mighty ocean billows foaming;
Torrents roaring, zephyrs moaning,
 Tell us " God is love."

Every blade of grass that's springing,
Every little bird that's singing,
In the woods the echo ringing,
 Tells that " God is love."
Every little insect creeping,
Every tiny floweret peeping,
To its proper season keeping,
 Whispers, " God is love."
Showers gently falling, rain in torrents pouring,
Summer's rose, and winter snows,
 The sun that shines above;
Rivers through the meadows flowing,
Lilies in the valleys growing,
Time of reaping, and of sowing,
 Tell that " God is love."

Every clime of every nation,
Every work in all creation,
And the gospel of salvation,
    Tell us "God is love."
Jesus left the throne in heaven,
And His life for ours was given,
That our sins might be forgiven,
    By the "God of love."
When thro' Adam's falling, sin for death was calling,
God came down, and so made known
    The plan devised above.
Pilgrims on their God relying,
Saints in glory, angels flying,
Jesu's praises, never dying,
    Tell us "God is love."

WE SEE JESUS.

Hebrews ii. 9.

In every line of every page,
Presented to faith in every age;
On the sacred field of Scripture revealed,
    We see Jesus.

The glory above His eternal abode,
Who spake but the word and the universe stood;
His Father's delight, beloved in His sight,
    We see Jesus.

And to do God's will, His counsels fulfil,
In the form of a man, the Holy One still;
The Heavenly Stranger laid in a manger,
    We see Jesus.

By sorrow surrounded, where sin had abounded,
The one before whom the foe is confounded ;
Tho Life and the Light, and Giver of sight,
 We see Jesus.

The eternal " I AM," the offered-up Lamb,
Enduring the cross, despising the shame ;
Put to death on the tree for you and for me,
 We see Jesus.

Now bursting the bands of death, with those hands
From which Justice received her fullest demands ;
Alive from the grave, almighty to save,
 We see Jesus.

Ascended again, past sorrow and pain,
Exalted by God for ever to reign ;
Receiving a name above every name,
 We see Jesus.

ON PSALM II.

" Blessed are all they that put their trust in him."—Ps. ii. 12.

WHAT meaneth this ?   The heathen rage,
Vain things the people's thoughts engage ;
And rulers in derision wild,
Have set at nought God's Holy Child.
Yet he is blessed, and he alone,
Who puts his trust in God the Son.

Kings of the earth, in impious pride
Are set ; but He shall them deride,
In heaven on high, who sits enthroned,
With righteousness and justice crowned.
His blessing rests on every one
Who puts his trust in God the Son.

The Lord shall His desire fulfil,
Who sits a king on Zion's hill ;
The heathen from their ignorant rage,
Shall be reclaimed, His heritage.
Forgiveness He will grant each one
Who puts his trust in God the Son.

He will destroy with iron rod,
Those who confess Him not as God ;
Be wise now, therefore, O ye kings,
Come unto Him whose sufferings
Have glory bought for every one
Who puts his trust in God the Son.

For fear He should in anger rise,
And send destruction from the skies,
Draw near :—The Lord of truth and grace,
Is waiting for thee to embrace
The hand once pierced for every one
Who puts his trust in God the Son.

ON PSALM XXIII.

Thou art my Shepherd, gracious Lord,
And I shall want no more ;
To me Thy rest Thou dost afford,
Thou dost my soul restore.

For Thy name's sake, by Thee I'm led
In paths of righteousness ;
Yea : in death's vale I need not dread,
Thy rod my Comfort is.

My table's spread by Thine own hand,
Before mine enemies ;
Mercy shall keep me till I stand,
Where my Forerunner is.

"LEAD ME TO THE ROCK THAT
IS HIGHER THAN I."

Psalm lxi. 2.

WHEN dead in my sins, and yet without God
Or hope in the world, I feared not the rod
Of just retribution, nor uttered the cry—
"Lead me to the Rock that is higher than I."

And e'en when the danger of sinking to hell,
With the angels of Satan in torment to dwell,
Affrighted my conscience ; it raised not the cry—
" Lead me to the Rock that is higher than I. '

I heard of His love who, for sinners like me,
Left the glory above to bleed on the tree ;
And He who, in mercy, gave Jesus to die,
Led " me to the Rock that is higher than I."

And there to my soul a refuge was giv'n,
In the cleft which therein was on Calvary riv'n ;
While for all things I learned this way to apply—
" Lead me to the Rock that is higher than I."

When the world, with its smiles, would draw me aside,
Or, frowning, would cause me my colours to hide ;
My God and my Father, who dwellest on high,
" Lead me to the Rock that is higher than I "

When the lusts of the flesh roll in like a tide,
To o'erwhelm and defeat me, O Heavenly Guide,
Thou Spirit of Truth—use the word, and thereby
" Lead me to the Rock that is higher than I."

When Satan, in subtle or undisguised rage,
With infernal spite would my weakness engage ;

Lord Jesus, his Victor, ascended on high,
" Lead me to the Rock that is higher than I."

When, finished my course as a pilgrim below,
To mansions of joy at Thy beckon I go ;
By the hand that was pierced,when for me Thou didst die,
" Lead me to the Rock that is higher than I "

" WATCHMAN, WHAT OF THE NIGHT ?"

Isaiah xxi. 11.

On Dumah's wall the watchman stands,
    In Judah's land by night ;
He waits the breaking of the dawn—
    A child of day, the light.
The sounds of mirth are silenced all,
    The stars assist his sight ;
From out of Seir he hears the call—
    " Watchman, what of the night ?"

And though the scoffer's granted time,
    His question to repeat,
The watchman's answer shews that hope
    High in his heart doth beat.
The watchman said, The morning comes,
    The night, too, comes apace ;
The morning, of my Lord's return,
    The night, on day of grace.

If yet ye will inquiry make,
    Enquire ye and return ;
Oh, come while it is called to-day,
    God's love no longer spurn ;

Else thou must have the scorner's doom,
    And never shalt see light ;
Should'st thou find this thy long, long home,
    Oh, what of such a night ?

" But sanctify the Lord God in your hearts: and be ready always
to give an answer to every man that asketh you a reason of the
hope that is in you with meekness and fear."

1 Peter iii. 15.

"BEHOLD, THE BRIDEGROOM COMETH."

Matthew xxv. 6.

The heavenly kingdom of the Lord,
We're told about in God's own word,
    In various ways defined :
A net, a sower and his seed,
A merchantman, and, as we read,
A Friend to help in time of need,
    The broken heart to bind.

In many parables, 'tis shewn,
How very near for every one,
    This kingdom has been brought :
By John the Baptist 'twas declared,
And Jesus, too, took up the word,
While old and young alike have heard
    The truths which so He taught.

How sweetly does the tender care
Of Jesus in the words appear,
    About the wandering sheep !
How richly, too, the Father's love,
The prodigal's return did prove,
And ev'ry heart in heaven did move,
    A holiday to keep.

But solemnly the virgins ten
Are used to shew the lot of men,
  Who mercy's day despise :
The midnight cry will come too late,
For those who in the scorner's seat,
Unmoved by mercy's voice have sat,
  Nor ope'd their sleepy eyes.

O ! then, before the Master come,
To shut the door and seal the doom
  Of those who know Him not ;
Awake and hear His gracious voice,
Bid all to make His love their choice,
His Father and Himself rejoice,
  When souls His peace have got.

"AND WHAT I SAY UNTO YOU, I SAY UNTO ALL, WATCH." MARK xiii. 37.

An Acrostic.

W ATCH ! for ye know not when your Lord doth come ;
A t midnight, cock-crowing, or break of day :
T hy lamp shines not so bright as other some,
" C ome, Lord !"—they louder cry—" no more delay,"
H e soon will come, and bid thee 'Come away.'

.

CAPERNAUM.

CAPERNAUM, Capernaum,
Thy day was bright, Capernaum,
When He who is the Son of God,
In Bethl'hem born, and then abode
In Nazareth, but thence removed
To dwell in thee, Capernaum.

Thy synagogue, Capernaum,
Thy homes and streets, Capernaum,
Were witnesses of what He said ;
At whose command the devils fled,
Who healed thy sick, and raised thy dead,
Thy lepers cleansed, Capernaum.

And thus thou wast, Capernaum,
To heaven raised, Capernaum !
Thy mercies did so far exceed,
But thou so little gavest heed ;
At last 'twill better be, indeed,
For Sodom, than Capernaum !

How like wast thou, Capernaum,
To those who now, Capernaum,
The Saviour's voice refuse to hear,
Who died to bring salvation near,
Whose resurrection shews so clear
His power to save, Capernaum.

His words declare, Capernaum,
Thy ruins shew, Capernaum,
Thy visitation-day is o'er,
And thou, alas ! wilt hear no more
His voice proclaiming on thy shore,
His tale of love, Capernaum.

MAGDALA.

BESIDE the sea of Galilee,
    There stands a little town ;
The Son of God its streets hath trod,
    And given it renown ;
At least it boasts, into its coasts
    Jesus himself came down.*

* Matthew xv. 39.

The rippling wave its shore doth lave,
  The oleander blooms,
Mid verdure seen of richest green,
  And fragrant with perfumes ;
The palm tree's crest, above the rest,
  Displays the victor's plumes.

A rich parterre in flank and rear,
  Revolving seasons find,
Or plowed or sown, or reaped or mown,
  While sheaves the reapers bind ;
Then oxen, o'er the laden floor,
  Tread corn for humankind.

Chorazin, nor Bethsaida, nor
  Capernaum supplies
This story rare and aspect fair,
  For traveller's ears and eyes.
Their wal's, once reared, have disappeared
  From underneath the skies.

Their favoured lot they valued not,
  When Jesus trod the street,
And bade the dead rise from her bed,
  And 'fore them all to eat.
Their ruins now, confused and low,
  The seeker's gaze do meet.

Forgiven much and loving much ;
  At Cross and Sepulchre,
Lo ! one appears, free from those fears
  His love has cast from her.
Who ask her name, hear her proclaim,
  " Mary of MAGDALA."

" Hunger: it's sharp for awhile ; but you buckle your belt a hole
tighter, and get over that. But, thirst! It's a terrible thing:
Thirst—

"YOU THINK OF THE WATER YOU ONCE
THREW AWAY."

ROBERT MOFFATT, D.D.

THE African desert or wilderness roaming,
  Pursuing his journey, the traveller goes ;
He sees not a torrent all gushing and foaming,
  But crosses a region where no river flows.
Himself and companions, all weary and thirsty,
  No shelter protects from the sun's scorching ray—
The fountain still distant and calabash empty,
  He thinks of the water he once threw away.

The African village surprised and surrounded,
  The terrified people endeavour to flee ;
Their every intention is crossed and confounded,
  The slave-hunter takes them his captives to be.
The rope round his neck and his hands tied behind him,
  The slave 'neath the whip, as he goes on his way,
In vain sighs for succour which cannot now find him,
  And thinks of the water he once threw away.

Outstretched on the field where the foeman has laid him,
  With sabre or bullet or splinter of shell ;
The soldier, a victim which one moment made him,
  In torture and anguish now lies where he fell.
The faintness and stupor the bleeding brought o'er him
  The smart of his wounds by departing obey,
And thirsting intensely, no succour before him,
  He thinks of the water he once threw away.

A river is flowing of pure living water,
  It comes from the temple of God and the Lamb:
The message is issued to every quarter,
  For all who are thirsty ; who hears should proclaim :
Who drinketh shall live and be savèd for ever ;
  Who hears and neglects it draws near to the day
When careless and scorners, where hope cometh never,
  Shall think of the water they once threw away.

THE THIRSTY TRAVELLERS.

THE sun had set on Palestina's land,
And crescent moon awhile the vigil kept;
As by her light, ere Jaffa's inmates slept,
The travellers, a feeble little band,
Through Jaffa's gardens started on their way.

Horse, mule and ass at roadside-fountain drink,
Then on the Ramleh road they keep their way;
Ere Ramleh's reached, the moon, of feeble ray,
Behind the western clouds doth also sink,
And air in coolness, night in darkness grows.

Thus mile succeeds on mile, and hour on hour,
Till Ramleh's walls and towers are far behind ;
Then thirst inspires the strong desire to find,
Or well, or fountain, or a prickly pear ;
But none there are, or darkness them conceals.

" When shall we quench our thirst?" "The muleteer
Is searching with a keen and practised eye."
The hope deferred, heart saddening reply,
Again and yet again falls on the ear ;
And thirst increasing is, and failing hope.

But now amid the deepest gloom of night,
Eleven becomes the little band of four;
Of Ramoth Gilead the governor,
And Nablûs Mufti with their turbans white,
And horsemen five their company unite.

Salutes exchanged, and free enquiries made,
" Whence do you come, and whither are you bound ?"
The thirsty hear the soul-refreshing sound,
" Would you drink water ?" Soon their thirst's allayed
From leathern bottle to the girdle joined.

So let the Christian with the Arab vie,
As this with earthly, that with heavenly store,
To fellow travellers to th' eternal shore,
Extend the draught, who drinks shall never die,
And point to CHRIST, THE SAVIOUR OF THE WORLD.

ALMOST ASHORE.

WHEN making your voyage, or outward or homeward,
    Though gain and repute would be lost by delay ;
Should you see from the deck on your larboard or starboard,
    With rudder and anchor both carried away,
A bark in distress and the breakers to leeward,
    Already her crew in the sound of their roar;
Stay not to consider who else may deliver,
    But take her in tow for she's almost ashore.

Mid cares and engagements, though never so many,
    A neighbour in trouble appears at your door ;
Dismiss not his story until you have heard it,
    Because he applied not a minute before ;
But spare at the least a few moments' attention,
    Although you have proved his unkindness of yore ;
And when you have heard and reviewed his narration,
    Then lend him a hand if he's almost ashore.

A A

Where the young and the friendless in scenes of temptation,
  Where children of error together abide,
Oh ! carry the news of a finished salvation,
  And tell of His love who for sinners has died.
Where the sick and the dying do wither and languish,
  Stay not till to-morrow to visit their door ;
That the balm of His name may dispel all their anguish,
  Of Jesus speak thou to the

ALMOST ASHORE.

SCRIPTURES QUOTED IN THIS WORK.

INDEX.

Memories

of

Grandma

Based on a true story of love,
loss, and memories

Stacie Gallerani

PAGE PUBLISHING
Meadville, PA

First originally published by Page Publishing 2026

ISBN 979-8-90251-002-4 (pbk)
ISBN 979-8-90251-004-8 (digital)

Printed in the United States of America

Dedicated to Mary C. Mello.

I t had been especially cold that winter—the topic of conversation amongst most adults in fact. As I recall, school had been cancelled half a dozen times in response to the frigid temperatures. Mommy wasn't fond of New England weather, especially that of Maine, but that was where Grandma lived—and she was fond of her. Jack and I, on the other hand, loved the winter. He was my little brother and best friend. Yes, Jack could be a pest at times, but we had lots of fun together. We spent much of our time frolicking in the snow; it never felt too cold to play. I remember my snowsuit well, as I wore it almost every day that winter. It was a purple two-piece little number with pretty pink-and-white flowers embroidered down the front. The jacket had a removable fleece liner that could be worn on its own. The coat was what my grandma called a "three in one." Strangers would look at her funny when she'd refer to it this way, but we all knew what she meant. It was a little big for me, but Mommy bought it on sale, and 5T was all the store had left. We both loved that coat—I, for the color and cozy feel, and Mommy, for the outstanding sale price. I remember that winter very well, though not for its weather or for the pretty little snowsuit but for the event that would forever change me.

The temperature had climbed to a whopping twenty degrees. It was a Thursday, and if it weren't for the Christmas break, I would have been in school. Instead, I woke from the sound of the telephone ringing. We hardly ever received calls that early in the morning. In a sleepy haze, I remember hearing Daddy and Mommy in the kitchen the night before.

"Looks like there's another storm heading our way," I heard Daddy say.

"How much are we going to get this time?" Mommy asked in a cranky voice.

"Forecasters say about a foot or so starting by late morning," Daddy replied with a matter-of-fact tone.

"Great," she whined. "That's just what we need—another layer of snow!"

I yawned, and after a long stretch, I jumped out of bed with excitement and anticipation of the snow event. As I pulled the drapes to one side to light the room, I could see the most beautiful fluffy snowflakes floating gently from the morning sky. I could hardly wait to share the exciting news with Mommy that the snow had begun to fall.

I tiptoed down the long hall that led to her bedroom, hoping to surprise her with a bear hug. As I entered the room and drew closer to where she sat quietly on the edge of the bed, there was a strange silence. With her back to me, I gently climbed up on top of the bed.

As I reached around to cover her eyes, I giggled. "Guess who?"

She gently placed her hand on mine, releasing my grasp from her eyes.

"How long does she have?" she inquired in a somber tone. I noticed my fingers were wet, and I quickly jumped off the bed in front of her.

With the phone in one hand, she reached for a tissue to wipe away her tears with the other. She motioned for me to stand close by, and as I did, she held me tightly. "I'll be there as soon as I can. I just need to make some phone calls first," Mommy stated before hanging up the phone.

I didn't say a word. I squeezed her as hard as I could and waited for her to speak.

After a few moments, she cleared her throat and said, "Grandma is very sick. I need to be with her."

"Can I go too?" I asked with hope.

"Children aren't allowed," she responded. "I'm sorry."

Daddy had left for work early, as he had every morning. Daddy was a computer software engineer. He worked an hour away from our home in a quiet little cubicle—a perfect job for a man of few words. He was of average height and build, with short blond hair and blue eyes. People always commented on how much Jack and Daddy looked alike.

Jack entered the room with a big smile. He woke up most mornings that way now that he was out of the crib and in a "big boy bed." Mommy didn't seem to notice though. She seemed anxious as she dialed the telephone.

"Who are you calling, Mommy?" I was curious to know.

She didn't seem to hear me.

After a few moments on the phone, she announced that Daddy would be home as soon as he could. "In the meantime, Mrs. Kindly is going to stay with you," Mommy told my little brother and me.

Jack was only two at the time and didn't seem to understand what was happening. But I did.

She arranged our clothes to be worn that day while we waited for our neighbor to arrive. People used to say I was a very nosy baby, but Mommy would always correct them and say I was inquisitive—but not that morning. I was too afraid to ask her what was happening, and Mommy offered little. The fear of something terrible happening to Grandma was too much for me to bear. Instead, I did my best to be a good listener and do all that she asked of me.

Mommy tried her best to hide it, but I could see the sadness in those big brown eyes of hers as she kissed and hugged my brother and me goodbye. "Remember your pleases and thank-yous," she reminded us. "I'll be home when I can." She told us she loved us and quickly made her way toward the door.

I watched her drive away as I stood by the living room window. The snow was getting heavier. I no longer wished to be out playing in the snow. All that I wanted was for Mommy to return and to hear that Grandma would be okay.

I spent hours by the window that day with the hope of good news. The heavy snow was piling up fast outside—much faster and heavier than expected. I could hear the rumblings of snowplows in the distance as I struggled to make sight of the road through the living room window. My heart was heavy and my body tired from the long wait. Jack was eager to play, but I was too worried to have any fun.

With his favorite teddy in one hand, Jack approached me with my favorite stuffed horse in the other. When that didn't seem to work, he brought some books for the two of us to look at. "Read to me," Jack pleaded. "*Pleeeaase?*"

I didn't really know how to read, but Jack didn't know the difference. I just looked at the pictures and made up my own words. It seemed to make him happy; and for a short while, it made me happy too.

After looking at several books, Daddy thought it best that we all play a game together. "Why don't we play Wheels on the Bus?" Daddy suggested. "I'll set it up if you'd like."

"No, that's okay, Daddy," I said politely. I knew that he was trying to coax me away from the frost-covered window. "I just want Mommy. When is she coming home? She's taking a really long time."

"I don't know," Daddy admitted, "but waiting by the window won't make her come home any faster, you know. How about some lunch? I'll make your favorite—pig's feet dipped in peanut butter with rhinoceros snout on the side."

Daddy had a way of cheering me up, and I laughed at that silly suggestion.

"No, thanks, Daddy. Maybe I could have a peanut butter sandwich with apple slices on the side instead."

The phone rang several times that day, and each time, I ran to it, anticipating Mommy's voice. I wasn't allowed to answer all by myself. She didn't trust that there would always be a kind person on the other side. I think Daddy was disappointed too each time he answered and realized she still hadn't called. I went to bed that evening missing her desperately and longing for her sweet smile and reassuring hug.

*****

I woke to the feeling of Mommy's soft lips on my forehead. "I always give you one last kiss before going to bed," she told us long ago. That night was no different. After a long emotional day at the hospital, she wanted nothing more than to crawl into bed and sleep away the emptiness she felt.

"I didn't mean to wake you," she whispered. "Go back to sleep."

It was dark, but I could tell that she was different. She wasn't her usual cheery self.

"Is Grandma okay?" I asked.

She took a deep breath as if to avoid the question. She sat down beside me and held her arms out for a hug. I had—what felt like—a million butterflies in my stomach as I held Mommy in my arms.

"She doesn't have to suffer anymore," she said, trying to hold back the tears. "She's in heaven now."

Although I didn't really know what that meant, I started to cry too. "Don't cry, Mommy. It's okay."

After a long silence, I asked, "What is heaven?"

"It's the most beautiful place you'll ever see," she explained. "There are blue skies and pretty flowers everywhere. All the stuff you love so much on earth is there with you in heaven. The best part though is that you can never get sick, and nothing bad ever happens."

"Never?" I asked in surprise.

"Never!" she reassured me.

"I want to go there. Are horses there too? I love horses."

"I'm sure there are lots of horses. But I'm not ready for you to go to heaven just yet."

"Why, Mommy?" I asked.

"If you go to heaven now, it will be a long time before I see you again."

"What?" I asked with tears in my eyes.

Until then, I had not truly understood what had happened. Warm tears trickled down my cheeks. As each drop fell to my pillow, I thought about what that meant. I had so many more questions, but they would have to wait.

Mommy drifted off to sleep.

As she had done so many nights for me, I now pulled the covers on top of her and kissed her on the forehead. "Good night, Mommy. I love you," I whispered. I snuggled up close to her, placed her arm around me, and fell fast asleep.

I woke the next morning and realized that she had returned to her own bed during the night. I sat up to listen for the slightest hint of movement from her bedroom. I carefully tiptoed into Jack's room, which was right next to mine, to check on him. The house was peaceful—as though it, too, were asleep.

As I returned to my bedroom, I thought about what Mommy had said the night before. I felt a sadness that I had never felt before—even greater than when I fell and skinned my knee or when I lost my favorite Barbie shoe at the mall. I thought about the last time I saw Grandma on Christmas Eve and the last hug I would ever give her. As if it were a movie in my mind, I remembered everything about that last night with Grandma.

*****

We arrived at her house that night—Mommy, Daddy, Jack, and me—as we had every year on Christmas Eve, only to see Grandma sitting quietly on her rocking chair.

As my brother and I approached Grandma with excited smiles, Mommy called out, "Merry Christmas! Where would you like the lasagna?"

She made it a habit of making lasagna every year to lighten the load on Grandma. Hosting that annual celebration for our big family was more work than her tired body could handle, and in order for Grandma to continue the tradition, she needed help preparing food.

"Lasagna?" Grandma blurted in confusion. "What is that for?"

"What do you mean? I always make lasagna on Christmas Eve," Mommy replied.

"When is Christmas Eve?" responded Grandma with a frown.

Mommy placed the lasagna down on the table.

As I walked closer to Grandma, I wondered why she sat undressed for the special occasion. She was a proud woman—much too proud to let others see her in such a way.

Family and friends were due to arrive shortly, yet she seemed unaffected by the fact there was much to be done. Grandpa was suffering from flu-like symptoms and wasn't much help to Grandma. He had his own ailments to deal with.

Clutching onto Mommy's hand tightly, I approached Grandma with hesitation.

"Give Grandma a kiss," she urged. "It's okay."

I half smiled and wrapped my arms around her. "Merry Christmas," I said in a shy voice.

Grandma's hugs were like soft, scented pillows wrapped firmly around my body. I could always feel the love bursting from her soul to mine. On that night, however, something was different. As her arms sat limp on her lap, I noticed how warm she felt despite the short-sleeve nightgown and housecoat she had on. The absence of sweet-smelling per-fume and unaffectionate greeting confused me. Mommy was aware that something was terribly wrong, and in her attempt to remove me from the situation, she invited my brother and me to place our presents under the Christmas tree.

The formal living room was my favorite room in Grandma's house during Christmastime. Entrances on both sides of the corner fireplace, large picture window, and sofa mirror made the room appear even larger than it already was. The deep-red wall-to-wall carpeting was the perfect backdrop for a Christmas wonderland. Crystal angels and ceramic mangers complemented the space nicely. The most spectacular sight, however, was the enormous Christmas tree hovering over a sea of beautifully wrapped packages. The freshly cut blue spruce adorned with delicate orna-ments sparkled in the glow of the colored lights. The tiny Christmas lights and raging fire were the only sources of light in the picturesque room. After setting our presents under the tree, I sat on the floor by the warm fireplace to admire the view. The rhythmic ticking of the grandfather clock was a comforting sound. While thoughts of what Santa might bring filled my imagination, so too did the mystery of my experience in the kitchen with Grandma.

It wasn't long before my thoughts were interrupted by the glare of flashing lights. An ambulance had come for

Grandma. I had never seen one that closely before, and I was startled by its presence. I ran to the kitchen where Mommy had been tending to Grandma to see what was happening. She looked worried as she explained to the two paramedics what had happened.

"Who are you?" Grandma asked the men in a worried voice. "Where are you taking me? I don't want to leave!"

While one paramedic knelt beside Grandma to help calm her, the other questioned Mommy. I was scared, and I knew Grandma was too.

I ran to her and rubbed her arm, hoping to ease her fear. "Don't be scared, Grandma," I told her. My heart was beating so hard I wondered if anyone noticed. "It's okay."

She looked over at me and said nothing. At that moment, I wondered if she recognized who I was.

Moments later, the ambulance took Grandma away. Mommy offered to stay at the house to clean up while other family members gathered at the hospital. She cleaned especially well when she was upset. The doorbell rang several times that night while Daddy entertained us in the living room with silly stories about Santa. Daddy was a good storyteller. It helped us not to worry so much.

The house was spotless by night's end as we locked the door behind us. As we headed home, I felt both anxious and excited. I wondered if Grandma was still scared and hoped that she'd be okay, but I also felt the happy anticipation of Santa's arrival.

******

Those were my last memories of Grandma. She wasn't the sweet, smiling woman I had known but a scared, confused stranger to me. Although it had only been a few days, I missed her deeply.

I could hear Mommy as she walked quietly toward my bedroom. We hugged for what seemed a long time.

"I miss Grandma," I cried.

"Me too," she said as she hugged me tighter. She invited me downstairs so we wouldn't wake Jack and Daddy. "I have something to show you," she said. "I have some pictures of Grandma I thought you should see." She opened an old shoebox.

In it were pictures of Grandma when she was a young girl. One of the pictures showed Grandma on a horse in front of her childhood home. She told me that it was common in those days for photographers to travel from home to home, offering their horse for a pose. She had beautiful shoulder-length platinum hair and sparkling hazel eyes. She wore her favorite dress that day, Grandma had told Mommy long ago.

"I look just like Grandma!" I said in surprise.

"Your father and I always wondered who you looked like," Mommy admitted with a smile. "Now we know."

We talked more about heaven that morning as Daddy and Jack slept.

"How did Grandma get into heaven?" I wanted to know.

Although she wasn't entirely sure, she thought the angels may have helped. "You know, Grandma is an angel now. Even though we can't see or hear her, she will always be around to watch over and protect us. All you have to do is talk to her and know that she is listening."

"Mommy, are you going to heaven someday?" I asked.

She smiled. "Not for a very long time. You and I have long lives ahead of us so not to worry. Just know that when it is your turn to go to heaven, I will be there waiting for you, and so will Grandma and everyone else that loves you that has ended their time on earth," Mommy reassured me.

That winter changed the way I looked at those I loved. I thought that Grandma would always be around for smiles and hugs. Although my heart remained heavy for a very long time, I knew Grandma was in heaven smiling down on me. I was only four years old that winter when Grandma died, but memories of her will never fade from my mind or from my heart.

About the Author

S tacie Gallerani was born and raised in New Bedford, Massachusetts. She has an undergraduate degree in education—pre-K to third—and a minor in psychology from Bridgewater State College. She also has a graduate degree in curriculum and instruction with a focus in literacy from Lesley University.

Stacie has dedicated her life to teaching first grade for the last eighteen years. Writing from the heart comes easy to her and is proud to share her heartfelt story of love, loss, and memories.